## Dear Cupid

"Julie Ortolon takes her wonderfully colorful and appealing characters on an unexpected journey of discovery."
—*Christina Skye*

## Drive Me Wild

"A wonderful debut novel." —*Romantic Times*

"A smart and funny story that I found very enjoyable to read." —*Rendezvous*

"Will drive readers to ecstasy . . . [a] superb romance. . . . Ortolon is a gem of a new author and readers will certainly want to watch for her future books!"
—*Romantic Times*

"A fun and completely captivating story. . . . Ortolon has given us believable characters with a wonderful range of personalities . . . Many of the scenes really sizzle!"
—*Romance Communications*

"Quick wit, snappy dialogue, sensuality that smokes, and a good story-line. This is one worth your time and will give you a pleasurable read." —*Under the Covers*

# Dear Cupid

## JULIE ORTOLON

St. Martin's Paperbacks

DEAR CUPID

Copyright © 2001 by Julie Ortolon.

Cover illustration by Chris Long / CWC International, Inc.

ISBN: 0-312-97871-5

Printed in the United States of America

St. Martin's Paperbacks edition / July 2001

St. Martin's Paperbacks are published by St. Martin's Press, 175 Fifth Avenue, New York, NY 10010.

10 9 8 7 6 5 4 3 2 1

*For Dad,*
*I miss you*

*Special Thanks to*

*M*Y agent, Laura Blake Peterson, for her years of faith and savvy advice. Editors Jennifer Enderlin and Kim Cardascia, for loving Mike and Kate nearly as much as I do. Author Cynthia Sterling, for her insights and encouragement.

And especially Cyndee DuHadaway, for friendship above and beyond the call of duty.

# Chapter 1

*Dear Cupid,*
*Do you believe in love at first sight?*
                              *Seriously Smitten*


*Dear Seriously Smitten,*
*Absolutely! But then I always enjoy a good*
*fairy tale.*
   *In the real world, things take a bit*
*longer. What appears to be love at first*
*sight is actually a subconscious recogni-*
*tion of a potentially compatible mate, a*
*premonition, so to speak, of what could be.*
*Only time will tell if the premonition comes*
*true.*

                                      *Cupid*

KATE needed a man. Any man. Well, maybe not *any*
man, she amended as she glanced about the gate area
of the Los Angeles airport. The businessman pacing
before the window looked too edgy; the grandfather
with the armload of Disney souvenirs too old; and the
two men in the corner appeared a little too interested
in each other for her purpose.

What she needed was a nice, reasonably attractive sort of man. Someone friendly. Approachable. Someone with whom she could flirt. That was all. Just flirt.

The last thing in the world she wanted was the emotional turmoil of a serious relationship. Romance, on the other hand, was an entirely different matter. Her job required a certain amount of romance in her life, or so she'd been informed that very morning by Gwen, the owner of *Gwendolyn's Garden,* the on-line magazine that ran her advice column.

She still couldn't believe Gwen had threatened to cancel her. She was Cupid, for goodness' sake! They couldn't cancel Cupid. Her column generated thousands of hits a month for the e-zine. Or at least it used to. As Gwen had pointed out, her popularity was dwindling—because her column simply wasn't fun anymore.

Now, however, was not the time for anger or self-pity. She needed to take control, to recapture the carefree spirit she'd somehow lost in recent years.

Turning her head, she saw a new passenger stroll into the gate area. Her skin prickled with interest at the sight of him, an odd occurrence since he wasn't her usual type. In the past, she'd gone for dark-haired men in Armani suits who wore power as easily as other men wore denim. That description, however, matched her ex-husband a little too close for comfort.

Which made this man perfect.

He had the sun-streaked hair and rich tan of someone who spent a lot of time relaxing in sunny places. The Hawaiian shirt and khaki pants gave him a casual, lived-in look that surprisingly appealed to her. As for his luggage, he carried a duffel bag: an old-fashioned, army-green duffel bag.

When he reached the ticket counter, he lifted his blue-mirrored sunglasses and smiled at the ticket agent. Kate's heart did something it hadn't done in years; it gave one hard thump against her ribs. The man had a devastating smile with perfect white teeth. Generous laugh lines winged outward from his eyes, marking him as older than she'd first thought. Late thirties, perhaps. As for his body, she couldn't quite tell if muscle or flab moved beneath the baggy clothes, but the shape had definite appeal, with broad shoulders that tapered down to narrow hips.

Just looking at him made some long dormant part of her stir to life. Her smile spread as he took a seat off to himself. She'd found her man. Now, all she had to do was catch his eye and prove she could still do what she once had done as naturally as breathing. Flirt his pants off—figuratively speaking.

Mike pulled off his sunglasses and stowed them in his duffel bag as he collapsed on a hard plastic chair. Dropping the bag at his feet, he took a moment to make sure his computer disks rested safely on top. Then he sank down in the seat to wait for his flight.

Exhaustion pulled his head back and closed his eyes. He was getting too old to put in these sixteen-hour workdays for weeks on end. What he wouldn't give to just pass out for the duration of the flight. Unfortunately, he had too much on his mind to give in to sleep—like the big gaping hole in his life where a wife and some children should be.

Settling deeper in the chair, he let his mind drift

back to the twenty-year high school reunion he'd attended while in L.A. What a reality check that had been! He still couldn't believe his former classmates had children in college, while he had yet to even get married. One of these days, he really needed to look into doing something about his lack of a personal life.

The problem was, he enjoyed his job a little too much. Make that way too much. As a special effects movie animator, he loved everything about his work . . . well, except the demanding schedule that left him little time for things like dating.

As his mind searched for possible solutions to the problem, a jangling thud sounded right before him. He tuned it out easily. Working on movie sets for the past twenty-odd years had taught him to tune out all manner of chaos. The bump on his leg, however, wasn't so easy to ignore.

"I'm so sorry," an anxious voice insisted. "Please excuse me."

He opened his eyes and found a woman crouched before him as she reached beneath his seat.

"How terribly clumsy of me," she said. With her head bent, her shoulder-length, coppery curls brushed his knee. Bending sideways, he saw her purse had fallen and spilled its contents at his feet. He leaned forward, intending to help her on her way as expediently as possible.

"I swear, I'm such a klutz today," she rushed on, gathering up pens and breath mints, a paperback novel, a pair of reading glasses, some loose change, a set of keys, and several business cards.

Shaking his head, he reached for a runaway tube of lipstick only to have his hand collide with hers. The lipstick tried to skitter away, but he grabbed it before it made good its escape.

"Gotcha," he said, chuckling. He lifted his head to address the lipstick's owner and found himself face-to-face with the most enchanting woman he'd ever seen. She had a bold, heart-shaped face with an impish nose, stubborn chin, and pouty lips that begged to be tasted. Gazing into her shamrock-green eyes, he felt his insides swirl, as if he were falling forward into a field of clover—a field where a man could lie back and rest with a woman snuggled to his side as he lazily watched the clouds float by. A smile slowly turned up the corners of her lips, and he realized her eyes tipped up at the corners as well.

"I really am terribly sorry," she said in a breathy voice that reached inside him and tied his stomach into knots of pure desire. "It's the flying, you see." She placed a hand over her chest. "Planes makes me very . . . nervous."

His gaze dropped to her hand, which rested right at the point of her V-collared red suit. He would never have guessed a woman with orange hair could look that good in red, but on her the combination staggered the senses. Or, perhaps his light-headedness came from staring at the breasts beneath her hand.

From what he could see, she had great breasts. Perfect breasts. The kind of breasts that could incite a man's lust, pillow his head. Or nurture his child.

His gaze snapped back to hers. She gave him a patient little smile—as if waiting for him to say something in return. Only, he couldn't remember her last comment, much less form a suitable response.

She laughed lightly. "Not that I'm stingy or anything, but I really don't think it's your shade."

"My shade?" he repeated, wondering what shade her breasts could possibly be that wouldn't suit him just fine.

"No, actually that's *my* shade," she said. "As in my shade of lipstick?"

She rose slowly to stand before him. The red suit hugged the kind of figure that had been in style back in the forties: full breasts, nipped-in waist, generous hips. Staring at that body, he wondered why fashion designers tried to convince women they should look like anorexic clothes hangers. This was what men wanted: Woman in her most powerful, elemental form.

When he continued to stare at her, she pointed to his hand. "You're holding my lipstick."

He glanced down. "So I am."

She started to reach for it. "How gallant of you to rescue it for me."

"Not so fast." He snatched the tube out of her reach. "How do I know it's yours?"

She raised a brow at such an obvious ploy, but her eyes sparkled with mischief. "Now, that is a dilemma."

"Let's see . . ." He drew the words out, enjoying the game, anything to keep her near. "I suppose I could have you describe it for me."

"All right." She tossed her head and his fingers twitched with the temptation to bury themselves deep within her fiery curls. Would her hair feel as hot as it looked? When she met his gaze head-on, her eyelids dropped to half-mast. "It's round," she said huskily. "And it's hard. And it's the color of passionate peaches."

All the blood rushed from his head right to his groin. God, what he wouldn't give to pounce on her right there in the airport. Numbly, he opened his palm and read the label on the end of the tube. Passionate Peach. "So it is," he muttered.

Her fingertips brushed his palm as she took the lipstick from him. Was that her hand trembling, or his? "I don't know how I'll ever thank you," she said.

His mind conjured up a few dozen possibilities.

With a final, knowing smile, she turned and walked away, her hips swaying to a seductive beat. He stared after her, determined to give her a salute of approval the moment she glanced back over her shoulder. But she never looked back. Even as she took her seat between two other waiting passengers, she kept her gaze averted.

He frowned, thinking it odd that such an accomplished flirt would leave it at that. Then he remembered the flutter of her hand, the heightened color of her skin. Either she'd been equally affected by their game, or she wasn't as bold as she pretended to be.

Before he could decide, the ticket agent gave first-class passengers permission to board. He started to reach for his duffel bag, but stopped when a white rectangle on the floor caught his eye. One of the business cards that had spilled from her purse still lay at his feet.

He picked up the card, hoping to learn her name, but the mug shot printed on the front proved a disappointment. The attractive blond woman who smiled back at him was not the woman he'd just met. Although returning the card would give him the perfect excuse to speak to her again. Better yet, the phone number was for the Lake Travis area, just west of

Austin, where he now lived. So, the mystery woman either lived near him, or knew someone who did.

His mind searched for the best way to return the card as he swung the duffel bag over his shoulder and headed for the ramp.

Kate pressed a palm to her stomach to still the jitters. She couldn't believe she'd dumped her purse on the man's feet like that. Not that she'd had much choice since merely dropping the purse hadn't fazed him. Oh, but once she'd gained his attention . . . Heavens, he had gorgeous eyes, and a slow sexy smile that made her insides flutter just thinking about it.

She averted her gaze to give her nerves time to settle, but from the corner of her eye, she saw the man disappear down the ramp. What was *he* doing boarding with first class? One of the main reasons she'd picked him was because he seemed so unassuming. She certainly hadn't pegged him as a man with money. Not that she had anything against money. She adored all the wonderful things it could buy. Unfortunately, wealthy, status-conscious men tended to put themselves and their work before family, which put them on her bad list—along with a lot of other men.

She frowned at that last thought, realizing that maybe Gwen was right. Maybe she had become too cynical to serve as the Dear Abby for the lovelorn on the Internet.

Memories from the meeting that morning rushed back over her. *Oh, God.* She slumped forward and buried her face in her hands. How could she possibly save her job as the expert on romance when she'd completely lost her faith in love? And what would she do if she couldn't save it? She had no other job experience. All she had were a stack of bills to pay and a seven-year-old son to feed.

"Are you quite all right, dear?" the elderly woman seated beside her asked.

"Hmm?" She lifted her head. "Yes, I'm fine. Thank you."

"Are you sure?" the woman persisted in motherly concern. "You look a bit flushed."

Kate felt her color go a shade brighter. "Really, I'm fine." More than fine, actually. Her body positively tingled with aftershocks of attraction for the man in the Hawaiian shirt.

Well, if nothing else, at least she'd remembered how it felt to flirt. And that's all the exchange had been. A passing flirtation. No need for embarrassment—even if she had let the exchange become entirely too blatant. She cringed upon remembering the phallic way she'd described her lipstick.

She was a mother, for goodness' sake. She had no business flirting with a stranger in an airport. She shuddered to think of the impression she must have given him. Her only comfort came from knowing she'd never have to see him again. At least not after she landed in Austin. In the meantime, she had to get on the plane—and with him seated in first class, that meant she'd have to walk right by him. She moaned again, and buried her face in her hands.

Mike studied the business card in his hand as he waited for the woman in red to board. On the back, he'd discovered a handwritten note.

*Kate,*
*Good luck in L.A. See you when you get*
*back.*

*Linda.*

The name on the front of the card was Linda Davis, so Kate had to be the woman carrying the card. Kate. A smile tugged at his lips. The name suited her. Kate with the saucy red hair and sweet green eyes.

Just then she appeared through the hatch and his stomach clenched. Never in his life had he felt such an instant kick of attraction to a woman. No, it was more than attraction. It was . . . a connection.

He quickly slipped the card into the breast pocket of his shirt, deciding to wait until the plane was in flight to return it. That way he could go back into the coach area and talk to her rather than simply hand it to her as she passed. Still, he wanted to catch her attention so he could once again feel the jolt that came from her smile. Only, she kept her gaze fixed firmly ahead as she walked by him.

Frowning, he turned in his seat and watched her move down the aisle, all the while willing her to look back. Instead, she took a seat halfway back, never once glancing his way. The longer he watched her, the more confused he became by her inconsistencies. Her stylish suit said Professional Businesswoman, but her tousled curls defied convention. As if sensing his gaze, she shifted nervously, not at all the confident woman who had flirted with him in the gate area. Could his instincts have been wrong about her? Maybe fate hadn't dropped a potential wife in his lap.

Just as his doubts began to rise, she turned to the young mother who sat across from her and her whole face softened with a smile at the sight of the child in the woman's arms.

There it was, the jolt from her smile that told him *she* was the answer to why he'd never married. Procrastination had nothing to do with it. He'd simply been waiting for *her*.

# Chapter 2

A falling sensation jolted Kate awake. She grabbed the armrest just as the plane's drop ended with a jarring bounce. Her heart lodged in her throat as she glanced around and saw several other passengers do the same. Beyond the windows, a streak of lightning sliced across a black sky.

When had night fallen? she wondered, looking at her watch. She barely remembered stopping in Albuquerque, and here they'd almost reached Dallas.

Her eyes went to the curtain that cut off her view to first class. *Is he still there?* The thought that the man might have left the plane at one of their stops should have filled her with relief in view of her embarrassing behavior. Oddly, though, regret stirred inside her at the prospect of never seeing him again. How strange to feel such a keen sense of loss for someone she didn't know. Or perhaps it wasn't. She knew all about the expectations, hopes, and dreams that filled one's mind upon meeting someone new. She just hadn't experienced them personally in more years than she cared to consider.

Overhead, the Fasten Seat Belt sign dinged and the flight attendants made their way down the aisle collecting cups and asking passengers to return their seats to the upright position.

"Oh, dear," the mother across from her whispered. "Do you think there's a problem?"

"I'm sure everything's fine." Kate smiled, hoping she looked more confident than she felt.

The plane took another hard bounce just as the captain's voice came over the intercom. He sounded surprisingly cheerful in contrast to the rising tension among the passengers. "Sorry about the bumpy ride, folks. Looks like we're in for a bit of turbulence as we make our final descent into DFW, compliments of that little thunderstorm you'll notice if you look out the windows to your left."

Kate glanced to her left as a blade of lightning cut through the storm clouds to the north. A stab of fear echoed in her stomach. Living in Texas all her life, she'd grown accustomed to thunderstorms—but watching one approach while twenty thousand feet in the air was a whole different matter.

"Now, before anyone gets alarmed," the captain continued, "the tower assures us we'll arrive at the airport well ahead of the storm. Unfortunately, we'll be the last plane to do so for a spell. All other flights have been canceled until further notice."

The murmurs of the passengers increased, nearly making Kate miss the rest of the captain's words.

"If the Metroplex was not your final destination, please go to the main ticket counter after you deplane to reschedule your connecting flight. On behalf of the airline, the crew and I would like to apologize for the delay in your travel and wish you a pleasant stay in Dallas."

*Pleasant stay in Dallas!* Kate gaped at the intercom. She couldn't stay in Dallas. She had a son who expected her home. And she'd promised Linda and Jim, the friends who were keeping him, that she'd only be gone one night.

All right, no need to panic, she told herself. As soon as they landed, she'd call Linda and let her know she'd be a day late. Which would put her another day behind in answering Dear Cupid e-mail. As if she weren't under enough pressure, the whole situation was going from bad to worse. In fact, it was terrible!

It was perfect. Absolutely perfect! Mike suppressed the urge to laugh as the plane descended toward the runway. Here he'd been racking his brain throughout the flight for a way to approach the woman in red—no, Kate, he reminded himself, her name had to be Kate—and now he had the perfect opportunity handed to him.

After the way she'd snubbed him while boarding, he'd nixed his first plan to go back into coach and simply introduce himself. No matter how he played that scene in his head, he never got a sense of rightness in his gut that told him "this will work." Instead, he pictured himself standing in the aisle like some idiot staring down at her with nothing to say. Or worse, blurting out something stupid like "Will you marry me?" God, what he wouldn't give for a good script-writer. Not that shyness had ever been a problem with him. He normally felt easy around women. With her, however, he felt as tongue-tied as a teenager with his first crush.

If he went back into the coach section, he'd blow it. He knew that the same way he knew when a special effect would or wouldn't work. He just *knew*. Just like he knew the woman in red was "it." His future wife. The mother of his unborn children. Or child, he amended. He was getting started a bit late in life to have more than one child. Well, two maybe, he decided as the plane touched down. Two would be good.

His second plan had been to wait until they landed in Austin, then strike up a conversation as they walked toward the baggage claim. He'd even worked part of it out in his mind. First, he'd hand her the card, then he'd mention the phone number and ask if she lived at the lake. From there, he'd figured he could wing it.

To be stranded together in Dallas, though, now that was far better than anything he could have arranged.

As the plane rolled to a stop, several passengers leapt to their feet. Overhead compartments popped open as people grabbed for briefcases and overnight bags.

"I need to call my wife," the businessman in the window seat beside him said, looking frantic at the thought. "If I don't get in tonight, she'll think the plane crashed, with me on it. You know how women are."

Mike snorted at the thought of any man claiming to know "how women are." He'd grown up with three younger sisters, and he still didn't have a clue. Tuning the man out, he reached for his duffel bag. He had to come up with a new plan before Kate came through the curtain.

"Do you suppose they'll put us up for the night?" the businessman asked. "Not at some fleabag, though, I hope."

Ignoring him, Mike craned his neck as the curtain opened, but with all the people filling the aisle, he couldn't see her. To his frustration, the flow of bodies carried him off the plane. He'd have stopped on the ramp to wait for her but the businessman, who'd been a total stranger mere moments before, seemed to have attached himself to Mike in that odd way people do in a crisis. He needed to shake the guy, and quickly. When they reached the gate area, he stepped to the right and turned to watch the departing passengers.

"What's wrong?" the man asked.

"Nothing, I, um . . ." Mike's mind raced. "Forgot something. On the plane."

"Oh?" The businessman glanced down at the duffel bag in Mike's hand.

"My sunglasses," Mike improvised. "Why don't you go on to the ticket counter, before they run out of decent hotel rooms?"

"Oh. Right." Fumbling for the cellular phone in his soft-sided briefcase, the man hurried off down the concourse.

Mike breathed a sigh of relief and turned back to the stream of departing passengers. Out of the corner of his eye, he caught a glimpse of orange hair heading in the other direction. He rose up to see over the crowd just as the throng of humanity swallowed up a shapely figure in a red suit.

Frantically he pushed his way forward, straining for some glimpse of that flame-bright hair. "Sorry! Excuse me! Pardon me!" Then he saw her, several yards up ahead.

"Kate!" he called, hoping like hell that really was her name. Her head turned and a frown creased her brow. Bingo, he thought, and raised his arm to get her attention. "Kate!"

Her gaze connected with his and her eyes widened. Color flooded her cheeks before she whirled around and increased her pace. He started after her, only to run into a small Asian woman loaded down with luggage. "Sorry," he said as he steadied her with one hand and reached for her fallen bags with the other.

The woman scalded him with a stream of Japanese

as he thrust the luggage back into her arms. He turned and jumped back as a cart cut in front of him, nearly running over his Reeboks. By the time it cleared his path, Kate had disappeared.

He took off at a jog, wondering why a woman would flirt so outrageously with him in L.A., then run from him in Dallas. And she had run, he had no doubt about that. If only he could catch her and explain . . . Explain what? That he thought he might be in love with her? Lord, he sounded like a nutcase, even to himself.

After several gates, the concourse opened up into a larger area with corridors leading off in several directions. His heart raced as he turned around, looking in every direction.

*No! She couldn't have disappeared.*

Yet, no matter how many times he turned, he saw no trace of her. She was gone. Vanished. He'd met the woman of his dreams—and lost her!

Or had he? Pulling the card from his pocket, he studied the phone number on the front. A smile settled over him. *Ah, Kate, you only thought you could get away.*

Kate peeked around the wall that hid the pay phones from the concourse and breathed a sigh of relief. She'd lost him, thank goodness. Only, why on earth had the man chased her? And how had he learned her name?! Could she have mentioned it while they were flirting? Not that it mattered. Once she was home, she could forget all about the forward way she'd acted with a total stranger.

Turning to the phones, she picked up the nearest receiver. More than anything, she wanted to be safely back in her little lakeside cabin with Dylan sleeping soundly in the loft. For tonight, though, she'd have to settle for a phone call to her son.

Tomorrow, she'd worry about getting her life in order—with or without any romance.

# Chapter 3

*Dear Cupid:*
*My boyfriend says he loves me, and that if I love him, I'll sleep with him. I've told him over and over that I do love him, desperately, but that I'm just not ready. The problem is, a lot of the girls at my school do put out. I'm so worried I'll lose him if I don't. What should I do?*

*Desperate and Worried*

*Dear Desperate and Worried,*
*You're perfectly right to say no until you're comfortable with the thought of physical intimacy. In fact, many school-age girls—and boys—share your conviction to wait. Polls show virginity is the in thing, so your classmates aren't as experienced as you might think.*

*As for your boyfriend, if he truly loves you, he'll respect your feelings and stop pushing. If he doesn't, you may need to look for a new boyfriend.*

*Cupid*

Kate reread the letter on the computer screen. The mild tone of her response to Desperate and Worried pleased her, since what she'd really wanted to tell the girl was that her boyfriend was an immature jerk who couldn't tell his heart from his hormones! She sighed at the small burst of anger. Obviously her attitude toward men still needed some work, but at least she was trying.

She saved the e-mail document to her send folder just as a knock sounded at the front door.

"I'll get it," Dylan hollered as he clambered down the ladder from the loft in the cabin's main room. A moment later, she heard her friend Linda's voice. Linda was more than a friend, she was also Kate's landlord and next-door neighbor.

Grateful for the interruption, Kate rose from the desk wedged into the corner of her bedroom and stretched her back. Though minuscule in size, the room perfectly reflected her personality. Peach pillows trimmed in gold tassels lay in a mound on the floral bedspread. The furniture ranged from Queen Anne to Louis XV and the artwork, mostly inexpensive posters bought from a craft store, depicted the works of da Vinci, Renoir, and Gainsborough. Though she'd decorated the room on a shoestring, she loved every old-fashioned inch of it.

"Hey there, big guy," Linda was saying to Dylan as Kate joined them in the room that served as living room, breakfast nook, and kitchen. "What are you doing home on a school day?"

A deep-chested cough cut off Dylan's reply.

"We had a little episode last night," Kate said by way of explanation, intentionally downplaying her son's frequent and terrifying asthma attacks.

Alarm flashed across Linda's face, but quickly vanished at Kate's warning look.

"Well, I don't know." Linda bent as far forward as her heavily pregnant body would allow. "You look pretty chipper to me, kid. You wouldn't be playing hooky, now would you?"

"Nah." Dylan giggled as Linda attacked his ribs with tickling fingers. The two made quite a picture, Kate thought, both as little as pixies, but Linda's healthy tan and blond hair contrasted sharply with her son's milk-white skin and jet-black curls. As for their laughter, the sound made her smile. Since moving to the lake, Dylan had slowly started coming out of his shell.

"Speaking of people who look chipper," Linda said to Kate as she straightened. "You're sure looking better today. Yesterday, when you picked Dylan up, you looked ready to collapse."

"I felt ready to collapse, and still do," Kate admitted as she headed for the kitchen area of the rustic fishing cabin that had been in Jim's family for years. Linda and Jim had even lived in it for the first few months of their marriage, until Jim built his bride a more suitable house up the hill. Since then, Kate had rented the cabin and been thankful for a place she could afford, no matter how small. "So, how about joining me on the deck for some iced tea?" she asked.

"As long as I can sit down to drink it." Linda sighed with one hand at the small of her back, making her pregnant stomach protrude.

"Me too," Dylan said. "I'm tired of sitting around inside."

"Hmmm, I don't know." Kate studied him. His breathing still sounded wheezy to her. She picked up the peak flow meter, which sat on the counter next to his numerous medicine bottles. The plastic tube allowed her to monitor the air flow to his lungs. "Let's see how you're doing."

With a dramatic sigh, Dylan came over and blew three times as hard as he could into the mouthpiece. Turning the tube sideways, Kate noted the final reading. "Sorry," she said, trying not to look too worried at the low number. "Not quite good enough to go outside in all those yucky pollens."

"Oh, Mom!" He slumped in disappointment. "Staying inside is boring."

"How about I let you play Goosebumps on my computer?" she offered.

His eyes brightened. "You mean it?"

"You betcha. But only while Linda and I are visiting. Then I'll need to get back to work. Okay?"

"Hot dog!" He dashed toward her bedroom with enough enthusiasm to make her laugh. Her smile faded, though, as she remembered how he'd struggled for every breath the night before.

"I never should have left him," she whispered, turning to fill two glasses with iced tea. "I know how any stress can trigger an attack."

"Ka-ate." Linda sighed in exasperation. "You're beating yourself up for nothing. He was fine while you were gone. Really."

"Are you sure?" she asked, desperate to allay her guilt.

"I swear," Linda insisted. "When I picked him up from school, you'd have thought the kid was on vacation. We stopped for burgers on the way home. Then he and Jim spent the evening in the workshop doing he-man stuff with hammers and saws."

"*Saws?*" Kate's heart dropped. They'd let a seven-year-old boy who couldn't tie his own shoes near finger-severing blades? And all that sawdust? No wonder he'd had an asthma attack.

"Would you stop it?" Linda gave her a stern look. "You keep saying you want Dylan to live a normal life, then you turn right around and try to seal him in a glass bubble."

"You're right," she said, trying to convince herself. "I just . . . worry."

"I know." Linda's look turned sympathetic. "But Dylan is going to be fine, and it's far too pretty a day to waste on worry." Taking one of the glasses, Linda led the way to the back deck.

The warm spring air flooded Kate's senses as she followed her friend outside. Sunlight dappled the stretch of land that sloped down from her cabin to the water's edge. Beneath a stand of oaks, a herd of deer munched on acorns and stripped the lower branches bare.

Settling in one of Jim's handmade wooden chairs, Linda propped her glass on her rounded belly, let her head fall against the chair back, and sighed in relief. "So, you want to tell me about your meeting with Gwen?"

Instantly deflated, Kate sank into the other chair. "She put me on probation."

"Probation?" Linda frowned.

"That's better than outright canceling my column." Kate shrugged.

"Cancel you!" A militant light flashed in Linda's eyes. "That's absurd. If not for you, Gwen wouldn't even have an on-line magazine."

Kate hid a smile at her friend's vehement reaction. They'd known each other barely three years, yet Linda was her staunchest supporter. In fact, they'd met when

Linda had written to her asking for advice on how to attract the eye of the building contractor who was remodeling the bank where she'd worked at the time. She'd claimed that every time she saw him with his mile-wide shoulders and tool belt slung low on his trim hips, her heart melted right into her knees. But if she tried to talk to him, he just stared at her as if she were an idiot.

Little had Linda known that Jim was also writing to Cupid, pleading for advice on how to ask out the pretty bank teller who looked so delicate that the mere thought of touching her with his big, callused hands scared the hell out of him.

If not for Cupid, they both claimed they never would have made it to their first date, much less gotten married. When they finally figured out the other one had been going to the same source for help, they'd laughed until their sides ached, then invited Cupid to the wedding.

Kate had been delighted by the invitation. While it wasn't the first or last she'd received, the wedding had been the closest to where she lived so she'd decided to attend. The three of them had been fast friends ever since.

"How can Gwen even think of canceling you?" Linda asked. "And after everything you've done for her. Why, you practically gave her the idea of starting the magazine."

"It's business." Kate made a valiant attempt to look as if she didn't care. In truth, the current strife between her and Gwen made her stomach hurt almost as much as it had during her divorce. Because it didn't feel like business. She and Gwen had been friends since they'd roomed together in college. "Gwen says my responses to letters have become more of a forum for male-bashing than romantic advice."

"Male-bashing!" Linda sputtered. "That's ridiculous. I've never known anyone who appreciates men more than you do."

"That may have been true, once." Kate glanced off toward the lake, fighting a sense of hopelessness. "Lately, though, I've had a hard time believing that romance ever leads to anything but heartache."

"What about Jim and me? Is that how you see us?"

"Heavens, no!" Kate turned back. "Seeing the two of you so happy together is the only thing that keeps me from losing faith completely. The problem is . . . I can't dash off pithy suggestions to women with serious problems anymore. I know the point of my column is to attract readers to Gwen's magazine, and thereby help her sell more lingerie and perfume ads, but I keep wishing it could be something . . . I don't know, more. I mean, how can I, in good conscience, tell some woman whose husband verbally abuses her to indulge in chocolate bonbons and a long, hot bubble bath? Those things won't make her problems go away."

"No," Linda agreed. "But reading your column, which is never that trite by the way, might make her believe that love does exist, and that she deserves to go after it."

"I wish I could believe that as easily as I used to."

"Well, what about the women whose only marital problem is boredom in the bedroom?" Linda raised a brow. "Let's face it, Kate, you have some very clever ways for couples to avoid that trap."

A short, bitter laugh escaped her. "Too bad I didn't take my own advice."

"Kate . . ." Linda growled.

"You're right." She held up a hand to forestall a lecture about blaming herself for her divorce. "I'm sorry."

Linda sipped thoughtfully at her tea. "Have you considered what you'll do? I mean, if Gwen really does cancel Dear Cupid?"

"I could always go back to school," Kate said, only half joking. Growing up as a professor's daughter, she'd always been more comfortable in the academic world than in the real one. Which was part of the reason she'd never had a "real" job; she'd practically made a career out of going to college. "Maybe I could major in something useful this time, like psychology."

"Psychology?" Linda laughed. "Since when is that a useful degree?"

"Well, it's more useful than the other things I've majored in, like art history or medieval poetry, especially if one wants to get a job as a counselor."

Linda waved the comment aside. "You're already a counselor of sorts."

"I meant a legitimate counselor," Kate clarified.

Linda cocked her head to study her. "You don't sound too thrilled about being a 'legitimate' counselor."

Kate realized her friend was right; she wasn't thrilled at the idea of doing anything but writing her column. Not only did it allow her to be home for Dylan, but she enjoyed hearing little snippets of people's lives, getting to know a few of them beyond that first letter, feeling that her advice had in some small way helped them find happiness. Lately, though, she'd started to feel like a fraud. What right did someone with a failed marriage have to give advice on romance to anyone?

She shook her head to dispel the sense of gloom. "I'm more worried about how I'll afford tuition if I do go back to school, not to mention little things like food and rent. I don't exactly have a plethora of job skills."

"Well . . ." Linda smiled. "There is one thing you could do."

Kate narrowed her eyes. "Linda Davis, what are you thinking?"

"That you could come to work for me."

"Absolutely not." Kate rose in a rush that startled the deer.

"Why not?" Linda asked.

"Because—" Kate paced before the rail. "It is not your responsibility to provide me with a job. Good heavens, you've given me a place to live for next to nothing and you baby-sit Dylan all the time for free. I've been a total leech since I moved out here, but I draw the line at taking your income."

"Would you quit!" Linda laughed and set her tea aside. "You won't be taking my income. Wife for Hire has generated more work than I can handle right now. And what with the baby coming, I couldn't possibly take on another account. You'd be helping me, Kate. I mean that. Truth is, I need you."

Kate studied her friend's face. She couldn't quite picture the Queen of Efficiency needing help. Still, Linda did have a baby coming. . . .

"It wouldn't have to be long-term," Linda continued, as if sensing her weakness. "You could simply try one account, see how you like it. Once I'm back up to full speed, you can quit, no hard feelings."

"What exactly would I have to do?" Kate asked warily.

"You mean, you'll take the job?"

"Maybe. But only if it doesn't involve anything remotely like bookkeeping."

The fear was legitimate, since Wife for Hire offered services that ranged from picking up dry cleaning to balancing the family checkbook. In the year since Linda had started the business, Kate had seen her walk dogs, shuttle kids to soccer practice, organize dinner parties, and decorate Christmas trees. The variety of work had a certain appeal, and Kate could easily understand why her friend preferred it to being a bank teller.

"Actually," Linda said as she pulled a slip of paper from the pocket of her maternity shorts, "I'm not sure what this job will entail. The call just came in this morning. He said he's a bachelor and, next to working moms, they make the best clients."

"Why, you little snake," Kate accused good-naturedly at the sight of the note. "You had this in mind before you even came down here, didn't you?"

"It never hurts to be prepared," Linda said primly. "Besides, the client specifically requested you."

"Me?" Kate's eyes went round.

"Apparently you recommended me to him." Linda flashed her a grin. "Nothing new there. Half the clients I've landed in the last year were referrals from you, for which I will be forever in your debt."

"Passing out a few business cards isn't exactly a strain," Kate pointed out.

"Maybe not, but when this guy called this morning and mentioned you, I said I wished I could talk you into working for me. He said he'd like to hire my service, but would prefer dealing with you since he already knew you."

"So, what's his name?"

Linda glanced at her notes. "Michael Cameron. Lives over in Lakeway," she added, referring to the affluent resort community that seemed like a separate world from the hodgepodge neighborhood where they lived.

"Michael Cameron." Kate tested the name. "Doesn't ring a bell."

"Well, he's expecting you today at one o'clock."

"Linda, I can't go today. Not with Dylan home sick."

"Hogwash. I'll watch Dylan, and it won't be any trouble at all since I plan to spend the day catching up on paperwork. I can bring my laptop down here and work. So, no excuses. Just go." She held out the note.

Taking it, Kate glanced at the address and raised a brow. Lakeway alone was exclusive enough, but this was one of the streets on which the real money lived. "Challenger Drive, eh? Pretty fancy digs for a bachelor."

"Honey, in this business, wealthy bachelors are a dream come true. So go get 'em."

# Chapter 4

*THE* moment Kate drove through the main entrance to Lakeway, nostalgia washed over her. The neighborhood reminded her so much of Barton Creek, where she and Edward had lived. Professionally landscaped lawns surrounded custom-built homes, herds of deer roamed along the golf-cart paths, and turtles sunned themselves on the banks of a picturesque pond.

But what tugged most at her heart were the basketball hoops and bicycles left in driveways. Those were the things she missed about her life with Edward, even more than the beautiful house, the designer clothes, and her spiffy red Miata. She missed the sense of safeness that came from living in an upper-class community, the feeling of raising her child in the American dream.

She'd left all that behind, though, the day she'd filed for a divorce.

Regret settled in her stomach, not for leaving Edward, but for her inability to give Dylan the kind of life he deserved. As much as she loved being Dear Cupid, the job didn't pay enough for her to raise Dylan the way she wanted.

That, however, was about to change. The more she thought about working for Linda, the more she liked the idea. After all, Wife for Hire had introduced Linda to all kinds of interesting people. Who knew what doors it might open for her? Maybe some opportunity would present itself that would enable her to become the independent, self-sufficient woman she'd always dreamed of being.

Her spirits lifted further as she topped a hill and there before her lay the wide expanse of Lake Travis. Its royal-blue water sparkled in the sunlight as its inlets stretched out among the rolling green hills. A lone sailboat drifted over the surface with the spring breeze filling its sails. Perched on the cliffs between her and the water, the million-dollar mansions of Challenger Drive offered their owners a breathtaking view. With a jumble of pastel stucco and white stone with terra-cotta tile roofs, the houses looked as if a slice of the Riviera had been dropped down in the middle of the Texas Hill Country.

Finding the address Linda had given her, Kate parked her battered Ford Escort on the street, which was level with the roof of the house. Getting out, she ran a hasty hand over her apricot silk pants suit with its epaulettes and big gold buttons and wondered if she'd overdressed. Life at the lake tended to be far more casual than her life as a society wife in Austin. Unfortunately, her clothes—like everything else—fell into two categories: BD and AD. Her BD, or Before Divorce, clothes bore names like Carol Little, Christian Dior, and Liz Claiborne. Her After Divorce clothes ran more toward Wal-Mart, Kmart, and Target.

Telling herself to stop worrying about how she looked, she started down the steep driveway, her high heels making the descent precarious. The white rock house had only one story that showed from the street. She imagined a second level and small yard climbed down the cliff at the back. And, far below that would likely be a boat dock for some outrageously expensive toy. A sailboat, she thought with envy. How lovely it must be to have the money and time to while away a whole day sailing—not to mention someone to while it away with. Someone who made her feel comfortable and good about herself.

Reaching the front door, she took a deep breath and rang the bell. Through the beveled and frosted glass, she saw someone come toward her and she pasted on a friendly smile. The door opened—and her stomach dropped to her feet at the sight of the blond man wearing a bright Hawaiian shirt. "Oh, my God!"

"We meet again." The man from L.A. grinned. He didn't seem the least surprised to see her, while her head spun with memories of her embarrassing behavior and her body heated with renewed attraction.

"What are you doing here?" she squeaked.

"I live here."

"I— What— How—" she stammered. He looked every inch as attractive as before, except the shirt sported neon shades of turquoise and yellow rather than blue and red.

"I'm glad to see you too . . ."—his grin grew as he lounged against the doorjamb—"Kate."

At the sound of her name, her breath rushed out of her lungs. "How did you find me?"

"Quite easily, actually." He pulled a card from his shirt pocket and handed it to her. "You dropped this in the airport."

As she took the card, her scattered thoughts came together with a snap. *He* was Michael Cameron. Her first client. "No. There's been some sort of mistake."

He gave her a teasing frown. "You mean you're not the woman who dropped her purse on my feet?"

"No! I mean, yes I am, but—" She pressed her

fingertips to her forehead. "Look, I apologize if I gave you the wrong impression. I'm usually not so . . ." The word "loose" came to mind, but she swallowed it down. "Forward. Now, if you'll excuse me—"

Panic kicked Mike into action the instant she turned to leave. "Wait a second." He leapt forward to block her way up the drive. "Where are you going?"

"I told you, there's been a mistake." She glared at him with the same green eyes that had teased him in L.A. "I'm not, you know . . . for hire."

"What?" He frowned in confusion, then laughed. "I don't want to hire you for *that*." She looked relieved but still nervous, and he sighed. "Why don't you come inside so we can talk?"

"I don't think so." She glanced toward her car.

"I promise, it's perfectly safe," he insisted. "And my job offer is legitimate." Well, perhaps offering her a job hadn't been his initial reason for calling the number on the card. While talking with the owner of Wife for Hire, he'd simply decided that hiring Kate was the easiest way to get to know her. After the way she'd run from him in Dallas, he feared she'd turn him down flat if he asked her for a date. As for the rest of his plan, the name of her friend's business had inspired that. "If you'll come inside, I'll tell you what I have in mind."

"No funny stuff?" She narrowed her eyes.

"Not even mildly amusing stuff. Besides," he said, "your friend Linda knows you're over here, right? So I'd have to be pretty stupid to try anything."

She mulled that over a moment, then nodded. "All right. I'll give you five minutes."

"After you." He waved an arm for her to precede him into the house. The moment she crossed the threshold, he breathed a sigh of relief. Five minutes wasn't long, but it was better than nothing. He just prayed his plan worked.

Following her down the single step from the foyer into the living area, he gave thanks that the maid service he used had come while he was in L.A. A comfortable sofa and overstuffed chair sat before a big-screen TV. To either side of the TV stood tower speakers any audiophile would sell his soul to own. At the far end of the room was the dining area, with a kitchen tucked off to one side. Or, at least, it would be the dining area if he ever got around to buying a table and some chairs. He discounted that small negative, though, since the wall of windows along the back of the house revealed an expansive deck that overlooked a swimming pool, barbecue grill, and plenty of furniture for eating one story below.

As she walked toward the windows, he fought the urge to ask her what she thought of his place. The impulse surprised him since he normally didn't care about such things. He had high hopes, though, that this woman would share his house with him, so her opinion mattered.

She barely took a second to glance around before she turned to face him. "All right. Let's hear it."

He hesitated, realizing the plan that had seemed so brilliant that morning now seemed a bit absurd. "It's kind of complicated. See, I'm, uh, looking for a wife."

Her eyes widened. Not a good sign. "Well, if you're looking at me, you're looking in the wrong direction, I'll tell you that right now."

"No, I don't want you to *be* the wife, necessarily. I, um . . . I want you to help me find a wife."

Her face went blank as if he'd wounded her, and for a moment he wondered if the straightforward approach would have been better. Except he wanted to spend time with her too badly to risk an outright rejection.

"Excuse me?" she said at last.

He took a deep breath and plunged ahead. "I've decided it's time I got married. Only, with my schedule I don't have a lot of time to look around. So, I want you to help me."

She laughed. "You're kidding, right?"

"Not at all."

"Why me? I'm no dating service."

He shrugged. "Your friend said Wife for Hire handles things like interviewing housekeepers and nannies, so I figure why not a wife?"

"Because that's not how it's done."

"Why not?"

"Because—" She spread her arms in a gesture that drew her top tightly across her breasts, distracting him. He'd thought she looked stunning in red, but the orange outfit she wore now nearly brought him to his knees. "This is not the Middle Ages, here. Nowadays, relationships are based on mutual respect, attraction, compatibility, not just personal gain and convenience. Couples generally meet, go out, fall in love, pick out china, set a date, that sort of thing."

He forced his attention back to her face. "I plan to love my wife. As for china, I'll let you—I mean *her*— pick that out."

Again, the wounded look flickered in her eyes. Then, she glanced around and muttered under her breath. "Well, I'll say this much. If anyone ever needed a wife, it's you."

"What's that supposed to mean?" He frowned.

She stared at him as if trying to decide if he was serious. "Your furniture," she said at last.

He looked around. "Yeah?"

"Well, it's not exactly— How do I put this delicately? It looks like rejects from Goodwill."

"Hey, my parents gave me that sofa when I graduated college." He tried to see the room from a woman's point of view. "All right, I'll admit, it's a little worn around the edges, but is that any reason to throw out a perfectly good sofa? It's just broken in."

"Have you ever heard of reupholstering?"

"Well, sure, but I figured if I ever got married my wife would probably want to redecorate, so why do it twice?"

She rolled her eyes. "Because—archaic as it sounds and may the feminists forgive me—few women want to marry a man who looks like he can't afford to support himself, much less a family."

"I can afford a family." He wondered where she'd gotten the idea he was broke. Did she think he'd won the house in a lottery or something? He'd made his first million writing animation software before he was twenty. Not that he'd tell her that, or she'd think he was a computer geek. "Besides, maybe I don't want a woman who'll marry me for my money."

"You're right." She held up a hand. "You're absolutely right. Unfortunately, initial attraction between the sexes is fairly superficial. A man asks a woman out because he likes the way she's built. The woman says yes because he has kind eyes and seems reasonably intelligent. Of course, a nice body and some decent clothes don't hurt."

"What, you don't like my clothes?" He looked down at his bright Hawaiian shirt and khaki pants.

"No. I like them fine." Color flooded her cheeks as her gaze traveled downward. "I'm just saying some women prefer a less rumpled package."

"I happen to like comfortable clothes," he offered reasonably.

"And there's nothing wrong with that. I mean, unless you're trying to impress someone."

"All right," he said. "As part of the job, you can pick me out some new clothes and redecorate the house."

She stared at him. "You're serious, aren't you?"

"Dead serious. If you're up to the challenge."

Her look turned wary. "And if I refuse?"

He hadn't considered that and had to scramble for a reply. "Then I wouldn't have very nice things to say about your friend's business, now would I?"

"That's blackmail!"

He shrugged, hoping she didn't call his bluff.

"Oh, all right!" she growled. "I'll take your ridiculous job, but only under protest."

"Great." Relief washed through him. "When can you start?"

"Tomorrow."

"Why not today?"

"Because I have things to do today!" she snapped as if plotting his murder had just been added to her list.

"Like what?"

"Look—" She stepped toward him, tossing her curls. "If I'm going to work for you, let's get one thing straight. My personal life is none of your business."

"Fine, I can live with that." *For now.* "Show up here first thing tomorrow and we'll get started on the Great Wife Hunt."

# Chapter 5

*HALFWAY* home, Kate pulled her Escort over onto the side of the road, dropped her forehead to the steering wheel, and waited for her insides to quit shaking. The last person she'd ever expected to see again was the man from L.A.

Oh, but heaven help her—she found him every bit as gorgeous as she had the first time.

Not that he returned that attraction, obviously. He'd come right out and said he wanted a wife, but did he even mention her as a candidate? No. Not that she blamed him. When men wanted to settle down, they did not look toward women who behaved as she had in the airport.

All right, so he wasn't interested in her, which was fine, she assured herself. She needed to concentrate on her job anyway—not a romantic involvement. Although that didn't keep his rejection from hurting.

Sitting back, she twisted her mouth in a smirk of self-disgust. She should be used to rejection after the last few years of her marriage. What she needed to do was get over that and get her life back on the positive, almost charmed course she'd enjoyed until recently.

*So, how to do that?* Tapping the steering wheel with one painted fingernail, she tried to think of what to do. It hit her all at once, the perfect solution: find

Michael Cameron a wife. What better way to prove to herself she still had what it took to be Cupid?

Although the man was going to have to pay for the threat he'd made to Linda's business. That had been a major mistake on his part. The question was, how could she accomplish both goals at once? Putting the car in gear, she contemplated ways to make him pay while she found him a wife.

The sound of car doors slamming jarred Mike from a dead sleep. He squinted against the morning light that poured through the windows facing the lake. Out on the deck, a mockingbird gave a rousing ode to spring. Somewhere beyond that cacophony, he heard the murmur of voices.

Kate.

A smile washed over him but faded abruptly at the shrill sound of the doorbell. Cringing at the noise, he fumbled on the floor for some clothes and managed to come up with a pair of shorts. He abandoned his search for a shirt when the doorbell pealed again. Dragging a hand through his hair, he padded out of the bedroom, across the living area, and up the step to the cold tile foyer.

He swung open the door, and there stood Kate, looking fresh and sexy in a bright yellow T-shirt and matching leggings. Morning sun sparked off the splashes of gold and silver paint across the front of the shirt.

"I'm sorry, did I wake you?" she said, eyeing him from head to toe.

"No, not at all." He yawned through the lie.

"You did say to come first thing this morning."

"Is it morning already?" He squinted past her toward the wide expanse of sky so blue the color stung. "So it is."

From the corner of his eye, he saw her gaze drift to his bare chest, linger a moment, then jerk away. He had to hide a smile at seeing that Kate wasn't as disinterested as she claimed.

"Wild night, I take it?" she asked.

He thought of explaining that he'd been working at his computer until four A.M., but scratched his chest and stretched a bit instead, just enough to flex his muscles. "Guess I can't keep up with the dancing girls the way I used to."

"Cute." She smirked. "Now, are you ready to get started or not?"

"By all means," he answered absently as his gaze lifted to the pickup truck parked at the top of his drive. "What'd you do, bring a bodyguard?"

"A building contractor," she explained with a suspiciously sweet smile. Behind her, a large, dark-haired man ambled down the drive, fastening a tool belt about his hips. "Jim, meet Michael Cameron. Michael Cameron, Jim Davis, my friend Linda's husband." She gave him a pointed look that silently added the words: *As in the Linda whose business you're so eager to destroy.*

"Call me Mike." He offered his hand in greeting as he summed the other man up in a glance. Jim Davis had a strong handshake, the body of a linebacker, and a directness in his gaze Mike liked right off the bat.

"Now," Kate said as she marched past Mike into the house. "I believe we'll start in here."

With a shrug, Jim followed the little general with the coppery curls across the living area. Feeling the first prickle of concern, Mike did the same.

"Last night, I was thinking about your house and I decided this wall really needs to go," Kate said, motioning toward the high-ceilinged wall that divided the dining area from the kitchen. "It closes the kitchen off too much and completely ruins the view of the lake for whoever's cooking."

Jim pulled a pad and pencil from his tool belt and began taking notes.

"Of course," Kate continued as she moved around the wall, "we'll have to redesign the kitchen, as well. Turn these cabinets into a breakfast bar. Maybe create an island in the center of the room."

"Excuse me," Mike ventured. "What are you doing?"

She turned to face him, looking entirely too pleased with herself. "Getting your house ready for a wife. Surely you don't expect the woman you intend to love for the rest of your life to cook in this place, do you?"

He looked around the perfectly adequate kitchen. "You're absolutely right. I don't know what I was thinking."

She seemed a bit disappointed at his easy acquiescence, but nodded in satisfaction. "Good. I'm glad to see I won't have to drag you along kicking and screaming."

He studied her as his brain slowly cleared of sleep enough to function. "Just one question, Kate. How much do you plan to make me pay?"

"Oh." She feigned innocence. "Is money a problem?"

"I'm not talking about money. I'm talking about the fact that you didn't seem too happy with me when you left yesterday and I'm wondering how much you plan to make me pay for whatever I did to upset you."

She had the grace to blush. Then, to his surprise,

mischief sparkled in her eyes. Her body moved subtly into a seductive stance that made his sleepy pulse hum. Even in the baggy T-shirt, he figured she could have a man whimpering in two seconds flat.

"That is the timeless question, now isn't it?" she purred. "How much is a man willing to pay to gain a wife? What about you, Mike?" She leaned toward him and her fresh, spicy scent reached inside his gut and pulled hard. "How much are you willing to pay?"

His gaze dropped to her breasts. A good question, he realized, but not one he cared to contemplate on an empty stomach. "If you'll excuse me, I think I'll scrounge some breakfast from my obviously deplorable kitchen while you two rearrange the walls."

Kate felt a little twinge of guilt as he moved past her. Jim's censorious look didn't exactly help. She stiffened her back, determined to see her plan through. "And new cabinet fronts," she decided. "Glass, I think. Definitely glass."

"No glass," Mike said as he pulled down a box of cereal and opened the refrigerator.

"Glass is very trendy," she pointed out. "It'll go with the open, airy look we want."

"No glass." Mike turned toward her with a gallon of milk in one hand and a box of Froot Loops in the other. "If you tear out that wall, then anyone sitting in the main room will be able to see straight into the kitchen. I don't want people sitting on my sofa discussing my groceries."

She glanced at the open cabinet behind him and struggled not to laugh. The shelves held a jumble of crumpled-up potato chip bags, boxes of Little Debbie snacks, and a few cans of soup. "I can see where that might be a problem. After you have a wife, though, your shelves won't be such an embarrassment."

Slowly, he set the milk down and opened his mouth to make some reply. The phone rang, cutting him short. He hesitated a moment, then snapped up the cordless handset. "Mike's Magic Shop."

She raised a brow. *Mike's Magic Shop?* Now that was interesting. Nearly as interesting as the view he presented. His bare chest, with its well-defined muscles and light sprinkling of blond hair, certainly could do things to a woman's bloodstream.

"Actually, I came up with an idea last night, but we'll have to coordinate it with makeup," Mike said, balancing the phone against his shoulder as he poured milk into his bowl. "I'd like to see the skin come off in stages rather than going straight from live action to the animated robot."

Kate tried to ignore him as he turned his back to dig in a drawer for a spoon. He had a very nice back, with smooth, golden skin over well-honed muscles. The man must do nothing but work out at the gym and lie around the swimming pool all day to get a body like that.

"Hang on. I've got some notes downstairs." He turned to her and whispered, "I'll be right back," then spoke once more into the phone. "Who did you say was doing makeup on this one?"

She scowled as Mike took his cereal and left the room, talking about fireballs, peeling skin, and soot-covered robots.

"Now why is it," Jim said in his slow, West Texas drawl, "I get the feeling this Mike fella ain't exactly thrilled with this here remodeling project?"

"Don't be silly." Kate waved a hand through the air. "He's dying to have his house remodeled. Why else do you think he hired me?" She tried not to fidget while Jim studied her. Hopefully her knack for decorating would weigh in her favor.

"I don't know . . ." he mumbled, shaking his head.

"Trust me, Jim, everything will be fine." Although maybe she should make Mike pay for the remodeling up front, just in case the second half of her plan—the actual matchmaking part—didn't go too well. When Jim continued to look doubtful, she searched for a way to reassure him. "Do you remember when you and Linda were dating and you asked for advice?"

"Yeah." Color crept up Jim's neck even as he smiled.

"When I told you to stop being so polite and just toss Linda over your shoulder and carry her off to bed, you trusted me enough to do it, right?"

"Scariest damned thing I ever did."

"But it worked, didn't it?"

"Yeah." His neck got redder. "Of course, you knew all along that's what Linda wanted me to do."

"Not exactly," she admitted. Her suggestion had been an educated guess, but then what woman wouldn't want some big, sweet guy like Jim to toss her over his brawny shoulder and play a little caveman? "I'm just good at guessing what attracts people to each other. Which is why I've made a career of advising people in such matters. This situation is no different, except that Mike came to me in person for advice on how to catch a wife."

"Oh, yeah?" Jim looked intrigued. "Smart guy."

"Maybe."

"One thing, though." Jim's frown returned. "How will remodeling a kitchen help him catch a wife?"

"It just will," she said with more conviction than she felt. Truth was, she'd come up with the remodeling project as a form of poetic justice for Mike threatening Linda's business, since paying Jim would indirectly pay Linda as well. Although having a fabulous, newly remodeled and redecorated house certainly wouldn't hurt his marriage potential.

"It's not that I doubt you when it comes to giving advice on dating," Jim said. "I just don't get how the two things relate."

"Jim, I'm telling you, this situation between me and Mike is no different than when you and Linda were dating."

He studied her a moment before his face lit up. "Oh," he said, glancing toward the stairs and back again. "You mean, you and he . . . Oh."

"No!" She held up a hand at the conclusion Jim had drawn. God, how embarrassed she'd be if anyone learned she found a man attractive only to learn he couldn't care less about her. "I didn't mean that at all. I meant, you just have to trust me."

"Uh-huh." He grinned. "I get it. And here Linda didn't even tell me you were dating. 'Bout time too."

"I'm not dating him," she said in desperation. "I'm not."

"Are you saying Linda doesn't know?"

"I'm saying there's nothing to know."

He winked at her. "Don't worry, I can keep a secret. If you don't want Linda to know yet, she won't hear it from me." Turning, he gestured toward the wall. "So, how much of this thing do you want me to take out?"

Kate opened her mouth to make further denials but closed it in defeat. Once Jim got an idea in his bull head, she knew arguing was futile.

So, instead, she turned her attention to the remodeling project. For a spur-of-the-moment idea, opening up the kitchen had definite merit, she decided as Jim gathered enough measurements to work up a bid.

"So," she asked a few moments later, "how long do you think a project like this will take?"

"Shoot, once I get a crew over here, we can knock this puppy out in six or seven days."

"Good." She nodded, silently praying he meant six or seven *consecutive* days, not one day a week for six or seven weeks, like he'd taken to repair the back deck of the cabin.

"Well, that ought to do it," Jim said, putting away his tape measure and notepad. They both looked around for signs of Mike.

"You go on," Kate said. "I know you have a crew working over by the golf course. I'll stay and wrap things up here."

"Uh-huh." Jim's grin held a wealth of sexual innuendo. "I can take a hint. Just one thing," he added as she walked him to the front door.

"What?" she asked warily.

He glanced toward the stairs and lowered his voice. "Go easy on him, Kate. I mean, this dating stuff is hard enough on a guy without you women pouring on the torture."

"Jim," she said with supreme patience, "I am not dating this man."

"Right." With a chuckle, he ambled off.

*"Arrgh!"* she growled in frustration and all but slammed the door.

Pacing the living room, she waited for Mike to come upstairs so she could go over the rest of her plans. At the opposite end of the house from the kitchen, she caught a glimpse of the master suite. The spacious bedroom offered a stunning view of the lake, and had its own access to the deck and pool below.

The furniture, however, left much to be desired. A king-sized water bed, chest of drawers, and single chair were all she saw in her one brief glance. A vision of Mike lying naked in the middle of the water bed sprang a little too easily to mind, so she turned away and resumed her pacing.

Ten minutes passed. *He does plan to come back upstairs, doesn't he?* She paced for another five minutes, feeling more dejected by the moment. After all, she knew she wasn't as attractive and exciting as she once had been, but was she this completely forgettable? *Maybe I should go looking for him.*

Not at all comfortable snooping through his house, she headed gingerly down the stairs. Before she reached the bottom, she caught the clicking sound of a computer keyboard. It was a familiar, comforting sound—one that often kept her company during the long hours of the night when she worked on her column or answered the endless flood of e-mail she received. She smiled, wondering what Mike would think if he ever found out he'd hired Cupid to help him find a wife—not that she planned to tell him. Her rocky job situation was none of his business.

On the bottom floor, she discovered a hall leading to two bedrooms. One was empty, but the other held a jumble of weight-lifting equipment. Closer to the stairs was a large, open room. The wall of glass revealed the back patio with its glistening swimming pool, barbecue grill, and neglected flower beds. But the room itself was what drew her attention. It was the only room in the house that didn't look Spartan. In fact, it looked very lived-in, like a big boy's dream room. Mobiles of spaceships dangled from the ceiling, while posters from *Star Wars, Back to the Future,* and

*Jurassic Park* covered the walls. Built-in shelves held an array of detailed models, awards, and books on animation.

She stared about her, remembering the conversation she'd just overheard. All of her assumptions about Mike being a lazy but rich beach bum slowly vanished as she realized he was in fact a special effects artist. A special effects artist who obviously loved what he did enough to ignore the rest of his house, and probably his life.

The clicking of keys started again, making her turn. She found Mike hunched over a computer keyboard. Not that she could see the keyboard for all the papers and books, videotapes, and computer disks piled on the desk and spilling onto the floor. To his side sat a drafting table with pencil drawings scattered across its surface. More drawings hung from thumbtacks in the wall, creating a cartoon storyboard. Oblivious to the clutter, Mike stared at the glowing screen as if in a trance.

Kate's temper, always quick to spark, ignited. "What are you doing?"

Mike jumped so hard he knocked his cereal bowl off the desk. The remnants of Froot Loops and milk spilled over a stack of notes. Cursing, he grabbed a T-shirt from the back of his chair to sop up the pastel-colored milk. "*Jeez,* you could warn a guy when you come into a room."

"Well, excuse me," she tossed back sarcastically.

"Oh, man." Mike lifted the once-white T-shirt, which he'd won from his favorite radio station for knowing the answer to the morning movie trivia, and stared at it in disgust. And people wondered why he wore so many Hawaiian shirts. At least with them, stains didn't show. Even if he accidentally washed one with something red, who could tell? "I loved this shirt," he moaned.

"Do you realize I've been waiting for you upstairs for half an hour?"

Confused by the whip crack in her voice, he glanced at the clock readout on his computer screen and wanted to kick himself. "Oh, Kate, I'm sorry. Really. I meant to come right back upstairs, but I needed to get this one fax off and—"

"S-sorry!" she stuttered, as if trying to come up with something scathing to say. As words failed her, color flooded her cheeks and fire sparked in her eyes.

"I guess I got sidetracked," he offered with a sheepish grin.

Her eyes narrowed. "Has it occurred to you that *this*"—she flung a hand toward the room at large— "might be the reason you aren't married?"

The comment confused him enough that he glanced about the room, trying to see it through her eyes. Most of it looked fine to him, except for the work area, which was admittedly its usual mess. "You mean because I'm a slob?"

"No! Because you're already married—to your work!"

"Oh, that." He breathed a sigh of relief that she hadn't said anything about remodeling his workroom. There were, after all, certain lines a man simply could not be expected to cross. And a workroom was sacred ground.

"If you're serious about wanting to get married," she said, "the first thing you have to learn is that some sacrifices have to be made. When a husband continually puts his career first, how can he expect his marriage to last? Nothing can survive that kind of neglect."

"I realize that," he ventured cautiously. "But, has it occurred to you that working hard is one of the ways a man shows his family he loves them?"

"God, I hate that excuse!" She balled her fists. "And that's all it is. When a man works eighty hours a week, it doesn't make his wife feel loved. It makes her feel ignored. And you!" She jabbed a finger toward him. "Are the worst. You're not even married yet, and you're already putting your work before your wife. Or did you think I could do this on my own? Just go out and hit some poor, unsuspecting woman over the head, drag her back here, and install her in your bedroom and kitchen while you stayed down here happily playing with your computer?"

"Whoa. Wait a second." He held up his hands. "I have no intention of neglecting my wife."

"Oh, yeah? Prove it."

"Excuse me?"

"Prove it," she repeated. "Right now. Turn off the computer and spend one day, one whole day, without doing any work."

He thought of the sketches he'd just promised to fax the director for the futuristic robot he'd been hired to create. A year didn't seem long enough to pull off the project, yet he only had three months remaining before the film went into final editing. All of the groundwork had been done, the major decisions made, but the actual animation process had barely begun.

One look at Kate's face, though, and he knew that if he said no, he'd lose any chance he had with her. His choice was that simple—pleasing Kate or getting the sketches faxed on time.

"All right," he said slowly, telling himself that one day wouldn't make that much difference. He could make up one day. Cringing, he hit the keys to save and close the file. Then he picked up the phone and called the director's mobile line. "Hey, Stan, this is Mike. About those sketches—I'd like to play with them a bit more and fax them to you tomorrow."

"Is there a problem?" Stan Kelly asked, then hollered at a key grip to move a boom stage left, not stage right. In the background, Mike could hear the special blend of noise unique to a Hollywood soundstage. Hammers banged while crew members shouted and actors ran through their lines.

"No problem," Mike said when Stan came back on the line. "I'd just like to smooth out a few rough edges." As he spoke, he glanced at Kate and noticed her wide-eyed look of disbelief. "I'll be sure and get them off to you first thing in the morning."

"Fine. I'll tell the art department to expect them tomorrow." Before the line went dead, Stan resumed yelling at the key grip.

Mike exhaled sharply as he set down the cordless phone. The idea of taking a day off left him feeling a bit lost. He glanced at Kate. "Well, I'm yours for the day. What are you going to do with me?"

She blinked once, then her face lit with a grin. "Shopping."

"Shopping?" He tried not to grimace. "So soon?"

"Absolutely. By the end of today, we'll have a whole new you."

Personally, he didn't see what was wrong with the old him.

# Chapter 6

$\mathcal{I}$ will not buy that shirt."

"Mike," Kate exhaled in exasperation. "There is nothing wrong with this shirt." Holding it against his chest, she could see it would fit him perfectly, even if the lack of color did make him look a bit bland. Still . . . "Every man needs at least one white dress shirt."

"Why?"

"Because—" She gritted her teeth, resisting the urge to strangle him. And here she'd thought Jim was stubborn? "Dress shirts can be very sexy. They convey an image of power, success, confidence."

"In other words, a man isn't successful unless he stuffs himself into a monkey suit?"

She took a slow, deep breath, then wished she hadn't as the masculine scent of his soap and skin filled her senses. He'd showered and changed into a short-sleeve shirt and navy slacks before they left his house. While the shirt wasn't precisely Hawaiian in style, it was a long way from conservative. She had to admit, though, the man looked great in bold colors. Unfortunately, she'd always had a weakness for the bold and dramatic. And the fact that they'd driven to the mall in his vintage orange Corvette hadn't done anything to discourage her libido.

She forced her mind back to the issue at hand. "You

hired me to market you as husband material. It doesn't take a genius to know that the first step in selling a product is to give it an enticing package."

"You're saying women find stuffed shirts enticing?" He looked baffled at the thought. He also looked completely out of place surrounded by walls of conservative gray suits.

"I'm saying that women are subconsciously attracted to power. Not a pleasant statement, but a true one."

"Power meaning money." He smirked.

"Sometimes, yes, but not always. For some women, power can come from intelligence or physical prowess or even artistic talent. Trust me on this one, I'm something of an expert."

"Part of your training as a Wife for Hire?" He gave her a teasing wink.

She shook her head. "Actually, one of my many majors in college was anthropology, so I'm basing this on what humans instinctually look for in a mate."

"What about you?" He leaned closer. "What kind of power attracts you to a mate?"

She flattened her hand against his chest to hold him off. A mistake, she realized, since his hard muscles felt entirely too good beneath her palm. "We're not talking about me. We're talking about women in general."

"I'm asking you, though." He covered her hand with his. The touch sent tingles down her arm. "What do you look for in a man, Kate?"

"Dependability." She jerked her hand away. "Maturity. Honesty. Affection. A sense of humor. And most of all, a man who values family." With angry jerks, she refolded the dress shirt and stuffed it back in the display case. "Which is why it really irritates me when men spout nonsense like you did earlier, about working hard being a man's way of showing his family he loves them."

He cocked his head to the side. "Let me ask you something. If you dislike workaholics so much, why are you trying to dress me up like a corporate monkey?"

"Because we're not talking about my likes and dislikes. We're talking about women in general. And— Where are you going?" She scowled as he turned and walked away from her.

When he refused to answer, she hurried after him through the mahogany tables stacked with sale items, down the polished marble aisle of the department store, and into the sportswear department.

"What are you doing?" she asked as he began riffling through a circular rack of brightly colored, long-sleeve shirts.

"Shopping." He pulled first one shirt then another off the rack until he held a fistful of hangers. "Isn't that what we came here to do?"

"Yes, but—" She broke off as a salesman rushed over.

"May I help you, sir?" the clerk asked a bit frantically as he watched Mike all but strip the rack of size-large shirts.

"Yeah." Mike dumped the whole load into the man's arms. "I'll take these."

"I— I'll put them in the dressing room." The salesman staggered slightly under the weight.

"No, that's okay, just ring them up." Mike moved to the shelves of casual slacks.

"Yes, sir!" The clerk beamed in the face of such a straightforward, take-no-prisoners approach to shopping.

Kate ground her teeth as the salesman trotted off. "I thought you agreed to let me pick out your new look."

"I said you could help me pick out some new clothes," Mike answered. "Not turn me into something I'm not."

"I'm not trying to turn you into anything," she insisted. Personally, she thought he looked darn near perfect the way he was, but she wasn't the potential wife they were trying to please. "I'm just sprucing up the package."

"Kate." He turned to face her, his eyes so direct, she squirmed. "I can think of only two times in my life when I've worn a white dress shirt. Both times were for weddings, and, quite frankly, if they hadn't been my sisters' weddings, I doubt I'd have worn them then."

"Well, dressing for a wife hunt is sort of like dressing for a wedding," she offered. Although she had to admit bright colors brought out the richness of his tan and the blond streaks in his hair.

"It's still false advertising," Mike said, pulling two pairs of slacks off the shelf. "I have no intention of lying to my wife, before or after the wedding. Now which of these pants do you like?"

Even at a glance, she could tell he'd picked one size too big. She turned to the shelves. "Try these."

"You sure?" He took the pants from her. "They look a bit small."

"Trust me, Mike. On this one thing, just trust me."

Putting the others back, he unfolded the pair she'd selected and held them to his waist. A mouth-watering image sprang to her mind of exactly how delicious he'd look wearing clothes that fit. She quickly turned away. "Okay. I don't suppose you'd consider a few ties to dress up those loud shirts you just bought?"

"Actually, I like ties. But I get to pick them out." He motioned to the salesman to come get the five pairs of pants he'd chosen, all of them in the size Kate had suggested.

"You know," she said, "I never would have pegged you as a clotheshorse."

"I'm not." He grabbed three more pairs of pants and handed them to the clerk. "I just don't see any reason to waste a lot of time on something that is basically cut-and-dried. I mean, who in their right mind wants to spend a whole day at the mall combing through every shop when you can walk into one good department store, get what you came for, and be done for the next five years?"

Kate rolled her eyes at such sacrilege. "Come on, we'll pick the ties out together while we discuss a game plan."

"Game plan?" he asked as she hooked her arm through his and dragged him back into the aisle.

"For finding you a date. Last time I checked, dating is the first step toward marriage." Reaching the lit cases of ties, she selected a conservative stripe. "I don't suppose you'd consider a dating service."

"About as much as I'd consider buying that tie." He shuddered.

"All right, no dating service." She held on to the tie and looked for another one along the same vein. "I guess we'll have to use the traditional approach."

"Which is?" he asked as he perused a section of psychedelic silks.

"Work, church, social gatherings."

He stopped his search long enough to glance at her. "I thought dating coworkers was considered politically incorrect."

"Only if it doesn't work out. And even then, it can be acceptable as long as you observe a few basic rules."

"What rules?"

"You pick someone who works *with* you, not *for* you, although they shouldn't work too closely to you, like in the same department. And you need to keep the initial flirtation very light and nonthreatening so the work environment won't become awkward if they're not interested. So, umm . . ."—she gave the selection before her undue attention—"are you interested in anyone you work with?"

"Hard to say since I've just started a new project."

"Project?"

"Movie project," he clarified. "So far, everyone I've met on this film is either married or male—not exactly my type on either score."

"Well, that's good to hear," she said, glad to learn he respected marriage vows. As for the other, she'd never thought for a moment he was anything other than a one-hundred-percent heterosexual male.

"How about this one?" He held up a tie-dye pattern so wild her head spun.

"Honestly?" She laughed, because the tie suited him so well. "I think it's great, but most women would take one look at that tie and run the other way." She sighed when he kept the tie and reached for one with flaming chili peppers. "Tell me about the people you've worked with on past movies. Have you been drawn to anyone in particular?"

He considered the question a moment, then shrugged. "Not in particular, really."

"I take it that means you've dated several coworkers." She felt her hackles rise.

"I'm not sure I'd even call it dating—exactly."

"And what 'exactly' would you call it?"

"You have to understand"—he turned toward her—"making a movie is sort of like joining a family. The crew becomes very close for the time they're thrown together, then they move on to the next project, sometimes together, sometimes not. There isn't a lot of time for anything as formal as dating in the middle of all that organized chaos."

"Not a lot of time for dating? Great!" She waved a hand through the air, fluttering ties. "That's just great! And since you're in the middle of a film right now, when exactly did you plan to squeeze in time to find a wife?"

"Kate . . ." He caught her hand and held it still. Her heart leapt as she stared up at him. All amusement had fled from his eyes. "One of the reasons I want a wife is because I need someone to do what you did this morning—pull my nose away from the computer and remind me there is a whole world out here that has nothing to do with the movie industry." His thumb moved over the inside of her wrist, making her pulse jump. "As much as I enjoy what I do, I want more in my life than that. I need more."

Staring up at him, she wondered if she'd been wrong; maybe he was interested in her. While the thought made her heart race, it also sent fear swelling up into her throat. She felt as if she were standing on the edge of a cliff with the wind trying to lift her off the ground. How easy it would be to leap forward with her arms spread just to see if she could fly. And how painful it would be to learn that she couldn't.

Stepping back, she eased her wrist free. "Yes, well . . . considering how much you enjoy your work, I think your best bet would be to marry someone else in the movie industry."

He looked ready to argue, then shrugged. "If that's what you think."

"When will you meet the rest of the crew?"

"This Saturday. Some of the cast and crew are flying in from L.A. to start the location shooting. The alliance is hosting a big Welcome to Texas bash out at the Lakeview Inn, where the crew will be living for the next month."

"The alliance?"

"The Austin Movie Alliance," he explained. "It's a group of local actors, producers, scriptwriters, and old crew dogs that meet every month to figure out ways to promote the film industry in Texas."

"Sounds like a fun group."

"They are. And before you even ask, the answer is no, I'm not dating, sleeping with, or interested in anyone in the alliance."

"Too bad." She frowned at her own sense of relief. "Although the party sounds like the perfect opportunity for you to scope out a potential victim—I mean wife."

"Cute," he said with a smirk, then his eyes lit on something behind her. "Now this is what I call a tie!"

She tried to move away when he reached behind her, but found herself trapped between him and the counter. His nearness engulfed her, bringing her senses to life.

"What do you think?" he asked, holding the tie to his chest.

Willing her heart to quit pounding, she stared at the tie. It suited him so perfectly, he'd be downright irresistible wearing it. "You absolutely cannot buy that tie."

"What's wrong with it?"

"It's a Tasmanian Devil tie."

"Yeah, isn't it great?" Grinning, he held out the end to study it upside down. With his head tipped to the side, she noticed his hair was blonder at the ends, and needed trimming. She curled her fingers against the temptation to run them through his hair. "This is the perfect tie to wear when we go to the alliance party."

"We?" She blinked. "What do you mean we? I'm not going."

"Of course you are." He gathered up the ties he'd picked, ignored hers completely, and motioned for the clerk, who had followed them from sportswear. "You don't even trust me to pick out my own clothes, so surely you don't trust me to pick up a date at a party by myself."

"Good point, but since you don't take my advice, it's not exactly a valid one, now is it?"

"Hey, I bought the size pants you suggested."

"I'm still not going."

"Why not?" he asked with that directness to his gaze that unsettled her.

"Don't you think taking a date on a wife hunt would sort of hamper your style?"

"You wouldn't be my date, precisely. You'd just be, well, tagging along as my . . . consultant. You know, in case I get tongue-tied and need a coach."

"Consultant?" She fought the urge to laugh. The man oozed confidence. No one could possibly need a dating coach less. "Come on, Mike, you're a big boy. I think you can handle an evening of mingling and flirting all by your lonesome."

"Scared?" He cocked a brow in challenge.

"Of you?" she scoffed. "Hardly."

"Then come with me."

She hesitated, far too tempted by his offer.

A smile tugged up the corners of his mouth, making him look boyish and sexy. "Come on, you'll have fun."

*Fun.* The word pricked a hole in her resolve. She couldn't remember the last time she'd done something just for *fun.* "Oh, all right. I'll go. But only if you understand I'm not your date."

"Certainly not. Now, how about something to eat? My treat."

"On one condition." She narrowed her eyes. "I get to pick the restaurant."

"Fair enough." He shrugged, then seemed to have second thoughts. "As long as it's not one of those pretentious places that puts weeds on a plate and calls it a salad."

"I thought you California types liked sprouts and field greens."

"Scurrilous lies and vicious slander."

She laughed. "In that case, you're going to love this place."

# Chapter 7

*You're* right, I love it," Mike said over the din of noise the minute they stepped into Paddy's Pub. Dark paneling and a green coffered ceiling gave the place the feel of an old Irish pub; a long, mirror-backed bar took up most of the back wall.

As Kate led the way between the crowded tables, she greeted several waiters and customers by name. The woman operating the gleaming brass beer fountain looked up and smiled.

"Kate!" the woman called, then laughed when she sloshed beer down the front of her Paddy's Pub T-shirt. "Hang on, I'll be right with you."

"Take your time," Kate called back and motioned toward an empty booth in the corner. "We came for lunch."

"I take it you come here often," Mike said as they slid into the corner booth upholstered in a faded cabbage-rose brocade. A stained-glass window beside them illuminated the scarred, wooden table.

"I have to. My cousin Mary Pat is the owner." She nodded toward the woman behind the bar.

"Well, your cousin has a great place." He looked around at the coat of arms over the unlit fireplace, the posters of Ireland, and pictures of people in famous locales around the world wearing Paddy's Pub T-shirts. If he didn't know they were in Texas, he'd swear they were in some neighborhood bar in Dublin. "Very authentic."

"It ought to be," Kate said with pride. "Most of it comes straight from London—paneling, bar, and all."

"London?" He raised a brow. "I would have guessed Ireland."

"My mother and uncle grew up in Ireland, but they both moved to London when they were in their early twenties."

His curiosity perked up at the mention of her family. "Oh? What took them to London?"

"Well now," she said, taking on an Irish brogue, "Uncle Paddy would be having a bit of wanderlust, wouldn't you know? And me ma, dear young lass that she was, fancied a better selection of suitors for herself than the lads back home."

He stared at her, enchanted. She was so fresh and animated when she let her guard down; and he realized this was the first time she truly had around him. "Is that where your parents met? London?"

"Yep," she said. "My father's a professor of medieval history at UT. He meet Mom while he was in England working on his doctoral thesis."

"When was that?"

She cocked her head sideways. "Are you really interested in all this?"

*I'm interested in everything about you,* he longed to say. *Every single detail from the day you cut your first tooth to the name of every boy whose heart you broke. I want to know your favorite food, what music you like, and how I can make you scream with pleasure in bed. Most of all, I want to know who put that wary look in your eyes and what I can do to take it away.*

He shrugged as he took a menu from between the bottles of malted vinegar and Tabasco sauce. "I figure, as long as we'll be working together, we might as well get to know each other."

"Makes sense." She shrugged. "Although I think it's more important for me to get to know you than the other way around, if I'm going to help you pick out the perfect wife."

"All right," he agreed amiably. "What do you want to know?"

"Tell me about this movie you're working on?"

"Ooo, dangerous topic." He leaned back with his palms flat on the table.

"Why's that?"

He narrowed his eyes. "First you tell me you don't like men who are compulsive workaholics. Then you ask me the one question that is sure to keep me talking about my job for hours, bore you to tears, and convince you I'm a total lost cause."

Her laugh surprised him. "Then I'd say it's the perfect topic, since I'm trying my best not to like you."

"Why's that?"

"No reason." She withdrew, her eyes haunted by old hurts.

Cocking his head, he tried to tease her back to him with a smile. "Is it working?"

"Maybe," she said with a reluctant grin that told him she liked him in spite of her efforts not to. But then, he already knew that. He could feel it in the electricity that arched between them each time their eyes met. "So are you going to tell me about your movie project or not?"

"That depends. Are you asking about the movie, or the project?"

"Is there a difference?"

"A huge difference," he said. "The movie is just what people see up on the screen. The real story is what goes on behind the scenes. Most people have no idea how many hours of work go into every minute of film footage."

"And what is your part of the production?"

"The best part." Enthusiasm shot through him as it always did when he talked about his work. "The movie is titled *The Seekers*. It's a sci-fi Western, sort of a *Terminator* meets the Wild West."

"*Terminator* meets the Wild West?" She laughed.

"Yeah." He leaned forward, folding his forearms on the table. "See, the seekers are these robots from the future that come back in time and kidnap women to help repopulate the planet. The main character is a woman from the present who is taken forward in time, then she escapes and tries to return home. Only, she overshoots her own time period, and winds up back in the Old West, where she meets up with the owner of a Wild West show."

"Does the robot go after her?"

"Of course." He smiled. "There won't be a smash hit without lots of danger and suspense, not to mention a few hair-raising chase scenes, some mind-blowing explosions, and a few million dollars' worth of special effects. And that is where I come in."

"You create the special effects, right?"

"Not all of them. They have whole teams of people working together on this flick." He rocked forward on his elbows and lowered his voice as if relaying a secret. "I, however, get to create the robot."

"Really?" She raised her brows playfully, but the interest in her eyes looked genuine. "That is impressive."

"Yeah." He held her gaze, enjoying the way he felt

simply sitting with her like this, talking. If only he could lift a hand and run a fingertip lightly over her cheek. Her smile faded slowly as if she read his mind. Rather than turn away, she went very still and her breathing turned shallow. Tension coiled deep in his belly. He opened his mouth to speak, not sure what he meant to say. "Kate, I—"

"Hey there, stranger," someone said from behind him, breaking the moment.

"Mary Pat!" Kate jumped, then rose with a nervous laugh to embrace her cousin.

Stifling his frustration, Mike stood as well to greet the bar owner. Though taller and slimmer than Kate, she had the same copper-bright hair, which she wore in a short, spiky style around features that reminded him of an inquisitive fox.

"How've you been?" Kate asked.

"Busy, as always," Mary Pat sighed. "About time you came by, though. I never see you since you moved out to the lake."

"Oh, pa-lease." Kate jokingly rolled her eyes. "You sound like Mom and Dad. Besides, it's not like the road only goes one way. You could always come see me."

"If only I had the time." Mary Pat glanced toward Mike and her eyes twinkled with curiosity. "So, are you going to introduce me?"

"Sure." Kate turned to Mike. "This is Mike Cameron."

"Cameron," Mary Pat said as she offered her hand. "A good Gaelic name if ever I heard one."

"As Scottish as they come." Mike winked as he shook her hand. "Though the blood's thinned a bit since my grandfather sailed out of Glasgow as a deckhand on a cargo ship."

"Oh, and a sailor too." Mary Pat looked delighted at that.

"Mary Pat." Kate laughed. "We're here to eat, not watch you drool."

"Too bad." Mary Pat grinned. "Although the special today is bangers 'n' mash. You like pub grub, Mike?"

"Absolutely," he answered.

"How about ale?" She narrowed her eyes in a way that reminded him very much of Kate.

"Are you kidding?" He grinned to let her know the answer was yes.

"Well, all right then. Have a seat." She hollered their order toward the kitchen, then turned back. "You two enjoy your lunch. I've got to get back to work. And Kate, next time you drop by, bring that handsome man of yours, Dylan. I haven't seen him in a gnat's age."

*Dylan?* Mike's mind stumbled over the name. *Who the hell is Dylan?* "I like your cousin," he said absently as he took his seat.

"Thanks." Kate chuckled. "I kind of like her too. Most of the time."

"So . . ." He drummed his fingers on the table. Dylan couldn't possibly be a husband, could he? No, he dismissed that notion. If Kate were married, she surely would have mentioned it by now. A boyfriend, then? That would certainly explain her insistence that they not become involved. "So," he started again, trying to sound casual. "Who's Dylan?"

"Hmm?" She glanced at him. "Oh, my son."

"Your . . . son?" His head dropped forward as his brain tried to function around that bombshell.

"Yeah." Her expression softened with pride. "He's seven, and the smartest kid in his class."

"Seven," he repeated numbly. He wasn't sure

whether he felt shocked or relieved to learn Dylan was her son, not her lover. "I, um, take it the father is no longer in the picture?" He regretted the question instantly as he watched the wall of wariness drop back over her features.

"Of course Edward is still in the picture . . . when he cares to be, which isn't often. We're divorced."

"I see."

She eyed him with cool detachment. "Do you have a problem with that?"

"No, no problem. I just didn't picture you as having a kid." *At least not one that isn't mine.* What an egotistical and ignorant assumption, he realized, as if she'd spent her whole life simply waiting for him to show up. God, he felt like a jerk.

She leaned back in her seat. "I take it then that you don't like children."

"No, I do," he assured her. "I love kids. In fact, I'd like to meet him."

"No." She shook her head slowly. "Definitely not."

"Why not?"

"Mike." She folded her hands on the table. "I think we need to get one thing straight. I am working for you, temporarily, because, quite frankly, I have no choice. My personal life, however, is my own. Understood?"

"Certainly," he assured her, even as the words "have no choice" repeated in his head. How could he have been so stupid as to blackmail her into working for him? He debated how to fix that blunder without her walking out on him. He had to say something, though. "Kate, I, uh, have a confession to make."

"Oh?" If possible, her expression became even more guarded.

"I . . . lied, yesterday, when I said I'd bad-mouth

your friend's business if you refused to work for me."

She studied him a long time, then nodded slowly. "I already figured that out. You're not cold-blooded enough to follow through with something like that."

He frowned in confusion. "But if you knew I was bluffing, why'd you say you had no choice about working for me?"

"Honestly?" Her expression turned thoughtful. "Mostly because I need the money."

"Oh," he said, not particularly liking the answer. He'd prefer she spent time with him because of the attraction between them, not because he was paying her.

Their lunch arrived, and Mike spent the rest of the afternoon contemplating the possibility that the attraction wasn't mutual. Maybe it was all one-sided, and he was setting himself up for a huge belly flop. By the time they returned to his house and parted company, he was more confused than he'd ever been in his life.

"Mom?" Dylan said that night as he settled into bed. "Am I ever going to see Dad again?"

Kate straightened from her task of picking up toys in the loft. "Of course you'll see him again, sweetie. Why wouldn't you?"

Dylan's narrow shoulders shrugged beneath his Winnie the Pooh pajamas. "Tomorrow's Friday, right? The third Friday of the month?"

"Oh, Dylan." She came forward and sat on the bed facing him. She'd completely forgotten which weekend was coming up. In the two years since their divorce Edward had so rarely taken advantage of his visitation rights, she'd even stopped expecting him to call. Reaching up, she brushed a black curl off Dylan's forehead. "I know it's hard, but you can't take these things personally."

His mouth twisted to the side, and her heart twisted with it.

"Dylan, I know I've told you before, but it really isn't your fault Daddy would rather work than spend time with you. He just . . . well, he just doesn't know how to have fun. Not like you and me, eh?" She tried a smile, but felt it slip away. Somehow, the mention of fun made her think of Mike. She realized she'd enjoyed being with him today—and that she hadn't enjoyed a man's company in a long time.

"I guess you're right." Dylan covered his mouth and coughed.

She tipped her head to study his face. He'd looked tired and pale since she'd picked him up from school. "How's your chest feel?"

"Okay." He coughed again, making her wince at the deep, gravelly sound.

"You think you need the nebulizer tonight?"

Rather than argue, as he usually did, he nodded. She tried not to show alarm at his easy acquiescence as she prepared the small machine that sat on the nightstand. Flipping the switch, she handed him the breathing tube and watched as he placed it in his mouth like an oversized straw.

"Which book do you want tonight?" she asked. From the time he was little, long before he could understand the words, she'd read to him while he inhaled the medicated mist.

"The Rabbit Book," he said around the tube, referring to one of his favorite books, which was actually titled *Guess How Much I Love You* by Sam McBratney.

She retrieved the worn volume from the jumble of

books on the rickety shelf and settled against the head-board beside him. The Mickey Mouse lamp enclosed them in a small circle of light. With the quiet hum of the nebulizer playing in the background, the rest of the world faded away as she read the words she knew by heart. Dylan's small, warm body leaned against hers as he lost himself in the story. He smelled of bruised grass and little-boy sweat and the Dial soap he'd used in a halfhearted effort before climbing into bed.

At last she heard him sigh and felt his body go slack. The tube slipped out of his mouth. She checked her wristwatch to mark the length of his treatment. Fifteen minutes. Just perfect.

Closing the book, she quoted the last line as she kissed the top of Dylan's head: " 'I love you right up to the moon—and back.' "

She turned the machine off and sat in silence, absorbing the stillness of the cabin. With her son's comforting weight against her, she should have felt content and full of life, and yet, she felt . . . a void.

She tried to place the source, knowing this unnamed emptiness was vaguely familiar. Then she remembered: The last time she'd felt it was in that year or so before she admitted her marriage was over. She'd known for some time that something was missing from her life, something profound, but she hadn't been able to name it.

Eventually, she'd figured out that what was missing was love.

Even so, she would have stayed with Edward. She'd sworn for better or worse, and she would have stuck to that vow. But the one thing she couldn't accept was his inability to love Dylan. She still didn't understand how Edward could resist sharing the joy in this miracle they'd created. And how could a man she'd once loved so madly turn out to be such a stranger? Had she made up the man she thought she married?

Falling in love with Edward Bradshaw her freshman year at UT had been the easiest thing she'd ever done, like a sweet, thrilling ride down a silken slide. He was a year ahead of her in school and a world apart from her socially, but he'd swept her off her feet with his Prince Charming eyes and that bad-boy grin. They'd been inseparable for three years, the perfect college couple from football games to rush dances. He'd proposed on his graduation night in the moonlit garden of his parents' Terrytown mansion.

Unfortunately, falling out of love had been a slow, agonizing process that tore at everything inside her, bit by bit, until all that remained was a million ragged pieces. Sometimes, she wondered if the pieces would ever mend, if she'd ever be able to see Edward, or even think of him, without the memories ripping her apart.

Her personal discomfort, however, was no reason for her to let him ignore their son, even if his absence made life less painful for her.

Easing Dylan under the covers, she tucked him in, then made her way down the ladder of the loft. The clock on the mantel read eight P.M., a time when even her workaholic ex-husband would be home from the office. Not that he would have quit working for the night, but he would at least be home.

She closed the door to her bedroom to keep Dylan from hearing and used the phone at her desk. As she listened to the ringing, she told herself to be calm, and above all civil. Just because Edward had failed once again to make arrangements for his visitation weekend was no reason to get into a screaming match.

After the fifth ring, the answering machine picked up. She closed her eyes to fight the tightness in her chest as Edward's voice came on the line.

"Edward," she said after the beep. "It's Kate. If you're there pick up." She pictured him at his computer, his hands poised over the keyboard as he debated answering. "Edward, please, this is important. We can't keep talking to each other through our answering machines."

She pinched the bridge of her nose as she waited. Still he didn't pick up, even though she knew in her gut he was there. "All right, fine." She let out a pent-up breath. "If you insist on avoiding me, we'll do this the hard way. I am calling to remind you that tomorrow is the third Friday of the month, yet you've once again neglected to tell me whether or not you'll be picking Dylan up from school. I assume that means you're too busy making money to bother with anything so trivial as your son."

She tried to leave it at that, she really did, but some vicious little demon that lived inside her refused to be silenced so easily. "Speaking of money, I keep meaning to call the attorney general's office about your dramatic increase in income since our divorce settlement so they can review the amount of your child support payment—"

"Kate, hi!" Edward's voice broke in, sounding completely thrilled to hear from her. "I'm so glad I caught you before you hung up. I was just walking in the door when I heard the machine."

*Yeah, I'll bet.* She rolled her eyes. "I was calling to see if you plan to take Dylan this weekend."

"Oh, hell, I'm sorry, I'm afraid I can't."

"Surprise, surprise." She heard the waspish sting to her voice, but couldn't seem to stop it.

"I tell you what," he said, in that smooth, urbane manner that used to make her melt like butter but now made her stomach curdle. "How about next weekend? I know it's not one of my appointed ones, but I happen to have a couple of tickets to the Longhorn game at Disch-Faulk Field and the client I was going to take bailed out. Dylan likes baseball . . . doesn't he?"

The very fact that Edward didn't know how much his son loved baseball infuriated her. "Just because he isn't good at sports doesn't mean he doesn't enjoy them. But so help me, Edward, if I tell Dylan that you're taking him to a Longhorn game only to have you cancel at the last minute—"

"I said I'd take him, didn't I?" Edward snapped defensively, losing some of his famous cool façade. *Why do we always bring out the worst in each other?*

"All right," she sighed, wanting to believe him, but fearing Dylan's disappointment at another letdown. "When will you pick him up?"

"Will ten A.M. Saturday be convenient?"

"Perfectly." She hesitated. "Do you want to keep him overnight?"

In the pause that followed she could almost hear Edward trying to think of a way to return Dylan directly after the game. That way, he could perform his fatherly duty without having to do anything strenuous, like communicate with his son beyond the confines of a ballpark. In truth, she hoped he would return Dylan right away, even as a part of her argued that Dylan needed to spend time with his father.

"Yes. I'd like to keep him overnight," Edward said at last. "I always look forward to spending time with the little guy."

*If only that were true.* "I know he'll enjoy seeing you. He misses you, you know."

"Well, you tell him he'll see me next weekend."

The minute she hung up, she closed her eyes and prayed she'd done the right thing. Even though her brain kept telling her that no force on earth would turn Edward into a doting father, her heart couldn't let go of that last thread of hope, for Dylan's sake.

Unbearably weary, she turned to her computer, determined to put in a few hours' work. Spending the day shopping with Mike had put her that much further behind. She had a column due on Monday that she hadn't even started.

Looking for inspiration, she scanned her incoming e-mail. The first letter to catch her eye was from a farmer's wife in Iowa who wanted to rekindle some spark of romance in her forty-year marriage. After reading the lengthy and heartbreaking letter, Kate realized the woman had suffered years of verbal abuse from a man who'd called her fat, dumb, and lazy so often the woman had all but forgotten her own name.

Kate hit the reply command and typed in three words: Dump the bastard.

Scanning farther down the list, she found a letter from a woman whose boyfriend of three years refused to marry her until she found a job that paid her as much as what he made because he feared she'd be a financial burden. Yet, at present, the man lived in her house, ate her groceries, and graciously let her pay all the bills.

Kate hit the reply key and typed: Dump the bastard. Then suddenly she realized what she was doing.

No. No. Wrong! Shaking her head, she emptied her outgoing mail basket. Responses like these were exactly why Gwen wanted to dump her. Her advice was supposed to be pithy, insightful, but most of all romantic!

With a sigh, she dropped her head into her hands. The problem was, after five minutes on the phone with Edward, she couldn't think of a single positive thing to say about the male portion of the human race. *Tomorrow,* she thought, shutting down her computer. *Maybe tomorrow some romantic inspiration will strike.*

# Chapter 8

$\mathcal{D}o$ you speak Spanish?" a desperate voice asked the minute Kate picked up the phone.

"What?" She thought she recognized the voice as Mike's, but couldn't quite imagine him being this rattled.

"Please tell me you speak Spanish," the voice begged. "Or at least tell me you know where to find your friend's husband."

"Who, Jim?" she asked, glancing at her watch. How had three o'clock arrived so quickly? She couldn't believe she'd worked at the computer all day and accomplished so little. "Isn't he at your house? I thought they were going to start tearing out your wall today."

"They are. They did! That's the problem. No, stop!" he shouted to someone else. "Don't touch that. Don't touch anything! Kate," he said into the receiver. "I need you. Now. Get over here."

With that, he hung up. She frowned at the dial tone coming from the handset, then glanced once more at her watch. As frantic as Mike sounded, he'd simply have to wait until she picked Dylan up from school. This late in the afternoon, she didn't even have time to change out of the baggy tank top and elastic-waist shorts she frequently wore when working at home. She just grabbed her purse, slipped on some sandals, and dashed out the door.

In the car, she did at least take the plastic clip out of her hair and swipe on mascara and lipstick. She felt a little foolish for caring how she looked to Mike, but then a woman with red eyelashes and pale skin had no business being seen in public with a naked face.

All thoughts of Mike vanished, however, when she pulled into the circular drive of Lake Travis Elementary. Dylan sat on the front steps with his backpack lying forgotten between his feet and his chin resting in both hands. All around him, children jumped and hollered as they dashed for parents' cars or fell into lines for the various after-school daycare shuttles. Her heart twisted a little when Dylan spotted her and rose slowly. With shoelaces dragging, he made his way to her car.

"Hi, sweetheart." She forced a smile as he climbed into the backseat. "How was your day?"

"Okay," he mumbled so low she could barely hear.

After he dutifully fastened his seat belt, she eased the car back into the long line of vehicles waiting to exit the circular drive. "Care to tell me about it?"

" 'Bout what?"

She glanced in the rearview mirror. "Whatever put that frown on your face."

He shrugged and turned toward the window.

*Okay,* she thought and suppressed the urge to question him further, or worse, stop and pull him into her arms and smother him with motherly affection. She wondered what childish insult he'd suffered this time. Being so much smaller, paler, and more awkward than other boys his age made him a natural target for ridicule. Life could be so cruel to those who most needed kindness.

"What would you think about stopping at Hamburger Haven for some fries and a Coke on the way home?" she asked, hoping to brighten his mood.

He shrugged again.

"Only one catch," she added. "I need to run by my client's house in Lakeway first. I think there might be a problem with Jim's crew."

That finally got Dylan's attention. "Will Jim be there?"

Her heart sank at the hopeful spark in her son's eyes. While Jim made a great substitute dad, he wasn't Dylan's father and never would be. "I don't think so, honey, which may be the problem." Dylan looked so dejected, she quickly added, "But, who knows. He might be there."

That hope died when she pulled into Mike's driveway and found no sign of Jim's truck. Climbing from the car, she heard Mike's voice as he shouted orders in stilted English. Even with the front door standing wide open, his voice sounded muffled, and a strange, pink haze drifted from the house.

"Sweetie," she said to Dylan when they reached the protection of the overhang by the front door, "can you wait for me here?"

Dylan nodded, his eyes going round at a stream of colorful language coming from within the house.

Cautiously, she stepped over the threshold and into a cloud of pink and white dust. Covering her mouth, she moved into the living room and her jaw dropped. While the ceiling in the main room remained intact, a whole section of ceiling in the kitchen had fallen, scattering chunks of white gypsum and pink insulation over the cabinets, floor, and the four construction workers standing beneath it. With white filters covering their mouths, they worked to brace what remained of the ceiling with two-by-fours.

"Good heavens," she breathed through her fingers.

Mike whirled at the sound of her voice, a red bandana tied over his mouth and nose. The eyes above it filled with relief. "Thank God you're here!"

"What happened?" she asked, her voice as muffled as his.

"What does it look like happened?" He flung an arm out to encompass the debris that littered the kitchen. "These morons tore down a bearing wall."

"No, that can't be," she said, trying to keep one eye on Dylan and survey the damage at the same time. "Jim and I discussed it. He assured me the ceiling joists in the kitchen ran the other way."

"Well, something sure as hell went wrong."

"Where's Jim?" she asked.

"A damned good question." Mike raked a hand through his hair. Pink and white dust drifted to the shoulders of his Eagles reunion T-shirt. "He comes in here, rattles off a bunch of Spanish to these guys, then tells me not to worry about a thing, they'll be out of here in a few hours. So I go downstairs to get some work done. The next thing I know, I hear these idiots shouting, so I run upstairs—and find this!"

Kate turned to the men who had just finished securing the two-by-fours. "Where is Jim?" They stared back at her, blank-faced. She tried again, using some of the limited Tex-Mex she knew. *"¿Dónde está el jefe?"*

This time she got a flood of response, none of which she understood. "Wait. Slow down. *No comprendo.*"

One of the men said, *"El jefe está en la casa en el*

*campo de golf.*" He made a motion with his body like a golfer hitting a tee shot.

"He went to play golf!" Mike hollered. "I'm going to kill him. I swear to God, the man is dead."

"No, wait." Kate waved a hand at him. "I think he said that Jim is at the house he's remodeling over by the golf course." At least she hoped that's where he was, or she'd help Mike kill him.

Mike's eyes glazed over as he stared at the gaping hole in his ceiling. "I can't deal with this right now. I have to finish inputting my wire-frame data. And the alliance wants me to help with the final plans for the party tomorrow night."

"It's okay," she placated. "Why don't you go on downstairs and let me take care of this."

After a bit more persuasion and soothing, he handed over his bandana and went back to his lair. *Jeez,* Kate thought, as she secured the makeshift mask into place. *What a mess.* At least Mike had managed to get them to brace what remained of the ceiling before the entire thing caved in. Now for the cleanup.

Turning to the workers, she motioned toward the chunks of gypsum that littered the floor. "We need to clean—I mean, *limpia, por favor.* No in *casa.* Outside." She racked her brain for the Spanish word for outside. *Afuera!* She pointed toward the front door. "Move all this—*esto—afuera.*"

To her relief, the workers began picking up bits of debris and carrying it out onto the driveway. As for the pink fiberglass insulation, it would likely take days for all of it to settle. After asking Dylan to wait right where he was, she made her way to the phone in what remained of the kitchen and dialed Jim's mobile number.

"We're sorry," a recording said. "The party you are trying to reach is not available at this time." Which probably meant Jim had once again forgotten to recharge the battery on his cell phone.

Grinding her teeth, she called Linda.

"Wife for Hire, Linda speaking."

"Thank heavens you're there," Kate breathed through the bandana. "I'm over at Mike Cameron's house and we have a major catastrophe on our hands." After hearing the situation, Linda promised to hunt Jim down and send him over.

Kate hung up and looked about her. This whole mess was her fault. She'd wanted to make Mike pay for a threat that hadn't even been real. Now it looked like she and Jim would be the ones paying, in a very real, monetary sense. An example of how she always managed to screw up everything. Well, lately, anyway. Her life hadn't always been one mistake after another, but in the last few years, she couldn't seem to do anything right.

As she bent to pick up some of the debris, she saw Dylan hurry toward her without even a hand covering his mouth. "No, honey, stay back."

"But I can help," he said.

"Dylan, no, it's too dusty in here." Lord knew what fiberglass would do to his lungs. Yet she couldn't very well expect him to stand in the doorway forever. "Come sit over here on the steps." She led him to the stairs by the foyer, well away from the kitchen and near the fresh air that came through the open door. "Hold your T-shirt over your mouth and nose. Can you do that for Mommy?"

"You never let me do anything!" he protested. "I'm not a baby, you know."

"I know that, Dylan," she sighed. "But all this dust

is bad for your lungs. Do you really want another trip to the hospital?"

Muttering under his breath, he stomped over to the stairs and sat with his back to her as he pulled the neck of his T-shirt over his mouth and nose. At times like these, he made her feel like the world's meanest mother. *It's never easy,* she thought. *Life can never, for one minute, just be easy.*

With a sigh, she gathered chunks of drywall and headed outside to dump them on the growing pile. By the second trip, a trickle of sweat had formed between her breasts. She picked at the front of her tank top in an effort to cool her skin, then returned to work.

Mike sat staring at his computer screen. He'd never considered himself a man who cared about material things, but the thought of the mess upstairs made him so mad he couldn't see straight. He tried to tell himself it was just a house; it could be fixed. Only, a house meant a lot more than just walls and a roof.

The house he'd grown up in certainly wasn't as nice as this place. And yet, when he thought of that clapboard structure in the hills of Santa Monica, he didn't think of the cracked driveway or the peeling paint. He thought of all the years of living that filled the rooms, the sound of sitcoms playing on the old RCA console in the living room, and the smell of his mom's chocolate-chip cookies baking in the stove she'd complained about for years. He remembered her tears the day his dad had surprised her with a brand-new Kenmore stove; and he could still hear the sound of his sisters' voices coming from the one bathroom the four of them shared. He'd listened in fascination over the years as they talked about everything from boys to the mysteries of makeup.

But most of all, he remembered the back deck that overlooked the ocean. How many nights had all of them sat on that deck with hamburgers sizzling on the grill as the fiery ball of the sun melted into the shimmering water? The day the real estate agent had shown him this house on Challenger Drive, the sun had been setting just like that over Lake Travis. He'd walked out onto the deck, looked across the water, and known this was the house where he wanted to raise a family of his own. He'd known it the same way he'd known that Kate was the woman he wanted to raise that family with. He'd just known.

Only Kate had knocked a giant hole in the middle of their house.

Before that thought could make him even madder, he tried again to concentrate on his work. He'd received approval on his sketches that morning, but wanted to get some more input from the special-effects supervisor before he started creating the skin that would cover the wire frame of the robot. Booting up his Internet search engine, he started to type in the studio FTP site so he could upload his file.

Behind him, something crashed to the floor. He bolted out of his chair and whirled to find a boy standing by the built-in bookshelves. A spaceship model from the first *Star Wars* film he'd worked on lay at the kid's feet.

"Holy shit!" He stared in disbelief at the broken pieces on the floor.

"I didn't do it!" the boy said frantically, his blue eyes wide with fear.

"The hell you didn't," Mike snapped as he came forward to inspect the gift that George Lucas had presented to him at the end of their first project together. The boy stumbled backward.

Mike drew up short, realizing he'd frightened the pint-sized intruder. Only, how had a kid gotten into his workroom in the first place? "Look, it's okay. I'm not going to hit you or anything." He bent down and retrieved the model. Relief went through him as he saw the break was clean. A little glue and some paint, and no one would ever know.

"I didn't touch it," the boy insisted. "It was just sitting there, right on the edge, and it just fell all on its own. Honest!"

Mike gave him a narrowed look. "All on its own, eh?"

"I'm not lying!" Red flooded the boy's cheeks. "It's just a stupid toy, anyway."

"It's not a toy," Mike corrected as he wondered again who the kid was and how he'd gotten into his house. "What's your name?"

"Why do you want to know?" The kid gave him a wary look that seemed very familiar.

Mike raised a brow. "Because you happen to be in my house, and I want to know what you're doing here."

"I'm with my mom," the boy said defiantly.

*Of course!* Mike recognized the suspicious expression now. Kate had given him that same look several times. He remembered her saying her son was seven years old, although this boy looked a bit small for seven. "Shouldn't you be in school?"

"School's out for the day." The boy smirked.

Mike glanced at his watch. "So it is."

"Wow, is that yours?"

"Hmm?" Mike followed the line of the kid's eye to the large monitor glowing from amid the piles of notes and drawings on his desk. With all the movie models and memorabilia in the room, the kid zeros in on a computer monitor? "Yeah, it's mine."

The boy stood silently eyeing the screen, looking as if he'd sell his soul to get at the slick, state-of-the-art computer, but would also cut out his tongue before he'd ask permission.

"You want to see it?" Mike finally asked.

"Maybe." The kid shrugged, trying but failing to look indifferent.

Mike studied him, recognizing a fascination with technology to match his own. "What's your name?" he asked again, remembering it was something that started with a *D*.

The boy hesitated, then glanced at the monitor again.

"If you want to see the computer," Mike said, "the least you can do is introduce yourself."

"I'm Dylan," the boy said at last.

"Glad to meet you, Dylan. I'm Mike." He held out his hand and saw the surprise flash across the boy's face. After a moment, Dylan gave him a good solid handshake.

"Ugh! You're stronger than you look," Mike grunted, hoping for a smile. The kid remained straight-faced and Mike sighed. "Come on, I'll show you the computer." Standing, he led the way to the desk. "You know how to operate one of these things?"

"Of course." Dylan rolled his eyes. "I have one at home I use all the time."

"Oh, you do, do you?" Mike hid a smile as he took a seat and moved his chair back enough for Dylan to stand between him and the keyboard.

"Well, actually, it's my mom's," Dylan confessed. "But she lets me play on it whenever she's not answering letters."

"Letters?" Mike's interest was piqued as he realized the boy could satisfy some of his curiosity about Kate. "I take it your mom has a lot of e-mail friends."

"They're not exactly friends."

"Oh?" Mike prompted.

Dylan seemed to sense his eagerness and warmed a bit. "You wanna see?"

"See what?" Mike asked.

With the ease of someone far older, Dylan used the mouse to select the search window, then typed in a Web address with two fingers. The address was admittedly short, but still Mike was amazed that a second-grader could be that proficient on a keyboard.

"There," Dylan said when the page came up. "That's my mom."

Confused, Mike glanced at the screen. Golden hearts and curlicues floated against a soft peach background. A chubby, winged cherub, in the manner of Raphael, hung above flowing script that read "Dear Cupid." The cherub's heart-shaped face, with its stubborn chin and mischievous eyes, bore a striking resemblance to Kate.

"Well, yeah," Mike said. "That does look a bit like your mom."

"No," Dylan said, pointing at the cherub again. "That *is* my mom. She's Cupid."

"What?" Mike glanced from the screen to the boy then back again. Taking the mouse in hand, he navigated through the Web site, skimming an article by "Cupid" on creative ways to celebrate an anniversary. Older articles covered topics on how to ask someone out, how to get through a first date, how to spice up a marriage.

The fact that Kate, who behaved at times as if men were the scourge of the universe, had written those articles struck him as the supreme irony. A chuckle started to build inside him just as footsteps sounded on the stairs.

"Dylan? Honey, where are you? Oh, there you are. Thank goodness. I've been looking everywhere." Kate came to an abrupt halt when she stepped into the room and found Dylan standing between Mike and the computer with Mike's arms going to either side of her son to reach the keyboard. "Dylan, what are you doing down here?"

"Hey, Mom, look at this cool computer," Dylan said. "Isn't it neat!"

Her eyes went to the computer screen and widened in utter mortification. "Dylan! What have you done!"

He gaped at her as she swept across the room, nearly falling into Mike's lap as she hit the close window command.

"It's okay, Kate," Mike said, steadying her with his hands on her hips. "Dylan was just showing me your Web page."

Kate jumped back and whirled to face him. Just as she feared, she saw laughter in his eyes. "Don't you dare say a word. I'll put up with other people making fun of what I do, but so help me, if you say one word against it, I'll—I'll—" Unable to think of anything horrible enough, she pulled Dylan against her and cradled his head against her stomach. Her son buried his face, as if on the verge of tears.

"Hey." Mike held up his hands. "I wasn't laughing at *you*. Although you have to admit, it is funny."

"What?" she demanded.

"That you're Cupid." His laughter spilled forth. "The woman who doesn't trust any man farther than she can throw him." He clamped an arm about his waist. "It's just too rich."

"I will not put up with this. Dylan, come on, we're

leaving." Taking her son by the hand, she headed for the door.

"I'm sorry, Mommy." Dylan's voice caught. "I didn't mean to make you mad."

Her heart twisted at the sight of his tears. "I'm not mad, sweetie. Well, not at you." She dropped to one knee to dry his cheek. "You didn't know any better. In the future, though, I'd prefer that you not show people my Web site. That's Mommy's secret, okay?"

"Why?"

"Because . . ." She floundered for an explanation. "It just is. Now, promise you won't tell anyone else."

"Okay." Dylan sniffed.

"I don't know what you're so embarrassed about, Kate," Mike said. "It's a great-looking Web site."

"No, I guess you wouldn't understand." She cast him a lethal glare over her son's head. What would he know about well-meaning family members who wanted to know when she planned to get a real job? Or a husband who publicly joked about her "little hobby" and privately commanded her to never embarrass him again by mentioning it to his colleagues? And all because her column involved romance. No doubt, if she wrote about any other subject, Edward would have proudly told everyone that his wife was a columnist. She'd long ago realized that nobody took love seriously, unless it was tragic, warped, or adulterous. And, of course, unless the novel, column, or article had been written by a man.

Deciding not to get into any of that, she rose with Dylan's hand firmly in hers and faced Mike. "I came down here to tell you that Jim has arrived. He's taking care of the problem so there's no need for me to stay."

"Wait a second," Mike called as she turned to leave. "What time do I pick you up tomorrow?"

"Tomorrow?"

"For the party."

She started to tell him again that taking a date on a wife hunt was a ridiculous idea, but sighed in defeat. "What time does the party start?"

"Seven o'clock," he answered. "But I doubt anyone will get there until eight or nine."

"Then pick me up at eight."

"You got it." He nodded. "Oh, and Kate," he called as she turned toward the stairs.

"What?" she growled.

A grin spread slowly across his face. "Wear something sexy."

Rolling her eyes, she left the room with Dylan in tow. Men were so predictable. Or most of them were. Mike, however, went beyond her comprehension sometimes.

# Chapter 9

$W_{EAR}$ something sexy," Kate snorted to Linda the following evening. "It would serve him right if I wore a burlap bag." Dressed in a floral satin bathrobe, she rummaged through her closet looking for something to wear. Something simple and conservative. Something befitting a dating coach rather than a date.

"I have to admit, your first account is certainly . . . unusual." Linda lounged back amid the mountain of peach and gold pillows on Kate's four-poster bed. "Since I started Wife for Hire, I've interviewed maids, nannies, landscapers, and housepainters, but I've never had a client ask me to find him a wife."

"I should have told him no," Kate said as she considered a black shift her ex-mother-in-law had talked her into buying. The outfit hung straight from her breasts to her hips, making her look forty pounds heavier. She held the dress before her and looked in the mirror. "This whole thing is completely absurd."

"So why did you take the account?" Linda tilted her head to study the dress, then made a face that expressed Kate's sentiments exactly. Black made her look like she'd been dead for a week. "Not that I'm complaining. I'm thrilled to have you working with me. Besides, I think Mike Cameron hiring you makes sense in a spooky, cosmic sort of way."

"Actually, you're right." Kate hung the black dress back in the closet since her ego refused to wear anything that made her look that bad. "It's enough to make you believe in fate, isn't it?"

"What do you mean?" Linda asked.

Kate continued digging through the closet. "Only that here I was, doubting my ability to be Dear Cupid, even before Gwen threatened to cancel me, which is all connected. Once you doubt yourself, pretty soon everyone will follow suit. The job with Mike is my chance to turn everything around."

"Turn what around?"

"My attitude." Her gaze landed on a skimpy gold dress way in the back of the closet. The dress was one of her favorites, yet she couldn't remember the last time she'd worn it. The cleverly darted silk accentuated her hourglass figure, and gave the illusion of being tight, when in fact, it flowed comfortably over her curves. The spaghetti straps and princess-cut neckline left her arms and a tantalizing hint of breast bare.

Holding the dress against her, she stepped before the mirror and wondered if it still fit. "If I can prove to myself that I still have what it takes to be Cupid, that confidence will come through in my articles and responses to e-mail, right?"

"And how will you prove it?"

She met her own gaze in the mirror. "By finding Mike Cameron a wife. The perfect wife." And if she wanted to wear a skimpy gold dress and do a little flirting of her own while she was at it, then by golly she would!

She headed for the dresser to find the right undergarments to wear with a spaghetti-strap dress. Thanks to her passion for lingerie and her discount through

*Gwendolyn's Garden,* she certainly had plenty to choose from.

"Wow," Linda said, watching her. "You didn't mention you wanted to be that wife."

"What are you talking about?" Kate glanced up, startled. "I'm not interested in marrying Mike myself."

"Right." Linda laughed. "Although it's about time you started dating again."

"I'm not dating him," she insisted as she took a seat at her Queen Anne vanity. A cheerful array of perfume bottles, jewelry, and makeup cases vied with family photos on its surface. Pointing her toes, she rolled the silk stockings onto her legs. "Trust me, Linda, there is absolutely nothing romantic going on between Mike and me. This is business."

"Too bad." Linda made a face that came dangerously close to a pout. "For a moment, I actually thought one of us had something romantic going on."

"What do you mean?" Kate stepped into the closet to exchange the robe for a bustier and French-cut girdle.

"Nothing," Linda mumbled.

Kate stuck her head around the door and frowned at her friend. "I know that look. Something is obviously wrong, so spill, woman."

"It's nothing," Linda insisted. "Except this huge stomach of mine! God, I feel so fat, I don't think I'll ever be thin again."

"Jeez, Linda, don't tell me you're letting that hamper your love life." Kate slipped the dress over her head. With a wiggle of her hips, the gold fabric settled about her, as light as a lover's whisper. *Yes!* she mentally cheered. It still fit.

"I'm not letting it stop me," Linda said. "But Jim

is. Do you know we haven't made love since the baby started kicking?"

"What!" Kate stepped around the door, slipping high-heeled sandals onto her feet. "But surely the doctor told you it was okay, as long as y'all don't get too rambunctious."

"She did. But Jim refuses to touch me. At first I thought he was just afraid of hurting the baby, but now I don't know." Her voice grew a bit desperate. "Kate, he spends all his time out in his workshop and he's made it very clear he doesn't want me to come out and visit with him anymore. It's like he doesn't want me around. What if he's having second thoughts about starting a family? Having a baby could change everything between us. What if he's not ready? What if *I'm* not ready?"

"Oh, honey . . ." Kate came to sit on the edge of the bed. Cupping her friend's chin, she stared into the frantic blue eyes. "I know for a fact that Jim finds you incredibly attractive—"

"I'm not attractive." Linda pouted. "I'm fat."

"You are not fat!" Kate growled. "You're pregnant with his child, and that makes you the most beautiful woman in the world to him."

"Then why won't he make love to me?"

"You said it yourself. He's worried about hurting the baby. So, what you need to do is reassure him that sex can be very healthy for the baby. In fact, every time you have an orgasm, it makes your uterus contract and gives the baby a massage. If you think about it, it really is incumbent upon him—as a caring father—to give you as many orgasms as possible. For the good of the baby, of course."

Linda gave a short, surprised laugh. "You're making that up."

"No, really, it's true. And what's more"—Kate wiggled her eyebrows—"the more your uterus expands to make room for the baby, the stronger your orgasms will be."

"Kate!" Linda moaned. "That's not the kind of thing to tell a horny woman who's gone without sex for two months."

"Maybe not, but Jim has gone without for just as long, so he's just as miserable as you are."

"You think so?"

"I know so." She tweaked Linda's nose. "In fact, that's probably why he can't keep his mind on his work. He's so hot for you he can't think straight. So, what you need to do is wait until Dylan goes to bed tonight. Then find something loose but sexy to wear. Put on some perfume, and offer to give Jim a back rub."

"Which will promptly put the man to sleep."

"Not a chance." Kate straightened her friend's bangs. "You are way too sexy to put any man to sleep. Especially one who loves you as much as Jim does."

"Oh, Kate." Linda leaned forward and gave her a tight hug. "Thanks. You always know the right thing to say."

"That's my job." Kate returned the hug. "Although if you wanted to repay me, there is something you could do."

"Oh?" Linda leaned back.

Kate lowered her eyes, uncomfortable with the sudden role reversal. Giving help was so much easier than asking for it. "Could you ask Jim to talk to Dylan tonight? You know, have him ask Dylan how everything's going at school and such?"

"What do you mean?"

"I don't know." Kate made a restless gesture with

her hand. "I think something's wrong. Only, Dylan won't talk to me. Maybe he'd open up more to a man."

"I'll be happy to ask Jim to talk to him, on one condition." Linda ducked her head to meet Kate's eyes. "That you quit worrying so much. You are a wonderful mother, Kate. I mean that. I only hope I'm half as good. But sometimes, not always"—she held up her hands—"sometimes, you do get the tiniest bit overprotective."

"I know, but it's so hard not to with Dylan. He's so small and awkward, I'm afraid the other boys pick on him at school."

Linda's brows snapped together. "Just because someone's small, doesn't mean they're helpless. And the more people try to protect them, the more they're going to resent it."

Kate blinked in surprise, then grinned in understanding. "Are we talking about Dylan here, or you?"

Linda blushed just as the doorbell rang.

"I'll get it!" Dylan hollered from the other room.

Kate jumped to her feet. "Oh, my goodness, he's here already? Linda, go stall him while I do something with my hair."

"Dylan can handle Mike." Linda laughed. "I'd much rather stay here and watch Cupid be nervous over a first date."

"I told you. It's not a date."

"Right." Linda smiled.

Dylan grabbed the door with both hands and swung it open. He expected to find Jim ready to take him to the big house up the hill where he and Miss Linda lived. Tonight, he was going to get to sleep over, so they wouldn't have to wait up for his mom to come home.

And Jim had promised Dylan he could help out in the workshop again. They were building a crib for the baby, but it was a big secret, just between them, 'cause they were both men, and men shared things that women didn't know about. Boy, he couldn't wait to see Miss Linda's face when they finished the crib. It was really cool.

Except, instead of Jim standing on the front porch, he found the man who had upset his mother yesterday. His shoulders slumped with disappointment.

"Hey there, Dylan." The man smiled. He looked really stupid standing there holding a bunch of dorky flowers.

"My mother isn't ready yet," Dylan replied sullenly. He'd known his mom was going out with the guy, which didn't make any sense. His mother didn't even seem to like him. So Dylan decided he didn't like him either. "You'll have to wait."

"All right," the man said. They both remained in the doorway, eyeing each other. "Mind if I come in?" the man asked.

"I guess not." Dylan turned and led the way inside.

Raising a brow, Mike followed. He'd accepted the fact that winning Kate wouldn't be as easy as he'd first assumed, but the last obstacle he'd expected was a seven-year-old boy. The mere fact that she had a son still had him reeling. To realize the kid didn't like him sent him further off balance. Kids always liked him. And he liked them. This kid, however, obviously required a little more effort to win over.

Taking a seat on a small camel-back sofa, Mike tried to decide if he should hold on to the flowers or set them on the coffee table. They'd been a last-minute impulse, and one he hoped he wouldn't regret. Across from him, the boy climbed into a wing chair by the rock fireplace. Neither of them spoke. Mike glanced about for some way to break the ice.

He wasn't sure what he'd expected for Kate's home, but the rustic cabin had surprised him when he'd driven up. The inside, however, suited her. Wisps of creamy gauze draped about the windows, softening the rough-hewn walls. A rug before the hearth added a homey touch, along with the colorful clutter of children's toys.

Family photos and breakable knickknacks marched across the mantel, well out of reach of a seven-year-old's curious hands. He squinted his eyes, trying to make out faces in the photos as he wondered at the names and stories that went with them.

"Are you gonna try to poke my mom?" Dylan asked.

"Excuse me?" Mike jerked his attention back to the boy, sure he must have heard wrong. "What did you say?"

"Are you gonna try to poke her?" Dylan scowled at him. "You know, with your binky."

His *binky*? From his experience as an uncle, Mike knew "binky" could mean anything from a pacifier to a penis. Somehow he didn't think Dylan referred to any of the more innocent options. "Who told you such a thing?"

"Jason," Dylan responded gravely. "He says guys always try to poke girls when they take them out."

"And who exactly is this Jason character?" Mike asked with mounting anger.

"Jason Haynie," Dylan answered as if any fool knew who Jason was. "His father plays in a rock band."

"Oh, yes, well, I can definitely see how that would make him an authority on dating."

Dylan waited a heartbeat. "So, are you?"

Mike studied the kid, tempted to tell him it was none of his damned business what he and his mother did. That, however, wouldn't win him any points with Kate or Dylan. And it suddenly occurred to him that, if he did manage to win Kate over, this kid would be his stepson. His stepson! Now there was a thought to unsettle a man. Even one who liked kids.

"I tell you what." Leaning forward, he braced his forearms on his thighs and met the boy's distrust straight on. "How about if I promise not to do anything with your mother she doesn't want me to do?"

Dylan considered that for a long time. Mike held his breath, hoping the boy wouldn't see the obvious loophole in the promise. Finally Dylan's brow dimpled. "You swear?"

Releasing his breath, Mike ran his right forefinger over his chest. "Cross my heart and may my hard drive crash tomorrow if I'm lying."

Dylan nodded. "I guess it's okay if you take her out then."

Mike struggled not to laugh. He'd thought fathers were a tough gauntlet to pass when picking up a date, but sons had them beat by a mile.

"Sorry to keep you waiting," Kate said as she breezed into the room.

"No problem," Mike answered, rising quickly on a wave of relief. "Dylan and I were just—" He froze as he turned and saw her. Good God, was it legal for a woman to look like that? Like pure desire gift-wrapped in gold silk? With her hair swept upward exposing her neck, he had an instant impulse to lean forward and sink his teeth in for a big bite.

She stopped short as well, staring at him as if equally startled. Self-consciously, he straightened the Tasmanian Devil tie he wore with a long-sleeved green shirt and black slacks. For one brief moment, he almost wished he'd bought one of those damned white monkey shirts.

"You cut your hair," she whispered.

"What?" He stared at her, not comprehending at first. "Oh, that." With a shaky laugh, he ran a hand through the shortened strands. Another impulse. "I figured you'd suggest it eventually, so I decided to get it over with." Feeling awkward and a bit foolish, he lifted the flowers. "Here. I um— Here."

"Oh." Kate went still. Before she could guard against it, a warm tingle slipped past her defenses and lodged in her heart. He'd brought her flowers, a huge colorful explosion of flowers wrapped in tissue paper and tied with a single red ribbon.

"I didn't know what you liked," he said with a shrug. "So I told the girl at the flower shop to give me one of everything."

Which was, of course, exactly what she liked, variety, color, and extravagant gestures. "Mike . . ." she scolded as she took them.

"I know, I know," he sighed. "I shouldn't have brought you flowers because this isn't a date. So, consider it practice—part of your job as my dating couch."

"Oh, well then . . ." Her heart softened as she inhaled their fragrance. "I suppose I could take them, for practice." She tried to keep her face from going soft and dreamy, only she'd forgotten how nice it felt to get flowers from a man, the way it made a woman's heart flutter. But then, she'd forgotten a great many things when it came to men. The last few years, she'd been an observer, an advisor, but never a participant in romance. She'd convinced herself that life was safer that way, less painful. But now she realized it was also less pleasurable.

"I'll, um—" She made a vague gesture toward the kitchen. "Just put these in some water."

As she moved toward the sink, she saw Linda come out of the bedroom, all curious eyes and friendly smiles. "You must be Mike Cameron," she said.

"And you must be Linda Davis." He shook the hand she offered. "I recognize you from your business card."

"I'm surprised you can. My face wasn't nearly so round back then. Not to mention the rest of me." Linda laughed.

"True," he admitted with a smile. "You are definitely . . . round."

"Which does not mean you're fat," Kate called from the sink as she filled a vase.

"Of course she's not fat." Mike frowned at her. "I didn't mean that at all. It's just that you women always look so . . . interesting when you're . . . you know, expecting."

"Interesting?" Kate asked, knowing she'd clobber him if he undid the pep talk she'd just given her friend.

Mike shrugged. "All glowing and maternal, like life-sized fertility goddesses." His gaze slid from Linda to Kate and moved over her body as if imagining her in a similar state. "Definitely interesting."

Heat fluttered low in her belly at the look in his eyes. "See?" She smiled at Linda, fighting to keep her voice from going breathy. "You're not fat."

Linda beamed at Mike. "I don't suppose you'd mention that part about fertility goddesses to my husband, would you?"

"Sorry." Mike laughed. "I'm afraid he'll have to figure that one out for himself."

Settling the flowers in the vase, Kate carried them to the breakfast table. Later she'd let herself get silly over them for an hour or so, arranging them, smelling them, but not now. Not in front of Mike. "Dylan, you be good for Miss Linda, now, okay?" She bent down for a hug.

"Okay." He flung his arms around her neck.

She absorbed the feel of him pressed tight against her body, let it calm the riot of other, more complicated emotions. "I'll miss you tonight."

"I'll miss you too." For a fraction of a second, he clung a little tighter, then stepped away to glare at Mike. "Remember what you swore."

"Scout's honor." Mike held up two fingers.

Kate frowned over that exchange as they left the cabin and descended to the gravel driveway. The ever-present herd of deer munched acorns under the stand of oak trees that hid the cabin from the road. The orange Corvette presented a jarring contrast to the rustic setting.

"So," she asked as Mike handed her into the passenger side. "You want to tell me what that 'scout's honor' business was about?"

"Not particularly." Mike chuckled before he closed the door and headed around the hood.

She watched him covertly, noticing how nice he looked in his new clothes. If only he hadn't cut his hair, she thought with an inward sigh. It looked more brown than blond with all the sun-bleached ends cut off. The longer hair had given him a rakish appeal that positively begged a woman to run her hands through it.

Realizing the direction of her thoughts, she pulled them up short and decided she was glad he'd cut his hair. Very glad. She needed to concentrate on doing her job, not indulge in fantasies about running her fingers through Mike's hair. Especially since that image led to a whole wealth of other fantasies about steaming up the windows of his sports car.

She forced her mind back to the subject at hand as he slid into the driver's seat. "Tell me anyway."

"Tell you what?" he asked.

"About the scout's honor thing."

"Naw-ah." He shook his head and brought the car to life with a twist of his wrist. "That's privileged information. You know—guy stuff."

Kate narrowed her eyes as they pulled onto the road. "And I'm his mother, which overrides any secret male pacts."

From the way Mike concentrated on driving, she knew he was doing a quick mental edit of whatever Dylan had actually said. "Basically, he wanted to know what my intentions were."

"And you told him . . . ?"

His grin turned wicked. "That I wouldn't do anything you didn't want me to."

"Oh, now that's reassuring." *And one of the oldest lines in the book.*

"It was to him," he insisted. "After all, what seven-year-old boy would believe his mother actually wants to do the horizontal boogie?"

"The horizontal boogie?" Her laugh surprised her, because it came so quick and easy.

"There." He nodded in approval at the sound. "That's better. You should laugh more often."

Her smile faded as she became aware of the close
quarters in the car and how near his hand on the gear-
shift rested to her thigh. Physical awareness tingled
along her skin. Shifting in her seat, she searched for
a safer topic. "Thank you for what you said to Linda."

"What, about her being round?"

"No." She shook her head at him. "About glowing
like a fertility goddess."

"And did you glow when you were pregnant?"

"No, I ate. And ate, and ate."

"I'd liked to have seen that." He said the words
with quiet sincerity. "Have you ever thought of having
another?"

"Baby?" she asked, startled, because she had been
thinking about that very thing lately. Watching Linda
these last few weeks, she'd thought about it a lot. "I
used to want one. When Dylan started walking, I used
to yearn for another baby to hold and fuss over.
They're so sweet when they're little."

"So, why didn't you?"

*Because by then my marriage was falling apart
around me. Even though I didn't want to admit it, I
knew it was ending. Even back then, I knew.* "Another
baby would have been a mistake," she said simply,
and felt her heart grieve a little for the children she'd
never borne. "Although sometimes I regret not giving
Dylan a brother or sister. I had one of each, both older,
and have always thought every kid should know that."

"Know what?" he asked.

"The noise and chaos of a big family, friends coming and going, fighting for the last piece of bread at
dinner."

"Waiting in line for the bathroom," he added.

"Ah, you have siblings too."

"Three. All girls. All younger."

Her eyes widened. "I bet you did wait in line for the bathroom."

"I could write a book about it." They both laughed, and for a moment, his gaze held hers before he turned his attention back to the road. "You know, if you still wanted to give Dylan that brother or sister, I might could be talked into helping out."

"Sorry." She shook her head at him. "You can't. Or have you forgotten you swore scout's honor to be on your best behavior."

"I only swore not to do anything you didn't want me to do." He raised his brows at her. "So, what do you say? You want to make a baby?"

She just laughed, deciding to be amused rather than offended at such a silly proposition.

# Chapter 10

$\mathcal{T}$HE distant strains of music, laughter, and voices caught Kate's ears the moment Mike opened the door to the Lakeview Inn. The festive sound drew her like an old, favorite song that she'd nearly forgotten. How on earth had a woman who so enjoyed people allowed her life to dwindle to little more than worrying over bills and taking care of Dylan?

"Sounds like we've got a full house already," Mike said.

"I thought the party wouldn't get going till later." She craned her neck to get a better look at the crowd that spilled out of a door at the far end of the lobby. Beyond them, a wall of glass offered a view of the fading sunset reflecting off the lake.

"I guess I forgot the schmooze factor," Mike confided close to her ear.

"The schmooze factor?"

"Yeah." He grinned. "Anytime there's a Hollywood director around to schmooze with, you can bet every wanna-be actor and scriptwriter within a hundred miles will be crawling out of the woodwork."

"Hey, Magic Man!" someone called as they neared the door to the bar.

"Hey, Ricky." Mike raised a hand in greeting as a man in a zoot suit detached himself from the crowd.

"I understand congratulations are in order."

"You better believe it." Ricky struck a pose with his thumbs behind his lapels. He had the kind of polished good looks that came more from grooming than genes. "You are looking at one gainfully employed movie actor—even if my first role off the stage is a two-minute bit part."

"Hey, even Kevin Wells had to start somewhere," Mike pointed out.

"True," Ricky admitted. "Speaking of, don't forget you promised to introduce me to him tonight—if he ever shows up. Rumor has it, he's holed up in his room pampering his voice."

"Kevin Wells?" Kate's eyes widened at the mention of Hollywood's newest box-office draw. "He's going to be here? Tonight?"

"Maybe." Mike shrugged as if meeting a movie star held little interest. "He plays the owner of the Wild West show."

"You didn't tell me that." His blasé attitude made Kate feel a little foolish for being so excited. But then, who cared, she decided. She was there to have fun and meeting a celebrity would definitely be fun.

"I thought I told you," Mike said absently, then he turned back to his friend. "Ricky, I want you to meet Kate. Kate, this is Richard Sanchez, president of the Actors' Alliance."

As they shook hands, Ricky leaned back to eye her up and down. "Great look. You in film?"

"Heavens no," she laughed.

"Kate's a writer," Mike elaborated, making her blink in surprise. No one had ever introduced her as a writer.

"Too bad," Richard said. "A little peroxide and

you'd be a dead ringer for Marilyn Monroe in that outfit."

Kate laughed at the outrageous compliment as the three of them moved through the doorway and into the dimly lit wonderland beyond. Overhead, hundreds of star-shaped silver balloons danced along the ceiling, trailing Mylar streamers that flashed like tiny rainbows in the colored lights. From the stage in the corner, a live band pumped out an energetic brand of boot-scootin' boogie-woogie.

The crowd ranged from the casually dressed to the flamboyant, their energy filling the room. Laughter vied with the music as old friends called out greetings and swapped news. A camera flash drew Kate's gaze to an area of the room that positively buzzed with excitement.

"Oh, my goodness," she breathed as she saw who stood at the center of the beehive. "Is that Rachel Lee?"

Mike glanced toward the leggy brunette wearing a whisper of a dress that made Kate's outfit seem like a nun's frock. "That would be her," Mike confirmed. "Being her usual low-profile self, I see."

"Is she in the movie?" Kate asked.

"The starring role, even if Kevin gets top billing," Mike answered.

"Magic Man!" someone called from the buffet table.

Kate raised a brow. "Your nickname, I take it?"

"More of a job title, really." He guided Kate toward the crowd of people hovering near the generous spread of Mexican food. "Frank," he said, smiling as he extended his hand toward a short, dark-haired man. "Welcome to Texas."

Frank juggled his plate of food to exchange hand-shakes. He had a soft white face and shrewd dark eyes. "I need to talk to you about a problem the animation team has run into. Maybe you could help them work out a bug in their program."

"Sure. Tell them to call me tomorrow. In the mean-time, let me introduce you to Kate Bradshaw. Kate, Frank Goldstein, the FX supervisor."

"It's good to meet you." She shook his hand.

"Frank's in charge of coordinating all the effects," Mike explained. "From animation, makeup, and mod-els, to special camera crews, and stunt teams, right down to the final film compositing to make sure we give the art department what they asked for."

"Sounds fascinating," Kate said, a little over-whelmed that anyone could pull off the things these people did for a living.

"Pain in the ass," Frank said, mopping up some ranchero sauce with a flour tortilla. "You should try coordinating crews strung out halfway across the country. And then Cameron here, best damned ani-mator in the business, turns traitor and joins the exo-dus from California to Texas. I'm asking ya, what's so great about Texas, for God's sake?"

"Is he complaining again?" a young woman asked as she joined them. She had a startling shade of burgundy-colored hair that perfectly matched the baggy lace dress she wore with combat boots. Though Kate thought her unattractive at first glance, she sus-pected a little makeup and some less frumpy clothes would go a long way—not to mention a more natural shade of hair. "I swear," the woman said, "you should have heard him on the plane out here. Bitching up a storm 'cause he couldn't get a bagel."

"Well, a man's gotta eat," Frank grumbled around a mouth full of tortilla.

"Frank's a real sensitive, cultured kind of guy." Mike winked at Kate. "Which is why we all love working for him."

"Yeah, yeah." Frank made a face, then waved his half-eaten tortilla between Mike and the woman. "I don't think you two've met. Cameron, Traci Hovick. Traci, Cameron the Traitor."

Kate watched Traci's face light up. "No, we haven't met. Not in person anyway. But gosh, I've admired your work since like forever."

"Same here." Mike shook Traci's hand, then introduced her to Kate. "Traci does some really kick-ass makeup effects."

"Horror flicks mostly," Traci elaborated, her eyes sparkling with enthusiasm.

"Sounds . . . interesting," Kate managed.

"Oh, it's great! I get to cut people up and drench 'em in blood. Of course I do monsters and aliens too, but mutilated bodies are my specialty. I get to do a really cool effect for this film in the final scene when an explosion burns the human skin off the robot that Cameron is creating."

"I see," Kate said, wondering why they needed a makeup artist for an animated robot.

"What about you?" Traci asked Kate.

"Hmm?" She blinked at the woman.

"Kate's a writer," Mike answered for her.

"Cool," Traci said.

"Now, if you guys will excuse us"—he dropped his hand to the small of Kate's back—"we haven't even made it to the bar yet. And from the looks of this crowd, it may take a while to fight our way over there." Drawing her near, he steered her through the milling throng.

"You have . . . unusual coworkers," she said.

Mike laughed. "Yeah, 'unusual' is definitely one word for them."

She realized that he had his arm halfway around her waist. The heat from his hand sent a shiver of pleasure over her skin. Before the heat could seep inward, she wiggled away. "Mike . . . I'm not your date, remember?"

"Oh, sorry." He found standing room for them at the bar and asked what she wanted to drink.

"White wine," she answered. "Why did you tell them I was a writer?"

"Because you are." Mike caught the bartender's attention and ordered wine for her and gin and tonic for himself.

"Not in the sense they thought you meant," she said. "You made it sound like I was a real writer, as in scripts or novels or something like that—not just an on-line advice columnist."

"Kate." Mike gave her an exasperated look as he handed her her wine. "I've read your work. Trust me, you are a real writer."

She narrowed her eyes at him. "Exactly how much of my Web site did you read?"

He cringed playfully. "You mean before or after you caught me?"

"Mi-ike!" She couldn't believe she actually stamped her foot.

"I don't know what you're so embarrassed about. It's a great site."

"It's just— Oh, never mind." She wasn't sure why having him read her column embarrassed her either, except it made her feel exposed. "Besides, it's not like I designed the site. Gwen has a Web master who takes care of all that."

"I was talking about the articles, not the site itself."

"Oh." A warm feeling blossomed in her chest at the thought that someone like Mike, someone who rubbed elbows with movie stars and Hollywood directors, would find her articles worthy of praise. "You really liked my column?"

"Mm-hmm." He grinned. "I especially liked the advice to men on how to talk sexy rather than dirty in bed."

The warmth shot right to her cheeks. "I happen to have a lot of men visit my site."

"I believe it. I'm just wondering where you were back when I was in high school. I could have used some of your dating pointers."

"Somehow I doubt that," she said. Although maybe she was wrong. Maybe Mike did need her help. Otherwise, how had such a charming and attractive man stayed single so long?

Sipping her wine, she let her gaze wander about the room. Several people in the crowd looked vaguely familiar, and she wondered if she'd seen them as minor characters in films. Then her gaze landed on a figure that seemed completely out of place: a cowboy who stood alone on the far side of the room, his shoulder propped against the wall. With his arms crossed over his chest, he watched the crowd from the shadow of his black Stetson. Being female, and still among the living, she couldn't help but notice how the white western shirt and black jeans hugged his tall, muscular body. He wore his long black hair in a ponytail that gave him an extra ounce of sex appeal.

Not until he turned his head, though, did recognition strike. "Holy cow!" She gripped Mike's arm in reflex. "That's Trey Evans."

"What?" Mike turned to look.

"Over there." Kate turned toward Mike so she wouldn't be caught staring. "See the man leaning against the wall? I think that's Trey Evans, the world-champion bull rider."

"So it is." Mike nodded.

"But what's he doing here?" Kate asked in disbelief. When she'd been in college, Trey Evans had been the heartthrob of her entire dorm. Not that any of them cared about the rodeo. They'd known him more from the TV commercials and magazine ads he'd been in. She vividly remembered the life-sized poster of him wearing Wrangler jeans, a black Stetson, and nothing else, that had hung in her suitemate's room.

"Actually, I'm surprised to see him here," Mike said. "He doesn't usually come to these things. You want to meet him?"

Her eyes widened at the thought. An offer to meet any other celebrity in the room would have pleased her rather than intimidated her. But this was Trey Evans, a walking female fantasy. "I— I—"

"Come on." Mike took her by the elbow and led her across the room. "Hey, Trey!" he called over the music as they drew close.

Kate scrambled for something remotely intelligent to say—anything that wouldn't make her sound like an idiot. Then the man turned to fully face her and she froze. A jagged scar slashed down one cheek from temple to jaw, pulling the corner of his eye down and his mouth up in a permanent snarl. He nodded in greeting as he shook hands with Mike.

"Trey, I want you to meet Kate, a friend of mine

who lives out here at the lake." To Kate he added, "Trey is playing Kevin Wells's stunt double."

"I'm, um, pleased to meet you," Kate stammered, trying not to stare as empathy squeezed her chest. *His face,* she thought, *his beautiful face.* She couldn't even imagine the physical and emotional pain he must have suffered from whatever accident had left his face so ravaged.

"So, where's Jesse?" Mike asked. "Since I know coming to something like this wasn't your idea."

Trey grimaced in agreement and nodded toward a cluster of women by the dance floor.

"Jesse!" Mike called.

A young woman lifted her head and smiled. At Mike's wave, she headed toward them with a coltish kind of energy to her gait. She wore a broomstick skirt, western-yoked shirt, and cowboy boots. Her dark hair swung in a thick braid down her back.

"Hey, Magic Man, good to see ya." Jesse thrust out her hand with the straightforwardness of a man. "I heard you were working on this dog-'n'-pony show." When Mike introduced Kate, Jesse turned to her with the same down-home friendly smile.

"So," Mike said to Trey, "I hear you actually agreed to leap from a train into a river—on horseback?"

Trey made a series of motions with his hands. Watching him, Jesse said, "If the ASPCA says I can."

"And what does your horse have to say about it?" Mike asked.

Again Trey moved his hands in sign language and Jesse spoke. "For enough carrots, that crazy horse'll do anything."

Mike snorted. "I still say they should use CGi to animate the whole thing."

"Not a chance," Jesse interpreted as Trey signed.

"You computer nerds can't have all the fun."

"Maybe not," Mike said. "But at least we don't risk our fool necks every time we create a special effect."

Trey started to sign again, but Jesse put her hand over his. "Enough shoptalk," she growled playfully at the former bull rider. "I came here to dance. And you owe me one, remember?"

Trey rolled his eyes toward Mike as if to say, *Women!*

Jesse just laughed. "He lost me a game of dominoes, so now he has to pay up."

"Well, that explains it." Mike laughed as Jesse grabbed Trey's arm and dragged him toward the dance floor.

Kate stood numbly watching them go. An odd blend of emotions swirled inside her. In spite of Trey's slight limp, he glided over the floor as only a born and bred cowboy could, with knees slightly bent and hips perfectly still. Jesse smiled up at him, adoration in her eyes, blind to his scar and so proud to be his partner she beamed. A lump formed in Kate's throat.

"He was trampled by a bull," Mike explained, in answer to her unspoken question. "Apparently he suffered some brain damage, which is why he uses sign language."

She thought of the commercials he'd made, and how the girls in her dorm used to sigh dramatically just at the sound of his deep, husky voice. "Will he ever be able to talk again?"

"Actually, his speech loss was only temporary," Mike said. "I've heard him talk a few times and he sounds fine to me, but apparently the stutter embarrasses him."

"Well, at least he has Jesse to interpret for him. Have they been together long?"

"They've worked together as long as I've known them."

"No, I meant *together*," she clarified.

"Together? As in *together*? Trey and Jesse?" He laughed. "Trust me, Kate, those two are more like brother and sister. Trey's known her since she was just a kid."

Kate looked back at the dance floor and noticed for the first time how Trey held Jesse slightly away from him, the way a man danced with a female relative. Her heart went out to Jesse. On a personal level, she knew too well the pain of not having one's love returned with the intensity it was given. Professionally, though, she wished she could pull the girl aside for ten minutes of advice on how to get the man to do the chasing.

"Perhaps someone should point out to Trey that Jesse isn't exactly a kid anymore," she said.

"Hmm?" Mike glanced at the dance floor as well. An appreciative look came over his face as if he were seeing Jesse for the first time. "You know, you're right."

Kate frowned at the admiring gleam that entered Mike's eyes. She felt illogically irked that Mike had noticed what Trey had not. "She's too young," she said.

"What, for Trey?"

"No, for you."

He looked at her, surprised, and then his expression turned mischievous. "Darn, are you sure? And here I was about ready to drag her off and marry her the minute she came off the dance floor."

"I'm afraid courting a wife isn't quite that easy."

"No kidding," he mumbled, then slipped his arm around her waist. "So, how about I dance with you instead?"

"Absolutely not." She leapt away, hating the way her heart fluttered every time he touched her. "You're here to look for a wife, not dance with me."

"Who says I can't do both?"

"I do." She scowled at him, wishing he didn't look so tempting in the soft, colored lights. "And since you hired me as your dating coach, the least you can do is follow my advice."

"All right," he sighed. "Coach me."

She looked around, searching for a course of action. Her gaze landed on a table where Traci and Frank had joined several others. "You should start by asking Traci to dance with you."

"Traci?" Mike looked dumbfounded at the suggestion.

"Sure." Kate shrugged. "She seemed impressed enough by you to be interested in a personal overture. Just remember to keep it light at first."

"You want me to come on to a woman who makes a living mutilating bodies?"

"Not 'come on' to her. Just test the waters to see how well you mix. Besides"—Kate patted his arm—"I don't think she meant any of that mutilation stuff literally."

"Yeah, well, if I start bleeding all over the dance floor, I expect you to come rescue me."

"What, you're not willing to bleed a little to get a wife?"

"Actually," he grumbled, "you'd be shocked to learn what I'm willing to do."

# *Chapter 11*

*Oops*, sorry," Traci said as she stumbled over Mike's feet.

"No problem. My fault." Mike dredged up a smile as he held the woman a bit farther away. He'd been trying off and on throughout the evening to teach her the Texas two-step. Not that he'd perfected the dance himself, but at least he left his partner's toes intact.

A burst of laughter drew his attention back toward the table. He narrowed his eyes at Kate and Frank, who sat with their heads together looking as chummy as old lovers.

"Sorry," Traci said again and Mike hid a grimace as pain shot up his leg. One more dance with Traci and he really would be bleeding on the dance floor. "I just don't get this two-step stuff, you know," she complained, studying her feet. "Why can't they dance like normal people around here?"

*Good question,* he thought as his gaze drifted back toward Kate. He imagined holding her in his arms as their bodies swayed to some smoky, soft-rock tune. Of course, at the moment, he'd settle for just getting her to smile at him as openly as she was smiling at Frank.

"Do you think it's working?" Traci asked.

"Hmm?" He glanced down and found his dance partner looking toward the table.

"Have you managed to make her jealous yet?"

His neck heated as he realized he'd been caught. The first time he'd asked Traci to dance had been to appease Kate, and to keep up the pretense of a wife hunt. Each time after that had been with a growing need to get Kate's attention.

"It's okay, I don't mind," Traci hastened to say. Her combat boot slammed against his foot. "Oh, sorry. I just hope it works before you lose all your toes."

"What's a few toes between friends?" He smiled, even though he'd never felt more miserable. When he'd invited Kate to the party, he hadn't planned on spending the evening watching her flirt with every man in the room but him. The song came to an end, and he and Traci instantly stepped apart.

"Like, maybe you should go back to dancing with Jesse," Traci suggested as they applauded the band. "At least when you do that, she notices a little. I think."

"I have a better idea," Mike said near her ear as they left the dance floor. "Why don't you ask Frank to dance? Sort of clear the playing field for me."

"Frank?" She blinked her owlish eyes at him. "You want me to dance with Frank Goldstein?"

He sent her a pleading look.

Traci's cheeks puffed as she exhaled. "All right. But only if the band plays some real music. This country shit is too out there, you know?"

Kate glanced up as they took their seats. For the barest instant, her smile faltered, then brightened as if she were intentionally turning up the wattage. "Having fun?" she asked.

"The time of my life," Mike insisted, kicking back in the chair as if he actually meant it.

"Glad to hear it." She looked so damned sincere, his ego took another nosedive.

"Yep, Traci here's a real natural at the two-step." He draped his arm around the startled makeup artist, and gave her a one-arm hug. "Isn't that right, Trace?"

Traci choked on her drink. "Yeah, a real natural."

"In fact, she was just telling me how she could dance all night to this music. Too bad my feet are wearing out." He nudged Traci, feeling only a twinge of guilt on behalf of Frank's feet.

With a sigh, Traci turned to the FX supervisor. "So, Goldstein, you want to, like, give it a whirl? This two-step sh—stuff is totally radical."

"Excuse me?" Frank frowned at her.

"Dance," she said between clenched teeth. "Do you want to dance with me?"

"Oh, well, I . . ." He looked at Kate, clearly reluctant to leave her side. Mike's sympathy vanished in a heartbeat. He hoped Traci annihilated the man's toes.

"Come on." Standing, Traci grabbed Frank's arm and all but hauled him out of his chair. As they left, silence fell at the end of the table where Mike finally sat alone with Kate.

"So," she said after a moment. "I take it things are going well with you and Traci?"

"Couldn't be better." Didn't she care at all that he'd spent most of the evening dancing with other women?

"I'm glad to hear it." She smiled.

"Yeah, I'm sure you are." He narrowed his eyes at her, looking for any spark of attraction. "After all, the sooner you shove me off on someone else, the sooner you'll be rid of me."

"That was the general idea." Her smile turned a bit brittle. "Now, if you'll excuse me . . ." She scraped her chair back and rose.

"Where are you going?" He reached for her hand on reflex. Was that hurt he saw in her eyes?

"Outside." She shook him off. "I need some fresh air."

As she hurried away, he forced himself to stay put. *Well, hell,* he thought. He'd certainly managed to clear the playing field—completely.

Kate gripped the rail of the balcony, tipped her head back and stared at the dazzling sky. *I refuse to be jealous,* she told herself for the hundredth time that evening. *I refuse!*

But the little green monster remained lodged in her chest, digging in with vicious claws.

She tried again to tell herself Mike was off limits. He'd hired her to do a job, and she was determined to do it to the best of her abilities. She had no business even thinking about getting involved with the man herself. Not when she was trying to get her life on steady ground. The last thing in the world she wanted was the emotional roller coaster of a relationship, no matter how much a man tempted her physically.

Especially since Mike was very serious about wanting a permanent relationship. While all she wanted was . . . well, *him.*

Her eyes drifted closed as she pictured his slow, sexy grin, his laughing blue eyes. She imagined him pulling her into his arms, their bodies brushing together. . . .

*What am I doing?* Her eyes popped open. Physical attraction was no basis for a relationship. She blew out a breath, wishing she could release the sexual tension inside her as easily as she released the air from her lungs. A walk, she decided. What she needed was a nice long walk that would put some distance between her and temptation.

Mike forced himself to wait a full thirty minutes before going after her. Stepping out onto the balcony, he scanned the dimly lit grounds, which sloped down toward the rows of bungalows that lined the cliff. *Where could she be?*

Descending the stairs, he took a stone path that meandered through the gardens. The sounds of katydids and splashing water filled the night as the music from the bar grew distant. Rounding the corner of a high retaining wall, he found her seated in a lounger by the swimming pool, gazing up at the sky.

He stopped for a moment, mesmerized by the sight of her bathed in moonlight. Behind her, a waterfall splashed down the side of the wall into the far end of the swimming pool. Potted flowers and ferns created the illusion of an enchanted lagoon.

He longed to go to her, to sink to his knees beside her chair and cover her mouth with his own, to cover her body with his body.

Shoving his hands in his pockets, he cleared his throat. "So, this is where you've been hiding."

She jumped at the sound of his voice, but shadows hid her expression as she turned to peer into the darkness that surrounded him. "Just getting some air," she said, her voice high with tension.

"It's a nice night for it." He came toward her, into the light, hoping to put her at ease. Before he could join her on the lounger, though, she scrambled to her feet. He stopped a short distance away and tipped his head toward the sky. "Great view."

"Yes, it is." He felt her study his profile, and forced

himself to stay still. The light from the pool danced about them, bathing everything it touched in blue.

"I'll never get used to all the stars here. Real stars," he clarified. "Not the kind that live in Hollywood Hills. Out in L.A. you're lucky to see any stars in the sky for all the city lights."

"Do you miss it? L.A., I mean."

"Sometimes." He lowered his gaze to smile at her. "But I like it here better. Here there's more room and less pretentiousness. That and no earthquakes," he added with a slow smile.

"No earthquakes," Kate repeated. Turning away, she wondered if he'd brought some of those tremors with him, for her knees had begun to shake. In the distance, she heard the band play the opening strains to the Mavericks' tune, "My Secret Flame." Mike came up behind her. Her breath caught and held as she waited for him to touch her, feared that he would even as she feared that he wouldn't.

"Dance with me, Kate."

She shook her head. "I already told you, we shouldn't. People will get the wrong idea about us."

"I don't see anyone here but you and me." His hands settled on her shoulders and the warmth of his touch relaxed her muscles. "Dance with me. I need the practice."

"You seem to need practice in a great many areas." She chided him with her eyes as she turned.

"Noticed that, did you?" He slipped his arm around her waist and drew her against him.

She turned her head, trying to concentrate on the music rather than how well his body fit against hers, how well they moved together. He was tall enough that her head could easily rest on his shoulder if she let it. As he danced her around the pool, the lyrics of hidden love played softly in the night air.

His hand moved up her back, drawing her closer. Against her better judgment, she settled against him, letting him fill her senses. *So this is how it feels to be held in his arms,* she thought. They danced toward the seclusion of the waterfall and his lips moved against her hair as he sang softly to the music. " 'My heart beats fast when I hear your name—you'll always be my secret flame . . .' "

The words sounded like a soft confession, straight from his heart. She closed her eyes, allowing herself to believe that he meant them. Was it so wrong to want, just once, to be the most important thing in a man's life?

His steps slowed as the song sighed into silence. They stood for a moment, neither of them moving. Slowly, she lifted her head from his shoulder and opened her eyes. His face hovered above hers as he cupped her cheek in his hand and lowered his mouth.

Entranced, she welcomed the first brush of his lips, so long awaited, so long feared. His mouth retreated and returned, as soft and hesitant as a young girl's dream. His hand slipped into her hair as he deepened the kiss. She tightened her arms around his neck, wanting, yearning. Emotions tumbled through her, too many to grasp.

He walked her backward and honeysuckle enveloped her as her back pressed against the vine-covered wall. Past and future faded. Nothing existed but now, the quiet splash of the waterfall and the glorious pleasure of his body molded to hers.

"Kate," he whispered hoarsely as his mouth trailed down her neck. His hands moved restlessly over her sides, as if wanting to touch her more intimately but not quite daring to try. She arched her head back, giving him access to her neck, wanting more, but fearing the very thing she craved. He pressed his lips to her pulse, kissing her neck with abandon. "You're driving me crazy in that dress. You know that, don't you?"

A hum of acknowledgment purred deep in her throat as she felt his arousal against her stomach. Resolve crumbled in the face of desire. She nudged him with her hips and thrilled to the sound of his quickly drawn breath. Her hands ran over his shoulders, his chest, down to his stomach, exploring the well-honed body that lay hidden beneath his clothes.

He took her mouth again, his kiss rough and ravenous. Her heart soared at his obvious hunger. *So, this was how it feels to be wanted. Truly wanted.* She lifted one leg along the outside of his. His hands moved to her thigh, pulling her hard against him. The dress bunched about her hips as he cupped and kneaded her bottom. Heat flooded through her. Their bodies pressed and moved together as the pleasure built.

"Christ." He broke the kiss, his breathing ragged as his forehead dropped to hers. "This was not a good idea."

"Hmm?" she murmured.

"I want you, Kate." With a knuckle beneath her chin, he tipped her face toward his, waited for her eyes to open. "And I'm tired of pretending that I don't."

The haze of desire receded enough for his words to sink in.

His gaze bored into hers. "I want you."

She shook her head to clear it. "Oh, my God," she whispered, horrified. "What am I doing?"

"It's okay." He brushed a kiss onto her forehead. "Don't get panicky on me."

"I'm not panicky," she said, her voice rising. "I—I just think you're right, that's all. This was not a good idea."

"Actually, it was a great idea, just really bad timing." The smile that flashed across his face was so endearing, her heart clenched. "A problem we could quickly remedy by leaving."

"Yes. Yes, I think that's an excellent idea." She scrambled out of his arms and staggered a few steps away. Pulling the hem of her dress down, she tucked a stray curl back into place. "I think we should leave."

He came up behind her, his arm going about her waist as he snuggled her bottom against the hardness of his groin. "I'll go get the car." His lips feathered kisses across her shoulder and her knees went weak. "We can be at my place in five minutes." His lips moved across her nape to her other shoulder. "Make that four."

She closed her eyes as her body longed to give in, to let him soothe the ache that lay deep inside her. "Mike, no. That's not what I meant."

"Hmm?" The sound rumbled against her back.

"I meant that I want to go my place." Closing her eyes, she swallowed against tears of frustration. "I want to go home—alone."

His body went still. Slowly he lifted his head. "Kate," he sighed. "I want to be with you, I won't lie about that, but I won't push for more than you're ready to give."

"You're already pushing!" She stepped away and turned to face him. "Don't you understand? I'm not interested in a relationship."

He had the gall to laugh. "That's ridiculous. After a kiss like that, you can't tell me you're not interested."

"All right, physically, yes, maybe I am interested. But that doesn't make it right."

"Right?"

"For me. This— You— Me—" She made a hopeless gesture with her hand. "It's all wrong. For me."

He stared at her a long time before resignation settled over his face. "All right," he said at last. "If that's what you want, I'll take you home."

"Yes." She swallowed again, not knowing if she wanted to sigh in relief or cry. "That's exactly what I want."

"I'll get the car, then."

She nodded, refusing to meet his eyes. "I'll meet you out front."

Without another word, he walked away. She bit her lip, fighting the urge to call him back. She'd made the right choice, dammit. They had no future together. Mike wanted more than she was ready or willing to give. Yes, she'd made the right choice. For both of them.

So why did it feel so wrong?

Mike wanted to kick himself as he drove Kate home. Of all the stupid things to do! He couldn't believe he'd kissed her like that. Not that kissing her was a mistake. That part was good. Fantastic, actually. She'd tasted exactly as he'd known she would, as if he'd known her taste all his life. But he should have left it there, one tantalizing kiss, just hot enough to give her something to think about, but not threatening enough to scare her off.

He glanced sideways. She sat perfectly still, staring straight ahead with a wide-eyed look that twisted his gut. In his thirty-eight years of life, he'd met a lot of women and certainly more than one divorcée, but he had never met any woman as gun-shy as Kate.

He gripped the steering wheel and fought the urge to ask her what the hell her ex-husband had done to make her so leery of men. How could anyone hurt this woman? In the short time he'd known her, he could already see that his first impressions were right. She was intelligent, funny, sexy. And he wanted her— more than he'd ever wanted anything. Yet, for the first time in his life, he didn't have a clue how to go after his goal.

"Look, Kate," he finally said. "I'm sorry about what happened back there—"

"It's okay," she hastened to say. "There's nothing to apologize for. I simply think we should keep things on a business level, since I am working for you."

"You're right." *Stupid, idiot, moron.* She'd told him specifically: You can date someone who works *with* you but not *for* you, and keep it light until you know if they're interested.

Well, he'd certainly broken both of those rules. "I didn't mean to push you into anything you're not ready for yet."

"What do you mean 'yet'?" Her eyes grew larger. "Please tell me you haven't put me on your mental list of possible wives."

"Oh, no!" he insisted, even though she was the only name on that list. "You've made it quite clear you're not interested in the position."

"Good." Nodding, she went back to watching the road.

"It's just that I thought in the meantime, we could, you know . . ." He trailed off, cringing at his own words. What a dumb thing to say. He held his breath, waiting to be flamed with an adamant refusal.

"No," she said at last, in a much quieter voice than he'd expected. He glanced over in time to catch the frown that dimpled her brow. "No, I don't think that would be a good idea at all."

Hope flared to life. Unless he mistook the signs, she was considering the possibility of an affair with him. And if he managed to keep his big mouth shut about his true intentions, who knew where that could lead?

When they reached her cabin, he pulled up under the grove of trees and cut the engine. She scrambled from the car, denying him the chance to open the door for her. Gritting his teeth, he followed her onto the tiny front porch. The porch light gave off a feeble glow, casting a faint halo over her tousled hair as she dug in her purse for her keys.

"Will I see you tomorrow?" he asked.

She looked up at him, frowning. "Tomorrow's Sunday."

"You're right, I meant Monday. I assume Jim will be by to fix the hole in my ceiling."

She bit her lip. "I'm sorry about your house."

He plowed his hands through his hair. "I don't care about the house." *I care about you.* "So, will I see you Monday or not?"

"I can't come until afternoon. I have too much work to do on my column."

"Fine. As long as you're there to keep an eye on the crew."

She nodded, without meeting his eyes. They stood there for an awkward moment, neither of them moving. More than anything, he wanted to gather her into his arms and indulge in a long, wet, good-night kiss.

Or, better yet, have her invite him inside. That, however, was not going to happen tonight.

He sighed in frustration. "Well, then, I guess I'll see you Monday."

Before he could make an even bigger fool of himself, he turned and headed back to his car. With every step, he vowed that the next time he saw her, he'd find some way to get her back into his arms and show her he was right for her—as right for her as she was for him.

# Chapter 12

*Dear Cupid,*
*Every time I try to do something romantic,*
*like buy my girlfriend flowers, she gets all*
*huffy and says I'm just trying to get into*
*her pants. I don't get it. Do women like*
*roses or not?*

*Confused*

*Dear Confused,*
*Most women adore flowers of any kind—*
*depending on who they're from and why*
*they're given. So, the question is, are you*
*trying to romance her heart or seduce her*
*body?*
*     If you are bent on seduction, take the*
*time to learn her fantasies and gift her with*
*pleasure. If, however, you strive to win her*
*heart, take the time to learn her dreams,*
*and offer a gift that shows your under-*
*standing and support.*

*Cupid*

Nodding in satisfaction after she finished her last letter, Kate shut down the computer and headed for the

Davises' to get Dylan. The sun had yet to burn off the dew that dampened her feet through the open toes of her high-heeled shoes. As much as she enjoyed the casualness of working at home, she liked church on Sundays for the chance to dress up.

"Is anybody home?" she called through the side door of the house on the hill.

"Up here," Linda called back.

Kate went up the half flight of stairs to the main level of the house. The large open area that combined the living room, dining room, and kitchen offered a view of the Hill Country and Lake Travis. She found Dylan already dressed for church and eating breakfast with Linda and Jim.

"There's my best boy," she said and kissed his sticky cheek. "Mmm, maple syrup. My favorite."

"Want some?" he asked, holding up a forkful of pancake.

"Maybe I'll just have you instead." He giggled when she made gobbling noises against his cheek. Just being near her son filled her heart with joy. "I missed you last night."

He bobbed his head in agreement, his cheeks bulging as he filled his mouth with pancake.

"There's coffee in the kitchen," Linda said. "And plenty of pancakes if you want some."

"I'll take you up on the coffee." Kate sighed, and headed for the cabinet to get down a mug. Even though she and Mike hadn't stayed out that late, she'd spent the remainder of the night staring into the dark, remembering the passion of his kiss and the hungers he had stirred within her.

"Did you have fun last night?" Linda asked from the table with enough innuendo to let Kate know she was asking about Mike, not the party.

Kate's hand tightened on the coffeepot before she forced it to relax. "The party was great. They had live music, tons of food, and the people! You've never seen such an eclectic crowd. You'd have loved it, Linda."

"Only I would have loved it alone. Jim hates parties." Linda made a face at her husband.

Smiling over her coffee mug, Kate watched Jim as she said, "Rachel Lee was there."

"Oh, yeah?" His eyes lit up. "As in the actual Rachel Lee?"

"The genuine article," Kate confirmed.

"Now, that's one party I wouldn't have minded going to."

"Jim Davis!" Linda batted her husband playfully on the shoulder. "Why don't you and Dylan finish getting ready for church?"

"In other words," Jim said to Dylan, "why don't you men get lost so us women can talk." Dylan giggled as Jim took both their plates to the sink. "Come on, partner," Jim said. "Let's go get the present you made for your mom."

"You made me a present?" Kate asked, delighted.

"Uh-huh. A wooden paperweight." Dylan nodded, his eyes wide. She gave silent thanks that he'd told her what the gift was, since some of them were difficult to figure out. "It's out in the shop," he said. "So you have to wait here while I go get it."

She smiled as her son dashed from the room with Jim lumbering slowly in his wake.

"That shop," Linda grumbled, clearing away the last of the dishes. "I swear I should get a case of dynamite and blow the thing to smithereens. Then Jim would *have* to spend some time with me."

"I take it your evening didn't go as planned?" Kate asked, concerned.

With angry jerks, Linda piled the dishes by the sink and turned on the water. "After we put Dylan to bed, Jim went right back out to that stupid shop, and stayed there so long, I fell asleep. So much for seduction."

"There's always tonight." Kate leaned her hip against the counter, sipping coffee as her friend loaded the dishwasher. "Speaking of Dylan, did Jim talk to him?"

"Of course he talked to him." Linda attacked the sticky plates with a food scrubber. "All he did last night was talk to your son, which saved him from having to talk to me!" She stopped abruptly, and closed her eyes. "I'm sorry. I didn't mean that to sound like a complaint against Dylan."

"I know you didn't. I'm just sorry you and Jim are having problems." Lord, if Linda and Jim couldn't be happy together, there really wasn't any hope left for romance.

"Yeah, me too," Linda said in a quiet voice that alarmed Kate more than any burst of anger. "And to answer your question, yes, Jim found out what's bothering Dylan."

"Oh?" Kate felt a skitter of nerves.

"You know the talent show the school puts on every spring?"

"Yes?"

"Apparently, Jason Haynie talked his dad into doing some sort of father-son routine."

"Oh." Understanding fell heavy on Kate's shoulders. "So now I suppose Dylan wants his dad to do a skit with him."

Linda gave her a sympathetic look. "He asked Jim for advice on how to talk Edward into it."

Kate's shoulders sagged. "We both know the chances of Edward agreeing are next to nil. Or worse, he'll agree, and then promptly forget about it, which will hurt Dylan far more."

"Or . . ." Linda began. "Jim could offer to do a skit with him."

"Jim? On a stage? In front of an audience?" Kate laughed at the image that sprang to mind. "The man would die of stage fright."

"But he'd do it. For Dylan."

"Yes, he would." Kate sighed, grateful for Jim's interest in her son, but concerned about the relationship becoming awkward. What would happen when the baby came? Would Jim still be as willing to play surrogate dad to a friend's child when he had a child of his own? "I don't know. I'll keep it in mind."

Linda nodded in understanding, then her eyes lit as she veered back to the original topic. "So, tell me about last night."

"I already did." Kate smiled, even as her stomach tightened.

"Details, Kate. I want details."

Shaking her head, Kate gave in, but strictly avoided any mention of her dance with Mike by the pool, or the heated kiss they'd shared. Or the fact that she'd lain awake all night wondering what to do about it. Even now, in the morning light, fantasies of what could have happened warmed her skin. She felt like the clichéd divorcée, hungering for a lover's touch, even as her battered heart cringed at the thought of emotional involvement. Worst of all, the inevitable question had wormed its way into her head: What if she could have the physical without the emotional?

She shook the question off, knowing such a shallow involvement was wrong for her and unfair to Mike. At

least she'd have a day's reprieve before she had to see
him again.

On Monday, the rain started just as Kate returned from
taking Dylan to school. With the sound of it drumming
against the roof, she booted up her computer and settled in to get some work done. She'd had an inspiration during the night for her next column: "Party
Flirting: How to Keep it Platonic."

With every sentence she typed, she felt more and
more as if she were lecturing herself rather than hand-
ing out advice to others. In hindsight, she saw a dozen
ways she could have handled the situation with Mike
differently right from the beginning. The question now
was, how to proceed from here. If only she had somewhere to turn for advice like her readers did.

The thought stopped her mid-sentence. "All right,"
she said. "So, what advice would Dear Cupid give to
someone in this pickle?"

Before she could come up with any words of wisdom, the phone rang. She answered it absently, her
mind still focused inward.

"Kate! Have you seen that thing on your Web
page?" the caller demanded.

"What?" She frowned, recognizing Gwen's voice.
"What thing?"

"That flying Cupid." Anxiety crackled over the line
like static electricity. "The Web master called me this
morning to tell me about it. I can't believe it!"

As Gwen went off on a tangent about computer
hackers and deadly viruses, Kate clicked on the book-
mark that would take her to her Web site. For the most
part, she tuned out Gwen's words. Even back in college, Gwen had been a knee-jerk alarmist who over-

reacted to any hint that she wasn't the one in control.

When the page finished loading, Kate stared in wonder at the new, animated graphic for her front page: a beautiful, charming, whimsical graphic. Rather than the stationary cupid stuck above the curlicue script, a da Vinci–style sketch of a cupid fluttered playfully around and through the letters. Then it swept downward and toward her, until it landed at the bottom of the screen with one forearm resting on the edge of the window and the other forearm raised so the chin rested in the hand—the classic pose of Raphael's angel from the *Sistine Madonna*. Rather than a serene, contemplative expression, though, this winged cherub looked straight at her and gave her a very cheeky wink.

Kate laughed in delight; the cupid looked just like her! Not in the manner of a serious portrait, but still the artist had captured her perfectly.

"And just what do you think is so funny?" Gwen demanded.

"It's wonderful," Kate breathed. If Gwen had gone to the trouble to have her page redesigned, then surely her job was once again on sure footing. "Oh, Gwen, I love it. Who did it?"

"That's precisely what I'd like to know. So I can have them sued."

"Sued?" Kate frowned. "Gwen, what are you talking about?"

"Some hacker broke into our Web site during the night and put that . . . that thing on your front page. Do you know what this means? Someone out there might have copied all the files in our database, our business records, our client lists. And for all we know, they left behind some time-bomb virus that could explode any second and wipe everything out."

"I don't understand." Kate tried to focus on Gwen's words. "Who would do such a thing?"

"Obviously someone who knows you, or at least knows what you look like. Which is another thing that worries me. God, Kate, for all we know, there's some wacko out there who's formed an attachment to you. Look what happened to Jodi Foster. And John Lennon."

Kate mentally weeded through Gwen's paranoia. "What makes you think the person knows me?"

"Well, look at the thing. It looks just like you."

Kate's gaze snapped toward the cupid. Not only did it resemble her, the animation was top-notch professional. "Mike," she breathed in disbelief.

"Who?" Gwen asked. "Are you saying you know who did this?"

"No, not for sure, but I have a suspicion." *And if it's true, I'm going to kill him.* How dare he pull a stunt like this when her job hung by a thread?

"Well, find out, for God's sake."

"I will, I assure you." She gave the cartoon one last look, her heart breaking at the thought that it had to go. "And I'll tell him to take the cupid off immediately."

"No!" Gwen shouted. "Tell your friend to stay the hell out of my Web site."

"Oh, don't worry, I'll tell him that." *And a whole lot more.*

# *Chapter 13*

*A* volley of thunder shook the windows of Mike's workroom. He glanced up briefly, distracted by the drama of black clouds hurling lightning and rain at the hills and lake. In the background, the radio he'd tuned in to the weather station offered a steady stream of alarming updates. He'd learned soon after moving to Texas that tornadoes could be as deadly and unpredictable as the earthquakes he'd left behind in L.A. With weather like this, he had a sinking feeling he wouldn't see Kate, or anyone else that day.

He turned back to the computer screen and tried once more to concentrate on work. He'd finished creating the 3-D robot, and had begun the tedious task of assigning keystroke commands for every movement of the hands, arms, legs, and head. Though time-consuming, the process required little concentration, which allowed his mind too much freedom to wander.

For the hundredth time, his thoughts went back to the scene by the pool. He never should have let the kiss get out of hand. From the beginning, he'd known to approach Kate cautiously. She'd obviously been hurt, and badly, for her to act with such frosty reserve.

He remembered how she'd been in L.A., feisty, sexy, confident. *That,* he suspected, was the real Kate—the Kate he'd fallen in love with the moment he'd laid eyes on her. The question was, how to get past the wounded Kate to the real woman she kept so carefully guarded? Did he push harder, or back off?

Over the low hum of the radio, he thought he heard the doorbell ring. He cocked his head, wondering if he'd imagined the sound. Who in their right mind would venture out in midst of a major thunderstorm? The sound came again, this time in a long insistent series of rings that demanded attention.

He hit the command to save his file and dashed up the stairs. He found Kate standing in the protection of the overhang with her arms wrapped around her middle, her body shivering. Rain poured off the roof like a gray curtain behind her while droplets glistened in her hair and darkened the shoulders of her tangerine-colored T-shirt-and-shorts set. Even so, the sight of her knocked the air from his lungs, as it always did.

"You idiot," he said, pulling her inside. "What are you doing driving in this weather?"

"What am *I* doing? The question is, what are *you* doing?" She shook her head, scattering raindrops over him and the tile floor. "Are you trying to get me fired?"

"Do you realize there's a tornado watch in effect?"

"Oh, for heaven's sake, Mike, it's springtime in Texas. Of course there's a tornado watch in effect. When they issue a tornado *warning,* then I'll get worried. Now will you answer my question?"

"What question?"

"What did you think you were doing, putting that animation on my Web page?"

"Saw it, did you?" He grinned. Even though the animation was relatively simple, he'd spent an entire day and half the night creating it for her. It was his form of an apology, he supposed, a kind of peace offering.

"Yes, I saw it!" she snapped. "And so did Gwen, the woman who owns the e-zine that sponsors my site. Do you have any idea how furious she is?"

"Why?" He frowned. "Because I gave you a present that would normally cost a few grand?"

"A few . . . *grand*?" Her face paled for an instant, before anger had the color flooding back. "Are you crazy? I didn't ask you to give me anything. Especially not something so, so—"

"Personal?"

"Outrageous!" Her hands flew, adding emphasis to every word. Her fire and energy completely enthralled him. "You broke into Gwen's Web site. For all she knows you corrupted her files, stole data, planted a virus."

"I didn't break into her site," he said defensively. "I broke into yours, and did some badly needed sprucing up. As for Gwen's accusations, I hope you know me better than to think I'd steal or destroy anything."

"Of course I do. But she doesn't." Kate placed a hand over her eyes as if to forestall a headache. "I can't believe you did this to me. Do you realize I could get fired over something like this?"

"That's nonsense. It's your Web site."

"No it's not." She dropped her hand. "I only write the articles. Gwen pays for the site. But even if it were my site, I resent your arrogant assumption that I would want you to go in and spruce it up, whether it needed it or not. God!" She strode away from him. "You're no better than Edward, thinking I'm too stupid or inept to take care of my own business."

"Wait a second." He followed after her but stopped when she whirled on him.

"Well, I have news for you, Michael Cameron, I'm doing just fine on my own, and I don't need any interference from you!"

"All right." He held up his hands in surrender, even as his fingers itched to touch her. "Do you think we could sit down and discuss this rationally?"

"I don't feel like being rational. I feel like throwing something!"

"I have some old dishes in the kitchen," he offered. "Since they're mismatched, you'll probably want to throw them out anyway. So, what do you say? Want to throw my plates in the fireplace? I'll even help, if you like."

She stared at him a moment, then shook her head as if amazed. "How do you do it?"

"Do what?"

"Make me so mad one minute, then make me want to laugh the next?"

"Family trait. Comes with the name. Now why don't you sit down while I get you a towel?"

He left her long enough to duck into the master bathroom. As he rummaged through the cabinet for a clean towel, he muttered to himself. "Great Cameron, just great. Do you think you could possibly do anything else to screw up your chances here?"

When he returned to the living room, he found her seated in the armchair rather than on the sofa, which denied him the chance to sit beside her. Not to be daunted, he knelt before her. "Here," he said, dabbing her cheek with the towel. "You're all wet."

"Mike," she complained, stilling his hand with her own. "Would you stop? I can take care of myself."

"Of course you can." He relinquished the towel, but remained where he was, just to be near her.

"It's important to me, you know. Taking care of myself."

"Why's that?"

"Because I spent too many years letting my parents and then my husband do things for me. Do you realize, I'd never even balanced a checkbook until two years ago?"

"There's more important things in life than balancing a checkbook."

"Not to me there isn't." She dried her forehead. "Which is why what you did really ticks me off. Being Dear Cupid is the only thing I've ever done on my own. Even if other people don't take it seriously, it's important to me. It's everything to me. If I lose it— If Gwen cancels me—"

"What do you mean? Do you really think she'd cancel your column because of what I did?"

"No, it's not you. It's . . ."

"What?" He took her hands in his to get her attention. "Talk to me, Kate."

She hesitated a long moment, then heaved a sigh. "Ever since I started having trouble with my marriage, I've found it difficult to be upbeat in my advice to others. That's something I'm working on, though, and the main reason I—"

"The main reason you what?" He ducked his head to meet her gaze.

"Flirted with you in L.A."

"I don't understand."

"Mike . . ." Pulling her hands free, she slicked her hair back, only to have it spring forward again in rebellious wet curls. "You have to understand, flirting is just something I do—something I learned when I was still knee-high. It was the natural, look-at-me ploy of a kid who could never get enough attention."

He rocked back on his heels to study her from an objective distance. He could picture her clearly as a child, with round cheeks and lively green eyes. "I can't imagine you having to work to get attention."

"When you're the baby of the family, and your older sister and brother are scholastic wonders and social overachievers, trust me, you have to work to remind people you're even there." She rose to pace before the windows. "The problem is . . . I haven't been very good at it lately."

"What do you mean?" He rose as well.

She wrapped her arms about herself and stared out at the lightning and rain. "Since the day I realized my marriage was over, I've, well, been a little down on men."

"Understandable." He nodded.

"Yes. And entirely acceptable, if I weren't Dear Cupid." She sighed. "That day in L.A., when we met, I had just come from a meeting with Gwen."

"And?"

"She threatened to cancel my column if I didn't turn my attitude around and become my old flirtatious self."

"I see." Some of the pieces began to fall together, and he wasn't sure he liked the picture they formed. "So you went to the airport, saw me, and decided to refresh your flirting skills."

She glanced at him over her shoulder as thunder rumbled over the house. "I just wanted to see if I still knew how to do it."

"Oh, yes. Trust me Kate, you definitely still know how to do it." He felt like a fool; something she seemed to make him feel on a regular basis. While he'd been blindsided by an instant attraction to an incredibly sexy woman, he'd been nothing more to her than an experiment. "Let me ask you this." He nailed her with a look. "Would any man have done?"

"No," she said, but the embarrassed flush of color in her cheeks made him wonder. "I was attracted to you, Mike. Still am, obviously."

"Are you?"

"Can you doubt that after what happened the other night?"

"Ah, yes. The other night."

"Speaking of . . ." She looked away again. "I've been doing a lot of thinking since then."

"And?"

"And . . ." She took a deep breath and let it out in a rush. "I can't work for you anymore."

"What?" His heart jolted and he moved around the sofa, started to reach for her, but stopped when she tensed. "What do you mean you can't work for me?"

"Well, don't you think it would be just a tiny bit awkward since you hired me to help you find a wife? After what happened . . . after we . . ." She made a helpless gesture but refused to look at him.

"Kissed?"

"Yes, I think it would be awkward."

"Why?" With his pulse racing, he laid his hand on her shoulder and tried to turn her. "Talk to me, Kate."

She turned enough to address the front of his Hawaiian shirt. "Because if we keep spending time together we both know what will happen. And that would be a huge mistake."

"How could something we both want be a mistake?"

"Because," she all but growled at him, "we're looking for entirely different things. You want something serious, something permanent, and all I want is—" She shut her mouth abruptly.

"What?"

"Nothing."

"Would you please look at me?" He cupped her neck and urged her chin up with his thumb. "Tell me, Kate, what do you want?" When her eyes lifted he finally saw what she'd been trying to hide: not mild attraction, but all-out desire. Strong enough and hot enough to match his own. But he also saw fear: felt both in the rapid pulse against his palm. "You don't have to be afraid, Kate. Just tell me what you want."

She shook her head in denial. "I don't want anything."

"Liar." He lowered his head, testing to see which would win, desire or fear. "You want this, don't you? As much as I do."

His lips brushed hers. She stiffened, but didn't pull away. He deepened the contact, testing, tasting. Her body relaxed a fraction, began to lean into him. With a murmur of defeat, she surged against him. He nearly shouted in triumph as they came together in a clash as volatile as the storm outside. Their tongues tangled, giving and taking with equal abandon.

"Yes," she sighed as her fingers slipped up along his chest. Her head dropped back as he kissed her neck. "I mean, no." He vaguely realized her touch had changed, that she pushed at his chest rather than clung. "I can't do this."

When he didn't immediately let go, she struggled to break free.

"What?" Fighting for air and reason, he loosened his arms, then tightened them when her legs buckled. She struggled harder. "Would you wait a second?" he said. "I'm not forcing you to do anything. Just talk to me, Kate."

"Talk?" Her eyes went from panicked to angry as she found her balance. "How can I talk? I can't even think when I'm near you."

"And you suppose I can?" He shook his head to clear it, then gave up. "To hell with it. We've done too much thinking already." He ran his hands over her back, felt the shudder that raced through her. "I say we stop thinking altogether."

"No." Her hands fisted in his shirt as she dropped her forehead to his chest. "I need to think. I have to, but you keep confusing me."

"Confusing you? Or scaring you?"

"You don't scare me." Her head shot up, revealing wide, frantic eyes.

"Oh, yeah?" He leaned in close. "Prove it. Kiss me, Kate. Stop thinking and kiss me."

"We shouldn't be doing this," she breathed as he laid a trail of kisses beside her mouth. She turned her head a fraction, letting their mouths brush. "It's a terrible idea."

"Speak for yourself." He cupped the back of her head. "I happen to think it's a brilliant idea." Tired of toying at the edge of the pond, he dove in headfirst, let himself drown in the textures and flavors of her mouth. He felt her go under with him, as her arms wound about his neck.

"Mike, wait." She struggled up for air. "This isn't fair to you."

"How could something I want this badly not be fair to me?"

"Because you want forever, and all I want is . . . now."

"Then take it, Kate." He took her hand and teased her palm with a kiss. He saw her eyes go heavy, felt her body tremble. "Seize the moment."

"As long as you realize"—her voice came out in a husky whisper—"this can't go anywhere. If we do this, if we wind up in bed together, we both agree it's just . . ."

"Sex?" He moved his mouth to her wrist, delighting in the rapid beat of her pulse.

"Yes." She met his eyes squarely, even as color rose in her cheeks. "There'll be no promise of happy-ever-after. No false commitment. Just what we have here and now."

His eyes hardened. "Fine. If that's what you want." He swept her into his arms.

"Mike!" she shrieked. "What are you doing?"

"Giving you what you want," he answered as he headed for the bedroom.

"You don't have to carry me. Besides, I'm too heavy!"

"The day a Cameron can't carry a woman to bed is the day I change my name." When he reached the master suite, he tossed her into the middle of the king-sized water bed. Her eyes widened as he climbed onto the bed and crawled toward her on all fours until he hovered over her. Beneath her, water sloshed, while lightning and thunder raged beyond the windows. She felt as if she'd been cast into a lifeboat on a storm-tossed sea. "You want mindless, emotionless sex? Then that's what I'll give you."

Her heart slammed into her throat, but before she could answer, his mouth came down over hers. Hard. Demanding. Excitement flared, blinding her in a white-hot rush. Yes, this was what she wanted, needed. Not the polite exchange between two people who shared their bodies because they shared a bed. When love died, sex became just another part of being married, like doing the laundry and paying the mort-gage.

This, however, was anything but polite. With savage efficiency, he pulled her top over her head and tossed it across the room. His mouth descended to the swell of her breasts above her lacy peach-colored bra.

Gasping, she arched beneath him, caught by a wild recklessness she'd only dreamed of, read about, written about, but never thought to experience herself. Waves of heat washed through her as his hands moved down her body, caressing every curve until he cupped her bottom and brought her hips firmly against his rigid arousal. "Touch me, Kate. However you want. I'm all yours."

Emboldened by his husky words, she slipped her hands beneath the shirt and discovered the body that lay beneath. She'd wondered about the feel of it, oh, how she'd wondered, and now she knew. Hard, heated flesh greeted her at every turn from the solid chest to the taut stomach. One of his thighs moved between hers, pressing and rubbing with deadly skill. She writhed within his embrace, thrilled by his strength and his urgency.

She lifted her hips as he removed her shorts. His eyes darkened when he discovered the lacy peach thong that matched her bra. When his gaze traveled back to hers, she saw amusement mix with approval. "I take it 'passionate peach' is your favorite color?"

A chuckle escaped her at the reference to the lipstick she'd dropped in L.A. How could any man be so arrogantly aggressive and light-hearted at the same time? The combination proved irresistible. "Absolutely," she said in her most sultry voice.

With a growl, he kissed her mouth, her neck, worked his way down to her breasts. Rather than remove the bra, he lowered the lace just enough to reveal the coral nipples that waited beneath.

"God," he said, shaking his head. "Do you have any idea what you do to me?"

"Perhaps you could show me."

And he did. With every touch, every kiss, he took her to places she'd only imagined—wild, wonderful places that left her breathless and greedy for more.

He shed his shirt, kicked free of his shorts and briefs. Her bra and thong quickly followed. Naked at last, they rolled together, a tangle of eager hands and desperate bodies until she pressed him to his back and straddled his hips.

"The nightstand," he mumbled against her breast as he flung one arm outward, groping over the sheet.

"What?" She frowned in confusion as he slowly destroyed her with his clever tongue on her nipples.

"I've got to . . . hang on. Don't go away."

Twisting sideways, he reached the nightstand, rummaged through the drawer, then came back with a small foil packet. A condom. Of course! She couldn't believe she hadn't thought of it herself and insisted upon it. She, who doled out lectures on safe sex, had completely forgotten the number one rule.

But then, she'd never had cause to use one before, had in fact never made love to a man who wore one. She watched in fascination as he rolled it on. Then he reached for her and her thoughts scattered.

"You want me, Kate?" he asked against her neck as his hands moved her hips into position. She felt his hard shaft press against her moist entrance. "Then take me. I'm all yours."

How could she have known that surrender from a man would thrill her so? How could *he* have known? She didn't care. She laced her fingers with his and carried his hands above his head, holding them there. Sinking over him, she took what he offered. Her head fell back as she gloried in the feel of his long hard length inside her, the power that it gave her. When she rocked against him, he followed her lead. The tension built slowly at first, than faster as she quickened the pace. It wasn't enough. And then it was too much. Too much feeling. Too much wanting. Too much everything.

In a final surge of energy and passion, they came together like a wave hitting a rocky shore. Thrust upward, airborne, they remained suspended in that perfect time and space, before they fell together back to earth, and into each other's arms.

# Chapter 14

*Mike* had lied. While the sex had been mindless, it definitely had not been emotionless. At least not for him. And, he suspected, not for Kate. She lay beside him, utterly boneless, with her leg draped over his thighs as she nestled her head into the crook of his shoulder. Her hair smelled of rain, and some floral-scented shampoo. Smiling, he allowed himself the luxury of running his hand over her soft skin.

This was not a woman who gave her body where she hadn't already given her heart. The thought warmed him even as it frustrated him—because he knew instinctively that she wasn't ready to admit it. In spite of what had just happened, too many barriers remained between them. He tightened his embrace a fraction, wanting to cling to the moment a little longer.

She raised her head and blinked at him, as if trying to figure out exactly how she'd come to be naked in his bed. He cupped her chin and stared straight into her eyes. "If you dare say that this was a mistake, or that it shouldn't have happened, or that it won't happen again, I may have to strangle you."

She burst out laughing, which at least took care of her confused expression. "Well, that's honest." Her laughter slowly stilled. "All right, I won't say it was a mistake. I'll simply say it was . . . inevitable."

"Yes." He relaxed enough to tuck a coppery curl behind her ear. Such soft hair, yet so vivid and unpredictable. "From the moment I met you, I knew I had to make love to you—not just that I would, but that I had to."

With a heavy sigh, she sat up, her back to him. "Mike . . ." She drew in a breath, preparing to say something more, when the doorbell rang.

They both froze.

Her eyes widened as she glanced at him. "Are you expecting someone?" she whispered, as if whoever stood at the door, in the midst of a thunderstorm, might hear her.

"Only your friend Jim," he whispered back.

"Ohmygod, I completely forgot." As if a starter had fired a gun, they both dove for their clothes.

"What am I going to do?" she asked. "I don't want him to find me here like this."

"It's okay. Don't panic. You were supposed to meet him here, remember?"

"Yes, that's right. But I told him I'd meet him this afternoon. What's he doing here so early?" She closed her eyes as color stained her cheeks. "I can't believe . . . It's not even noon, and we just—"

"Yeah." He grinned in pure male satisfaction. "We certainly did."

"Don't you dare gloat." She scalded him with a look as she pulled shorts over her thong. "Or I swear, I'll beat you."

"Promises, promises." He bent forward and pressed a quick smacking kiss to her mouth. "You're cute when you blush."

"I'm embarrassed when I blush."

"Yeah, I know." He sat on the bed to pull on his Reeboks. "Which is what's so cute—the woman who wrote all those articles on how to have a healthy sex life embarrassed to be caught in bed before noon."

"I'm a mother, for heaven's sake." She pulled on the T-shirt. "And that's my best friend's husband I'm about to face. He'll take one look at me and *know*."

"Kate." He laughed. "It's not like it's written across your forehead." She gave him an exasperated look as she pulled on her shoes. He had to admit, someone would have to be a blind fool to look at that flushed face and those swollen lips and not know. "All right, but so what? You're entitled." Standing, he took her by the shoulders. "As for being a mother, there wouldn't be very many second and third kids running around if mothers didn't do this sort of thing." He kissed her forehead. "Now, wait here while I answer the door."

"No!" She grabbed his arm. "Are you crazy? He knows I'm here, my car's out front. If I hide, it'll just look worse."

"Then what do you suggest?"

The doorbell rang again. "You go down to your workroom," she said as they headed across the living room. "I'll answer the door."

"On one condition." He squeezed her hand. "That you don't run off without coming downstairs."

"All right. Yes, whatever." After one more quick kiss, he darted past the glass door and disappeared down the stairs.

*Thank God for frosted glass,* Kate thought as she took a moment in the foyer to compose herself before she opened the door. "Jim," she said with a bright smile. "I wasn't expecting to see you here so early."

"With this weather, I couldn't do any work at the other house, so I figured what the heck." He came in shaking off rain. "Damn but it's rainin' like a son of a bitch out there." As if suddenly struck by a thought, he looked at her. "So, what are you doing here so early?"

"I, uh . . . Mike wanted me to look around and give him some suggestions about . . . window treatments for his workroom, which is why we didn't hear the bell the first time it rang. We were downstairs. Looking at his windows."

"Uh-huh." Jim nodded knowingly. "Didn't hear the bell the first time it rang. You know, Linda and I have had that problem a time or two."

She cringed as she realized how inane her excuse sounded—if she hadn't heard the bell the first time, how could she have known it rang more than once? "So—" Clasping her hands together, she turned toward the kitchen. "Now that you've gotten the mess cleaned up, are y'all ready to start the actual work?"

"Just as soon as I pick up the materials." He headed through the dining area, pulling out a notepad. In the kitchen, he looked up at the gaping hole. "You know, this really wasn't my crew's fault. Whoever built the house didn't attach the ceiling to anything. The only thing holding it up was the wall. So, when that came down, so did the ceiling."

"I'll be sure and tell Mike. I wouldn't want him to think I'd hired an inferior contractor," she teased.

"Thanks." He flashed her a shy smile as he scribbled a note on his pad.

"Speaking of . . ." She made a vague gesture toward the stairs. "If you don't need me up here, I'll just . . . go talk to Mike some more . . . about those window treatments."

"Sure, fine. I'll be out of here in a second." He nodded distractedly, still jotting down notes. "Oh, and Kate?"

"Yes?" She turned back.

He grinned at her. "Your shirt's on inside out."

"I am going to die," Kate said as she reached the bottom of the stairs. "I swear to God, I have never been so embarrassed in my entire life."

Smiling, Mike turned his swivel chair to face her. Vivid color stained what little of her face he could see, since her hand covered the upper half. "That bad, eh?"

She lowered her hand to glare at him. "I told you he would know."

"Read it on your face, did he?" Mike's cocky grin faded in surprise as she whipped her shirt off over her head.

"That, and my dang shirt's on inside out!" Her breasts jiggled enticingly within the confines of her lacy peach bra as she fixed the shirt and jerked it back on. "How on earth could you have let me answer the door like that?"

"Huh?" He shook his head.

"I can't believe that we— That I—" Her breath came out in a hiss of exasperation.

"Kate," he said calmly. "Come here."

"Why?" She gave him a wary look.

"Just come here." When she obeyed, he took her hand and pulled her off balance so she landed in his lap.

"Mike!" She laughed and wiggled to escape.

"Careful," he warned as her round bottom rubbed him in some very interesting places. "You're about to get yourself into trouble."

"Oh, no." She went still. "I think one embarrassing incident per morning is my quota."

"That's better." He sighed and draped his arms

about her hips. "Now, first of all, you have nothing to be embarrassed about. You are a grown woman who's entitled to a personal life. And secondly"—he grinned—"how much fun would the world be if we always behaved ourselves?"

"You're right," she agreed. "But only to a point." Slipping from his lap, she moved safely beyond his reach. "If there was something more between us than lust, I would only be mildly embarrassed at being caught in bed with you. But, we both agree there isn't anything between us but that."

"So?" He shrugged, as if she hadn't just kicked him in the gut.

"So . . ." She took a deep breath. "I really do think I should turn your account over to Linda. Especially now."

"Why?" His voice rose, and she held up a hand.

"You hired me to help you find a wife. In light of what just happened, I don't think I'm the best person for the job."

"I didn't hire Linda. I hired you."

"To help you find a wife."

"Forget about the wife thing, would ya?"

"Are you saying you no longer want to get married?"

"I'm not saying anything. I just—" He rose to pace. "I thought you said you needed the money from this job."

"I do, but—"

"No buts. Look, I'll admit that hiring you for a wife hunt probably was not one of my better ideas." He crossed to her and took her hands. "So, how about if we simply stick to remodeling the house?"

"But Linda could do that just as easily—"

"I said no buts. I don't want Linda. I want you."

He pulled her close and took her chin between his thumb and forefinger. "I mean that, Kate. I want you."

"I know. That's the problem. Only, I won't sleep with you again, not if I'm working for you."

"Does that mean you want to sleep with me again?" A smile tugged at her lips, giving him hope. "Maybe."

"Fine, then stick with the job at least till the kitchen's done. When you're on the clock, I'll keep my hands to myself. However . . ." He covered her mouth with a slow, toe-curling kiss. Her body relaxed against his, making his pulse leap. He wrapped his arms around her and, cupping her bottom, he pulled her snugly against him, so she could feel exactly what she did to him. She responded by pressing even closer.

He sucked her bottom lip into his mouth and pulled slowly away. "If you decide to clock out for an afternoon—or morning—of mutually satisfying, uninhibited lovemaking, be sure and let me know."

"I'll, um . . ."—she blinked as if to focus her vision—"keep it in mind." Then, with a dazed look, she headed for the stairs, mumbling something about having to get home.

He let out a breath the moment she left. "Let's hope you keep it in mind. Lord knows I will."

# *Chapter 15*

*Dear Cupid,*
*Is it true what they say, that a man and woman can never be just friends? In my case, I'm afraid it is because I've done a really stupid thing. I've fallen in love with my best friend. A part of me wants to tell her how I feel, but another part doesn't want to risk losing what we have. What should I do?*

*Friend in Love*

Kate sat back and stared at the letter on her screen, incredibly touched by the plight of Friend in Love. A few weeks ago—no, a few *days* ago—she would have fought the urge to speak from her own fear and say: "No. Don't. Don't risk your heart. Don't risk yourself."

Now . . .

Now, she found herself more tempted with every letter to tell readers: "Yes! Go for it! Open your heart, no matter the risk, because life without at least the chance of love is so desperately empty."

*Empty.* She sighed. The word described the way she'd felt for years, since long before the divorce. That, at least, had certainly changed since Mike had

burst into her life. Since then, she had felt many
things: angry, amused, frightened . . . happy. Alive.

He made her feel alive.

In the five days since they'd made love— No, not
love. Her stomach jumped even at the thought of that
word. Pressing a hand to her jittery belly, she amended
that to: in the five days since they'd tumbled onto his
water bed together, she'd felt very much alive. She
felt it every time he looked up from his work to slay
her defenses with one of his lethal grins; every time
he sent her heart reeling with a heated look from
across a room, even if that room was crowded with
construction workers.

They hadn't had a single moment alone all week.
She'd timed her visits that way to give herself some
room to breathe. And yet, she never doubted that he
knew the instant she walked into a room, whether she
was there to show him fabric and wood samples for
the barstools she'd picked out, or a catalog of dishes
and glassware. She could almost feel the tingle of
awareness that passed through his body when she was
near, because it passed through hers as well.

That wonderful feeling of awareness was something
she hadn't felt with Edward since the early days of their
marriage, if even then. And now she wondered if the
absence of that awareness was what had killed her marriage rather than Edward's obsession with work. Mike
certainly cared as passionately for his career, and
worked as many hours as Edward did, perhaps even
more, but with Mike, she never felt ignored. Or worse,
invisible. Edward had made her feel invisible.

Pushing her personal thoughts aside, she leaned forward to answer the letter, then noticed the time readout
on her monitor. Nine fifty-five A.M., Saturday. Good
heavens, how had the morning slipped by so quickly?

"Dylan," she called, saving the e-mail to answer later. "Are you finished packing the toys you want to take this weekend? It's almost ten o'clock and your father will be here any minute."

"I'm trying to decide," he called down to her in a panicky voice that made her smile. For the past two days, he hadn't been able to think of anything but his big weekend with his dad. Thankfully, when she'd called Edward last night, he'd assured her the plans were still on. So, maybe he was finally willing to make an effort with Dylan.

"He's here!" Dylan shouted from the loft just as she entered the cabin's main room. Her stomach lurched as it always did at the thought of facing Edward. "Daddy's here! He really came!" Dylan clamored down the ladder.

"Dylan, wait!" She rushed forward and grabbed him before he could dash out the door. With shaky hands, she tucked in his shirt and ran her fingers through his hair. "Remember what we talked about?"

"I know." Dylan rolled his eyes. "Don't talk Dad's ear off, or get too excited 'cause it gets on his nerves. Play it cool, right?"

"Right." She gave him a thumbs-up sign, determined that things would go well this weekend, for Dylan's sake. "Now, go tell your father hi."

With a loud whoop, Dylan charged out the door and leapt from the front porch just as Edward climbed out of the sleek black Lexus. "Hey, Dad, you want to see my new computer game? Mom got it for me, 'cause I made an A on my math test. It's really cool and I already beat her highest score."

"Still the little egghead, eh, Dill-man?" Edward held his hands out; not to greet his son, but to fend him off before he could scuff the Italian loafers.

Watching from the porch, Kate held her breath, silently willing Dylan to slow down. Instead, he continued in a headlong rush about his new computer game. His breath turned ragged with excitement. *Oh, please don't let him have an asthma attack this weekend,* she prayed. At least Edward was smiling, which she took as a good sign. Everything would work out fine. Dylan was older now, so maybe they'd find some common interest to form a bound. After all, lots of men had difficulty relating to infants and toddlers but managed just fine with older children.

Her heart warmed as Edward reached out a hand and rumpled his son's hair. They looked so good together, even if Dylan was a paler, thinner version of what his father must have been at that age.

"So," Dylan asked, bouncing up and down on the balls of his feet, "you want to come in and see it?"

"Some other time, perhaps." Edward glanced at his watch. "Right now we need to run if we're going to have time to eat lunch and still make it to the game."

"We're really going to a baseball game?" Dylan asked. "We're going to see the Longhorns?"

"Certainly." Edward gave him a smile that appeared only a little forced around the edges. "And afterward, I'll take you to see your Grandma Anne and Grandpa Henry."

"Ah, Dad . . ." Dylan's shoulders sagged. "Do we have to go see 'em?"

"They're your grandparents, Dylan." A touch of impatience entered Edward's voice. "Of course you'll want to see them. Now go get your things before you make us late."

Kate bit her tongue to keep from echoing Dylan's sentiments about visiting his grandparents. Just because she'd never gotten along with her in-laws was no reason why her son couldn't.

With the resilience of youth, Dylan's enthusiasm returned full force as he rushed inside for his things, leaving the two adults alone.

Edward hesitated a moment, then removed his sunglasses and came to stand at the bottom of the stairs. The sunlight added a sharpness to his angular features. "Hello, Kate."

"Edward," she said, looking down on him from the added height of the porch. He jiggled the keys in his pocket, and for the first time, she wondered if these meetings distressed him as much as they did her.

His gaze flickered over the yellow sundress she knew complemented both her figure and coloring.

"You're looking good," he said at last. "In fact, I believe you may have finally lost some of that weight you gained from having Dylan."

"Why, thank you, Edward," she said politely, even though she knew he meant it as a clever insult rather than a compliment. He always had to get in a few digs. His ego demanded it since she was the one who'd left him. Today, however, she was determined to let his remarks roll off her back. "Come inside while I write down the instructions for Dylan's medicine. He's been a bit wheezy today, so you'll need to watch him closely."

"Are you sure he's up to this?"

"He's up to it," she said, wondering if that was concern that had flashed across Edward's eyes or hope for an excuse to cancel the weekend. Turning, she led the way inside.

"I can't believe you're still living in this dinky place," he said as he stepped over the threshold. "I'd think, with the amount of child support I pay, you could afford better."

"It suits me." She smiled as she rechecked the bag of medicine she'd packed along with the nebulizer. Truthfully, she longed for the day when she could afford a real house where her son could have a room of his own. As for Edward's child support, they both knew it didn't come close to what he should be paying. But then, Edward was a master at making himself look poor on paper when it suited his purpose.

As he crossed to the window that looked out over the lake, she wondered what had ever happened to the college boy she'd fallen in love with, the one who had been so liberal and a bit rebellious: the one who had actually cared about something other than himself.

"You know," he said, ducking his head to see up the hill. "I bet the land around here would be worth a bundle if someone tore down all these shacks and hauled off the mobile homes. Maybe put in a gated community with a greenbelt along the waterfront."

"Dabbling in real estate these days?" she asked.

"It's a thought." He shrugged.

Shaking her head, she pulled a pad and pen from a kitchen drawer and began writing down instructions. "Here's a list of Dylan's prescriptions and how each one should be taken. I assume you remember how to use the nebulizer?"

He gave a sigh of exasperation as she hefted the machine off the counter. "Is it necessary for me to lug that thing around? He's only staying with me one night."

"And you know as well as I do that a lot can happen in one night. I want you to promise me that if he starts wheezing, you'll make him use it."

"Of course," he said as he took the machine from her.

"I've also written down Linda's home number. If for any reason you can't get a hold of me, she usually knows where I am."

Taking the note, he gave her a curious frown. "Is there any reason why you wouldn't be here?"

"Oh, I don't know . . ." She trailed a hand through the air. "Maybe I have some hot plans, since I'll be a free woman all weekend."

"I see." A line formed between his brows.

"Jealous?" she asked in a falsely sweet voice.

"Why wouldn't I be?" His gaze met hers, and held. "Just because things didn't work out for us doesn't mean I stopped loving you."

A bitter laugh escaped her, because she saw the words for what they were. Edward flattered people so effortlessly, not because he cared about them, but to bind lesser mortals to him so they'd be ripe for using when the time came. Well, she'd had enough of being used when she'd learned the phrase "I love you" was the cruelest one ever spoken when it wasn't true.

"You find that funny?" His expression turned confused at the sound of her laughter.

"No." She found it incredibly sad. And somehow, that sadness helped quiet the churning in her stomach.

"Okay!" Dylan shouted as he struggled down the ladder with his backpack over one arm and a stack of books and toys under the other. "I'm ready."

Kate turned to give him a hug. "You have fun at the game, and don't eat too much junk food, okay?"

"Okay. See ya." Dylan wiggled out of her arms and hurried for the door. "Come on, Dad!"

With a resigned sigh, Edward carried his own load toward the car. "Dylan, wait," he called. "Wipe your feet before you get in. Jeez, I just had the leather upholstery cleaned."

Kate went to stand on the porch, calling a final good-bye as Edward loaded the nebulizer and Dylan into the backseat. Everything would be fine, she told herself as they pulled out of the drive and the car disappeared around a row of cedar trees and a rusted barbed-wire fence. She remained on the porch a moment, her heart already aching to have her son back even though she'd wanted him to have this weekend with his dad.

When the sound of the car had faded, she went inside, feeling at loose ends. As much to get her mind off Dylan as anything else, she settled back in front of the computer to answer the letter from Friend in Love. She labored over her response, striving for just the right tone, the right blend of caution and encouragement. When she'd finished, she read her response one last time, nodded in approval, then signed on-line to send it and the other responses waiting in her to-be-sent folder.

In the last few days, she'd felt as if she'd finally gotten back in the swing of things. She'd felt more confident in the power of romance. Even more, she'd begun to believe again that love could last—for some people. She smiled a bit as she typed in her Web address to see if they'd posted her latest article on role-playing between lovers.

To her surprise, a line of text appeared on the screen saying "Address Not Found." Assuming she'd typed it in wrong, she entered the address again. The same message appeared. *Could the phone lines or server be busy?* She typed in the main address for Gwendolyn's Garden, just to check. The site came up fine, although she noticed they'd changed the front page and had forgotten to include the little Cupid icon that linked the main page to her site. Curious, she typed in her site address again, and received the same message: "Address Not Found."

She sat a moment, staring at the screen as a sense of foreboding settled over her. Reaching for the phone, she dialed Gwen's office in L.A., knowing her friend would be at work, even on a Saturday.

"Gwendolyn's Garden. Gwen speaking."

"Gwen?" she said, somehow relieved by the mere sound of her friend's voice. "This is Kate."

"Kate? Oh . . . hi." Gwen sounded a bit uncomfortable, but not alarmingly so.

"I just went to access my page and got some silly message about the address not being found."

Silence.

"Gwen?"

"Oh, dear." A heavy sigh came over the line, and the bottom fell out of Kate's stomach. *God, no, please no.* "Kate, I— I'm sorry. I told the Web site manager not to upload the changes until I'd talked to you personally, but you've been out the last two days, and I didn't want to leave a message about something like this. I guess he got tired of waiting."

"W-what are you talking about?" Kate asked even though she knew. She pressed a finger to her lips to keep them from trembling.

"I'm saying that at our last staff meeting, we all decided that the page needed a little revamping, something fresher. You know, younger, trendier. The whole cupid concept is becoming passé."

"We? What do you mean 'we'?" Gwen was the sole owner of the magazine. While she might, on rare occasions, ask her staff for their opinion, all decisions were ultimately hers.

"It's nothing personal, Kate. In fact, your site seems to be gaining hits again."

"I don't understand. Is this because of what happened last Monday with the animation?"

"No, of course not. Although I am still angry about that."

"Then what? You said if I eased off the male-bashing, you'd keep my site going."

"I know. And you've done an excellent job this past week. In fact, I really loved your last column on role-playing."

"Then why did you take it down?" she demanded as anger swirled with disbelief.

"Kate," Gwen sighed. "The truth is, even though your number of hits are up, your site isn't generating sales for our advertisers. People are signing directly on and off your page, without even browsing the rest of the site."

"And that's my fault?"

"In a way, yes. You've known from the beginning that the purpose of your column was to draw new people to the site and encourage them to splurge on some romantic notion. It was never intended to be something people took seriously, and certainly nothing that could stand on its own. Plus, our last survey shows your demographics are all wrong. You attract too many older married women and men, when our magazine is targeted to a young singles crowd."

"So, you're dumping me. Just like that."

"I'm sorry. Really. But I don't have a choice."

"No choice? How can you say that?" The trembling settled into Kate's bones, shaking her whole body. "You hold all the choices and all I hold is the short end of the stick."

"Kate, don't do this. It's business, all right? That's all it is—simple business."

"Fine, Gwen," she snapped, on the verge of tears.

"Whatever you say. If it salves your conscience to say this isn't personal, then you do that. But the truth is you can't stand knowing my site is more popular than yours. You never could stand to be one-upped. This isn't business. It's you and your inflated ego."

"*My* ego?" Gwen sputtered. "What about yours? You're the one who had to go and take herself seriously when all your articles were supposed to be was a little fluff to help sell lingerie and bubble bath. If you'd kept it light and fun, this wouldn't have happened."

"If that's what you want to believe, I guess that's your choice too. I'm not going to argue about it. I'll just find someone else to sponsor my site." Although who, she had no idea.

"Kate, wait!" Gwen called, then sighed in frustration. "I don't want to end things this way. We've been friends too long."

Kate closed her eyes, trying to push the pain away. Gwen was right. They had been friends a long time. Which made this slap in the face even worse.

"Kate?" Gwen asked. "Are you okay?"

"I'm perfect, Gwen. How else would I be? Now, if you'll excuse me, I have to go." She hung up the phone and dropped her face into her hands. *Oh, God!* She'd lost her column. Even though she'd seen it coming, she felt as if Gwen had reached inside her chest and ripped out something vital.

Lifting her head, she swiped the tears from her cheeks. She refused to sit here and indulge in a crying jag. That wouldn't solve anything. She still had one job left, one that would last a while longer since Mike kept adding to his list of things he wanted her to do.

The thought of going over there suddenly held infinite appeal. Not that she wanted to go running into

Mike's arms like some wounded child needing comfort, she assured herself. She just, well . . . needed something to do. Jim had told her the drawer pulls she'd picked out had come in yesterday and that, if he had time, he meant to install them today. She wanted to see how they looked, that was all. Anything to get out of the house.

Mike stumbled into the kitchen, bleary-eyed from lack of sleep, and nearly tripped over Jim.

"Jesus!" Jim exclaimed, jumping up from his crouching position before the cabinets. "I didn't think you were here. You didn't answer when I rang the bell."

"No problem," Mike assured him, as his heart settled back into his chest. Even though he'd given the contractor a key, he couldn't quite get used to construction workers coming and going on their own. He'd be glad when this phase of Kate's project ended and she got down to picking out living and dining room furniture. "I probably slept right through the bell."

"Long night, eh?" Jim asked, moving aside an assortment of doorknobs and drawer pulls so Mike could get to the coffeepot.

"Yeah," Mike sighed, thinking with satisfaction of the work he had accomplished as he scooped grounds into the filter. The robot was shaping up into a horrific bit of work—frighteningly fluid and lifelike. When finished, it would scare the pants off the audience. "You working alone today?"

"It's Saturday," Jim grumbled, obviously in a surly mood.

"Already?" Mike mentally counted the days since he and Kate had made love. "So it is," he said, amazed at how quickly the week had flown by. "I take it your crew doesn't work on the weekend."

"Most of them have families, so I give them the weekends off." Jim shrugged and moved on to the next drawer.

Since he needed to wait for his coffee to brew, Mike took a seat on one of the stools Kate had picked out for his new breakfast bar. He had to admit, now that the kitchen project was almost over, she'd been right about knocking out part of the wall. The open look made the kitchen seem larger and brighter. For countertops, she'd selected native Texas granite that went great with the pickled-oak cabinet fronts. For drawer pulls, she'd found copper knobs in a Texas star motif.

He couldn't wait to see what she did with the rest of the place. With luck, he'd be able to come up with enough projects to keep her around until she finally admitted they had something more important going on between them than physical attraction. How any woman could look at him as she did at times, with those hungry, admiring eyes, then insist she wasn't interested in a relationship boggled his mind. *Time,* he reminded himself. *Give her time.*

He turned back to watch Jim. "Speaking of families, why aren't you home with yours?"

"I don't have a family," Jim grumbled as he tightened the screw on a drawer pull. "What I have is a pregnant wife."

"Doesn't that qualify?"

Jim looked up from his work. "You ever had a pregnant wife?"

"No, I, uh, can't say that I have." Mike chuckled. He did, however, remember some of the tales his brothers-in-law had told when Kim and Kelly were pregnant. There had been days when they, too, had fled from the house to preserve their sanity. Although, he noticed as he reached around to pour his first cup of coffee, Jim looked a bit more uptight than Bryan or Larse ever had. "So," he ventured, "what is it today? The crying tizzy about being too fat, or the hundred-and-one projects she wants you to do before the baby comes?"

"If only it were that easy." Jim gave the screw another twist, coming dangerously close to stripping the treads. "Linda's never looked better than she does right now, and as for projects, I'd build her a whole damned house if it would make her happy." Sitting back on the heels of his work boots, Jim let out a heavy sigh. "This, however, I have no idea how to fix."

"And what is 'this'?"

Jim rummaged through the pile of hardware for another drawer pull. "She thinks I don't want the baby."

"Ah," Mike said, sounding far sager than he felt. "I assume you've told her that you do?"

"Well, of course I've told her." Wielding the screwdriver, he tightened the next drawer pull into place. "I'm making her the baby crib, aren't I? Every night, I spend hours out in the shop working on the thing. And what does she do? Breaks out bawling and accuses me of avoiding her."

"Hmm." Mike mulled that over as he sipped the scalding coffee. The situation was clearly more complicated than he'd thought. "How about getting her to talk about, you know, how she's feeling and everything? My sisters' husbands seem to think listening to them go on about their bodies and the baby and making a big deal over all that confusing stuff they get at baby showers helps. Women are big on talking about things."

"I don't know." Shaking his head, Jim grabbed another drawer pull. "Right now, I don't think anything will help. I might as well just stay out of her way until this whole thing is over."

Mike frowned, thinking something sounded wrong with Jim's logic, but damned if he knew what it was. When it came to women, logic rarely applied. "Yeah, you're probably right."

"So." Jim eyed him. "You got any more rooms you want me to tear apart and put back together?"

Mike started to laugh, but realized the man wasn't joking. In fact, Jim looked frustrated enough to tear apart a whole house with his teeth. "I'm afraid you'll have to ask Kate on that one."

As if on cue, the front door opened. "Jim?" someone called. Mike straightened as he recognized Kate's voice. "Are you in here?"

"Speak of the devil," Jim muttered to Mike before raising his voice. "In here, Kate."

The minute she rounded the corner, Mike noticed her pale complexion. He tried to catch her eye, to give her a smile before he said hello, but she didn't even look at him.

"I, uh." She bit her lip. "I thought I'd come by and see how those handles look."

"I'm putting them on now," Jim said. "Want to see?"

Mike frowned when she stepped around him as if he weren't there. "Oh. Yes. They look fine. Just f-fine." Her voice broke over the last word.

"Kate?" Mike came off the bar stool. "Are you crying?"

"N-no," she sniffed. "Of c-course not."

"Hey . . ." He settled his hands on her bare arms and turned her toward him. "What's this? What's wrong?"

"Nothing, I—" She covered her mouth with one hand.

Mike looked to Jim, but the man held up his hands as if to say "Leave me out of it." Not knowing what else to do, Mike led Kate to the living room and urged her to sit on the sofa. "Here, sit down." His hands fluttered about her shoulders as he perched awkwardly beside her. "You, um, want to tell me what happened?"

"No." She sniffed as fresh tears spilled down her cheeks.

"Okay," he assured her. "You don't have to talk if you don't want to."

"I lost my job!" she wailed.

"Your job? What do you mean? With Linda?"

"*Nooo!* With Gwen. I'm not Dear Cupid anymore."

From the corner of his eye, Mike saw Jim head for the door, apparently choosing to take the high road and abandon him to deal with this on his own. He felt panicked at the thought. His usual way of dealing with a crying woman was to find another woman to figure out what was wrong, then make himself scarce.

"I can't believe she'd do this to me," Kate managed through sniffles. "After all the years we've been friends. I even helped her get started by writing most of the copy for her first magazine. And she didn't even pay me." She ran the back of one hand over her cheeks.

"Kate?" he asked, dreading the answer. "Is this because of the animation I loaded on your site?"

"No. At least she said it wasn't." She took a breath that seemed to settle her nerves. "Do you know what I think? I think she canceled me because she's jealous. She as much as said my site was getting too popular."

"But that doesn't make sense. If your site was so popular, why would she cancel it?"

"Because more people are signing on to read my column than to buy her advertisers' lingerie. So, of course she has to eliminate the competition. She's such a *bitch*." Kate's eyes widened at her own words. "I didn't mean that."

"That's okay." As far as Mike was concerned, any woman who made Kate cry *was* a bitch.

"I'm sorry." She brushed at her cheeks, then frowned at her wet fingertips. "I can't believe I'm being this way. Friend or not, Gwen has a right to cancel my column if she wants. Besides, she's right about what she said."

"What's that?"

"That I take the column too seriously."

"What's wrong with taking it seriously?"

"I don't know." She shook her head, looking broken and defeated. "I can't think straight right now."

"Okay." Patting her shoulder, he glanced around for something that would magically make her feel better. "Hey, I have an idea."

"What?" She rummaged through her purse and came up with a tissue to dab at her eyes.

"I've been working like a dog around here all week. What do you say I take the day off so you and I can go sailing?"

"Sailing?" She frowned. "Mike, no, I've taken up enough of your time already."

"Hey, it's the weekend, isn't it? Surely I'm entitled to a weekend off every now and then." A ridiculous statement, since he rarely took any time off in the middle of a project. "We can even take Dylan with us. What do you say?"

"Dylan's spending the weekend with his father."

"Oh, yeah?" He tried not to look too happy about that. "Well, in that case, how about an overnight sail?"

"Overnight?" Her eyes widened. "Are you serious?"

"Sure. I do it all the time. In fact, there's this great cove a few miles up the lake. We'll drop anchor, do a little swimming, grill hot dogs, watch the sun set. It's the perfect cure for anything that ails you."

"I don't know." She bit her lip. "It's already nearly noon, and we'd need to pack food, and I'd have to go home to get a swimsuit."

"Not to fear. We'll stop at the marina and get everything we need, including a swimsuit for you."

"I can't afford a new swimming suit!" She looked horrified at the expense.

"I'll pay for it."

"You will not!"

"All right." He held up his hands. "We'll skinny-dip."

She smirked at that suggestion, even though he thought it a perfectly reasonable solution.

"Come on," he coaxed, deciding to play on her soft heart. "I could really use some downtime. You'd be doing me a favor."

"Are you sure?"

He gave her a wicked grin. "Do I look like a man who isn't sure of what he wants?"

"All right, then." She put a hand on his chest before he could stand. "Just don't get any ideas, though, that this changes things. We're still not dating."

"Absolutely not." He held his hands up in a gesture of surrender. "You just want me for my body. I understand completely."

She managed a teasing smile. "Well, it is a very nice body."

"Same goes, sweetheart." He dried her cheeks with his thumbs. "Same goes."

# Chapter 16

"Here, Kate, take the wheel while I untangle those mooring lines."

Kate glanced over from the cushion in the cockpit of the thirty-four-foot Catalina where she'd been enjoying the sun on her face. Before she could tell Mike she didn't know how to sail, he stepped away from the giant chrome wheel, leaving her no choice but to grab it.

"What do I do?" she asked, sliding into the space he'd vacated at the very back of the boat.

"Just hold her steady." He pointed straight ahead, as he nimbly stepped over all the contraptions that cluttered the deck. "Keep the bow aimed to the left of that point there, where the shore juts out."

That sounded easy enough, she decided, until she felt how the wind tried to turn the wheel to the right, which would send them crashing straight into the rocky shore. Gripping the wheel with both hands, she aimed for the point Mike had indicated.

The sun beat down on her back, exposed by the sapphire-blue one-piece swimsuit she'd found on sale at the marina's store. The suit came with a colorful scarf that tied about her hips and went a long way toward slimming her generous figure.

From somewhere off to the left, a Jet Ski raced toward them, looking as if the rider meant to run right into the back of the sailboat. Instead, the Jet Ski veered off to hit the small wake left by Mike's boat. It leapt into the air, landed with a splash, and spun about to do it again.

Kate turned back to watch Mike. He possessed a sureness to his movements she couldn't help but admire. The same wind that filled the sails buffeted his Hawaiian shirt, which he wore open over a pair of dark blue swim trunks. His hair had already grown a bit from its recent trimming, and she felt sure that by the end of the day, the blond sun-streaks would have returned full force. At least now, after watching him work the sails and unfathomable other things onboard, she knew he came by his tan naturally.

With his legs spread for balance, he bent forward to untangle some lines. The sight distracted her for a moment, long enough that when she glanced up, a large motorboat had appeared directly in their path.

"Mike?" she called nervously, but the high-pitched whine of the Jet Ski drowned her out. "Mike," she called more loudly. "There's a boat up ahead. What do I do?"

He continued messing with the mooring lines at the front of the boat, completely oblivious to the danger. "Mike!" she tried again with rising anxiety as the motorboat came closer, taking on the proportions of the *Titanic*. If she turned right, she'd crash straight into the shore. But turning left would take her even more into the motorboat's path. Still, that seemed a better choice than smashing into the rocks, since she'd hopefully clear their path before they collided.

"Michael!" she shouted one last time. When he still didn't look up, she jerked the wheel left, and imme-

diately realized she'd made a mistake. The sailboat
turned sharply, dipping onto its right side. She
screamed, sure they would tip over. Somewhere over
the noise of the Jet Ski and the motorboat that was
frantically blaring a horn and turning to go between
her and the shore, she heard Mike holler as he lost his
footing. He managed to grab the mast before he flew
into the lake.

"Jesus, what are you doing!" he yelled. "Look out,
we're coming about! Pop the jib sheet. Release the
boom!"

Now that the motorboat was passing safely to the
right—with a great deal of cursing from the passengers—she tried to correct her mistake by turning the
wheel back. It was too late. The large, horizontal beam
swung over her head. Wind snapped the sail into place
with a jarring force that threatened to flip the boat in
the opposite direction.

"Let out the mainsail!" Mike yelled as he fought
against the front sail that had engulfed him like a
shroud. "Pop the jib sheet!"

"What's a jib sheet!" she hollered back as he finally
battled his way free of the sail and scrambled into the
cockpit. With one smooth flip of his wrist, he jerked
on a line, and the contraption that held it taut released
its hold. The line fed out, allowing the front sail to
move to the opposite side of the boat. He did the same
to the line that held the big beam in place. Both sails
fluttered and went slack as the boat settled neatly into
an upright position, slowed, and died in the water.

Standing in the cockpit and breathing hard, he
turned to face her. She cringed and waited for an explosion of male temper.

"I, um, I take it you've never sailed before," he
said, very calmly.

"Well, no, not exactly."

"Ah." He nodded. "Well, then, first lesson. Sailboats can't maneuver as fast as a motorboat, which gives us the right of way. In other words, we're supposed to hold steady, and let the motorboats go around us."

"But they were about to hit us."

"Trust me, Kate, they would have passed safely on our port side if you hadn't tacked right into their path."

"Oh." She squirmed. "Sorry."

"No, no, that's okay." He ran both hands through his hair, a useless gesture in the wind. "My fault. I should have asked if you knew how to sail before I turned the helm over to you."

"Perhaps we should let you take care of the sailing part of this weekend." She started to slide away from the wheel.

"What, and deny you all the fun? Don't be ridiculous." He took the seat behind the wheel. "Come on and I'll show you how it's done."

"No, Mike, really—" Before she could express her opinion on just how *un*fun she'd found the last few minutes, he took hold of her waist and settled her before him with her bottom wedged between his thighs.

"Now the first thing we need to do is find the wind. So, take hold of your port sheets—"

"What's a sheet?"

"One of the lines that controls your sails," he explained, gathering two of them in hand.

"You mean these ropes?"

"Kate." He chuckled. "There are no ropes on a sailboat."

"Then what the heck do you call all those?" She waved a hand at the dozens of blue-and-white nylon ropes trailing all over the deck.

"Once a rope is cut and attached to something on a sailboat, it becomes a line, which can also be called a halyard or a sheet, depending on what it's attached to. The halyards raise and lower the sails, the sheets control their side-to-side motion."

With surprising ease, he tightened two of the sheets. The mainsail and jib—as he called the front sail—magically filled with wind. Gracefully, the boat eased forward. He set the main sheet in a cleat, then handed her the jib sheet.

"Here," he said near her ear. "Take this, and get a feel for the wind."

She was about to ask what he meant, but the minute she took hold of the line, she understood. The sail tugged playfully against her hand, like a frisky mare asking for more rein.

"Now, if you ever get scared and want to slow down, simply let your lines out."

"And what if I want to go faster?"

"Tighten the sheet and turn closer into the wind. Not all the way, just close enough so you're riding the edge of it."

With one hand beside hers on the wheel and his other hand guiding hers on the sheet, he helped her find the edge of the wind. The boat leaned sideways as it picked up speed.

"What do I do if we start to tip over?" she asked.

"We won't," he assured. "A good, sturdy vessel like this is virtually impossible to ditch."

"Virtually?" Her voice rose as the boat leaned farther to the side. They both leaned in the opposite direction as counterbalance.

"Trust me, Kate. Unless you'd rather take things slow?"

Not sure what she wanted, she held their course,

feeling the wind tug against her hands. The more the boat leaned, the faster it sliced through the water. At some point, the fear of flipping over shifted to exhilaration, followed by a thrilling sense of freedom.

Mike gradually turned over control and moved to the high side of the bench where he could watch Kate. Everything about her delighted him, especially the memory of their trip into the marina's store. She'd taken one look at the prices of the swimsuits and her eyes had bulged. If he hadn't slipped the store clerk his credit card and convinced her to tell Kate all the swimwear was half off, he never would have talked Kate into buying one. And though he would have preferred she'd purchased one of the skimpy two-piece numbers, he had to admit she looked great in the bright blue suit she'd selected.

Gone was the pale anxiety from that morning. In its place he saw an expression—part fear, part wonder—that reminded him of how he'd felt when he'd first started sailing with his dad. There was nothing quite like the feel of a good solid vessel responding to your slightest touch, of flying over the water on nothing but the power of the wind.

The breeze shifted subtly and Kate adjusted instinctively.

"You have the feel for it," he observed.

"For what?" She glanced toward him then turned back to keep her eye on the lake traffic.

"For sailing." Reaching for the bag of supplies they'd just bought, he pulled out the bottle of sunscreen. "Not everyone does," he said, squeezing lotion into his hand. "Are you sure you've never done this?"

"Never. Oh, that's cold." She sucked in a breath as he applied the lotion to her shoulders.

"Sorry." He hid a smile as he squeezed more lotion

onto her back and felt her body shiver beneath his hands. The tropical scent of coconut rose up from her sun-heated flesh. "With this white skin of yours, you'll be red as a lobster by the end of the day."

"Actually, I don't burn. I don't tan either. I just freckle." She made a face. "So, what about you?"

"I never freckle."

"No, silly, how long have you been sailing?"

"Since before I could walk." Shedding his shirt, he squeezed lotion on his own shoulders and sucked air in through his teeth. Kate was right; it was cold. What'd they do, keep the stuff in the refrigerated cases with the beer? "But then, I'm a Cameron, so sailing's in my blood."

"Oh, that's right, you said your grandfather sailed out of Glasgow on a cargo ship. I assumed you meant a freighter, though, not a sailing vessel."

"I did." Mike reached into the ice chest. "You want a beer or a Coke?"

"Coke for now," she answered. "I'm holding out for that bottle of wine you bought to go with dinner."

Grabbing a beer for himself and a Coke for her, he settled back to enjoy the day. The sky stretched overhead, with just enough clouds to cool things off while sunlight shot sparks off the water. The wind off the starboard bow was strong and steady; the woman at his side a pure pleasure. In all, a perfect day. "Even though my grandfather started out on a freighter, sailing has always been the old man's secret passion, especially after he settled in California and started his own shipping company: Cameron Shipping—'We sail the world for you.' "

"The old man?" She cocked a brow in disapproval.

"His choice, I assure you—as in *The Old Man and the Sea*."

"What about your father? Is he into sailing?"

"Absolutely." Mike looked about to check their heading. Although Lake Travis was large, its long, winding course through the rolling hills required a great deal of tacking back and forth to navigate. "We need to come about, pretty soon. Think you can handle it?"

"I don't know." Her eyes widened a bit, but she looked willing to try.

"I tell you what. Why don't I take the wheel while you handle the sheets?" He talked her through the maneuver, which they pulled off with surprising ease. "You want the wheel back?" he asked once they'd set a new heading.

"No." She let out a nervous laugh. "I'd rather sit back and watch for a while." Scooting along the bench, she leaned her back against the cabin and stretched her legs out on the cushion to catch the sun.

"So, where were we?" he asked, distracted by the trim shape of those feminine ankles and calves. Women had such intriguing dips and curves; an endless landscape to be thoroughly explored.

"You were about to tell me about your father." She tipped her head back, looking peaceful and relaxed as the boat settled into a steady rhythm.

He smiled in satisfaction, since that had been the point of the day, to help Kate get her mind off what had happened that morning. He still wanted some more details on the subject, but decided to wait until later.

"My father," he said, drawing his attention away from her legs. "Now, there's a man who loves to sail. In fact, in his rebellious youth, he ran off to Hawaii to crew on a charter boat."

"Hawaii?" Kate cocked a brow. "How exciting. Did he stay there long?"

" 'Bout ten years. He worked his way up to serving as first mate on one of the first big commercial yachts, the kind with luxury cabins, a dining galley fit for royalty, and a lounge with live entertainment."

"Ooo." Kate's smile turned dreamy. "Wouldn't that be wonderful? To sail around the islands on a ship like that?"

"Yeah," he agreed, as an image came to mind of sailing with Kate in Hawaii—not on some crowded luxury yacht, but on a small, chartered vessel for their honeymoon. On the way home, they could stop in Santa Monica so he could show her off to his family, maybe fly Dylan out so he could meet his new cousins.

The thought of Dylan dimmed the fantasy a bit, since Mike still wasn't used to the idea of taking on another man's son as his own. Pushing the thought away, he concentrated on his story. "That's where Dad met my mom, working on that ship."

"Oh?" Kate prompted.

"She was the headliner in the lounge, and a hell of a singer."

"Oh, really?" Her attention perked up at that. "Does she still perform?"

"No." He shook his head. "Mom gave up the stage when she found out I was on the way. She and Dad had been married less than a year, having the time of their lives, both of them living for the moment with little thought for the future. Then, wham, here I come along and change everything. I guess having a baby has a way of making a man think about the future, big time."

"Believe me," she laughed, "it has a similar effect on women."

"I imagine it does."

"So what happened?" she asked.

"Dad moved back to California and went to work for Cameron Shipping."

"And your mother?"

"She became a full-time mom to me and my sisters. I pretty much took that for granted growing up, but now I wish she hadn't."

"Why's that?"

He shrugged, glancing at the gauge at the top of the mast to check the direction and speed of the wind. "I think it's just as important for kids to see their parents pursue their dreams as it is for parents to see their children succeed."

"I never thought of it that way." She cocked her head, studying him. "Speaking of children, you must have made your parents proud with your success. You're very talented."

"Thank you." He smiled, pleased.

She leaned forward. "Just from the little animation you did for my Web site, I can see how good you are."

"I thought you didn't like the graphic."

"I liked the graphic just fine." She gave him a repentant look. "In fact, I loved it."

"Even if it got you in trouble with Gwen?"

She shrugged. "I wish now I'd told Gwen to stuff it and leave your cupid alone. Well, it's too late for that now. But I hope it's not too late for me to say thank you. It was a wonderful gift."

"You're welcome." He felt his chest expand with pride as their gazes held.

"But tell me about your parents," she said, settling back. "Are they happy with your career choice, or did your father have his heart set on you going into the family business?"

"Honestly, I don't know what Dad expected me to do." Mike shrugged. "By the time I was old enough to go to work in a shipping yard, I was already making money as an animator."

"And how old was that?"

"I was fourteen when I worked on my first movie."

"Fourteen!" Her eyes widened, making him grin.

"Back then, we were all pretty young. I think the average age of most special effects crews was between eighteen or twenty."

"That's incredible."

"You have to understand, CGi barely even existed until recently. In the beginning, we just made it up as we went along, writing our own software and gluing spaceships together from whatever model parts we could pick up at the local toy store. It was fun, exciting." He smiled at the memory. "And it's never stopped being that way."

Her face softened as she looked at him. "I think it's so great that you love what you do."

"Yeah, I really do love it," he said. *As much as you love being Dear Cupid.* And he'd be damned if he'd stand by and watch her give up her column just because some woman out in L.A. couldn't take the competition.

# Chapter 17

"*M*IKE?" Kate called up through the hatch of the sailboat's cabin. "Where do you keep the salt and pepper?"

"Look in the cabinet over the sink," he called back from the cockpit where he was lighting the grill attached to the stern pulpit. Since she'd wrinkled her nose at the thought of hot dogs, they'd opted for chicken kebobs instead.

Late that afternoon, they'd found Mike's cove and dove in the cool water for a refreshing swim. She couldn't remember the last time she'd felt so carefree, floating about on air mattresses, splashing water at Mike, then shrieking obligingly when he swam toward her to the theme from *Jaws*.

With her swimsuit now dry, and the scarf tied back around her hips, she rummaged through the galley in search of condiments. "I'm not finding them," she called through the hatch.

Mike's head appeared, backlit by the golden-peach sunset. "Try the shelf over the dining table."

"Dining table," she muttered, moving around the counter to the eating area. On the shelf over the U-shaped booth, she found all manner of nautical flotsam, including models of old sailing ships, gadgets and tools she couldn't begin to imagine the use for,

and pictures. There amid the sailing notions and what-
nots, she found three framed photos bolted to the wall.

"Did you find it?"

She glanced over her shoulder as he came down the
ladder. "Is this your grandfather?" she asked.

He leaned over the counter to see what had caught
her attention. "Yeah," he breathed, his face warming
with a smile. "That's him. Crusty old sea dog, isn't
he?"

Actually, she found him very handsome in a rug-
ged, weather-beaten way. He held an infant in his big
callused hands that looked as fascinated with him as
he was with the child. "Is that you?"

"Heck no, that's my baby sister, Carly the Brat."
Undisguised affection tinted Mike's voice as he rummaged through the icebox for the bag of preseasoned
meat. "She's fourteen years younger than me, and
spoiled rotten."

"Oh, and I'm sure you had nothing to do with spoil-
ing her." She cast him a sideways smile, enjoying the
sight of him with his windblown hair and freshly
tanned skin.

"Hey, I'm her big brother. I'm entitled."

"So who's this man standing with you here?" She
pointed to a photo of a much younger Mike holding a
sailing trophy and bottle of champagne with a slender,
darkly exotic–looking man.

"My dad."

"Really?" She looked closer. "You don't look anything like him."

"My grandmother's Polynesian. Dad and my two
middle sisters take after her, Carly looks like my mom,
and I'm a throwback to my Scottish grandfather."

"Yes, you are," she agreed, imagining how he'd
look in his later years. The image had definite appeal.

Then she looked at the final picture and her smile faded at the sight of the stunningly beautiful woman in the black-and-white glossy photo. A long fall of pale hair framed intoxicating eyes, arrogant cheek-bones, and a pouty mouth. A movie star, she assumed from the illegible autograph sprawled in one corner after the words. "To Mike, with all my love."

"An old girlfriend?" she asked coolly.

"Bite your tongue." Mike shuddered playfully. "That's my sister, the Brat."

"Oh." She blushed at her momentary lapse into jealousy. "Your favorite, I take it."

"What makes you say that?" he asked, slicing open the package of meat.

"She's the only sister whose photo you carry on your boat. And not just one photo, but two." She waved to the picture of his grandfather holding the infant.

Mike chuckled. "She's my only sister with a big enough ego to give me an autographed picture of herself for Christmas."

"Still, you have it here alongside your father and grandfather."

"The kid's got spunk." He shrugged. "She knows how to piss you off and make you laugh all at the same time."

"Kind of like you?"

"Like I said, family trait."

"Is she a movie star?" Kate turned back to gaze at the beautiful young woman.

"She wants to be. Unfortunately, she's hit the mid-twenties mark and hasn't managed more than a steady career in commercials and a few supporting roles in some minor films. Still, she hangs in there, waiting for her big break."

"You're obviously proud of her."

"I'd rather she be proud of herself."

Kate turned and studied him, seeing layers to his personality she hadn't fully noticed before: supportive, faithful, optimistic. "You're a good brother, aren't you?"

"I'd like to think so." He grabbed the skewers. "Now, let's eat."

Mike smiled as Kate handed him her empty paper plate. There was something very satisfying about cooking for a woman.

"That was wonderful," she sighed, with a hand over her stomach.

"Thanks to you." He brushed a kiss to her cheek before he tossed their used plates and plastic forks into the makeshift trash bag. "I would have settled for hot dogs, but I'm glad you talked me into this."

He sat sideways on the bench with one leg bent behind her so she sat between his thighs. With their dinner plates out of the way, he gathered her close and leaned back. It pleased him when she turned as well, to rest her back against his chest and plant her feet on the bench. Overhead the stars winked in time to the slap of the water against the hull. The dark silhouettes of hills surrounded them on three sides, enfolding them in their own world.

"I'm glad you talked me into this sail," she said. "I can't remember the last time I enjoyed myself so much." She shifted to smile at him over her shoulder. "Thank you."

"You're welcome." Reading the invitation in her eyes, he dipped his head and let their lips brush, retreat, brush again. His eyes drifted closed as the kiss deepened and he wondered if they would make love tonight. He'd promised earlier in the week not to push her. Yet with every day that passed she seemed more comfortable in his presence, more receptive to the idea of them as a couple. Tonight, her body made all the subtle moves that told him she was definitely open to the possibility.

Arousal tightened his groin. He started to deepen the kiss even more, but made himself pull back. They had all night, and simply holding her in his arms was too enjoyable to rush things. He lightened the kiss, let it end with a few last nibbles before settling back to gaze at the stars. The mast rose like a tall cross against the lavender sky, its halyard pinging softly as the water rocked the boat. "You know, Kate, I've been thinking."

"Oh?" She sounded dreamy as she joined him in stargazing.

"As popular as your column is, have you ever considered starting your own site?"

"Actually, yes I have. But I decided against it."

"Why?"

She stretched languidly against him, exposing all manner of interesting curves to his touch. He caressed her ribs, letting his thumbs brush the underside of her breasts. "I don't have an aptitude for all that computer stuff, and I don't have the money to pay someone else to do it."

"Well, if you're interested . . ." He ran his fingertips down her sides and back up. "I could do it for you."

"No. Not that I don't think you'd be wonderful at it, but no."

"Really, it would be fun." He circled her waist with his arms and cuddled her close. "I could expand the animated cupid so it appears on each page, only different each time. Oh, and I know—"

"Mike, no."

"I could do some sort of shooting arrow whenever you click from one page to the next, and—"

"Mike, I said no." She twisted to face him. "It's incredibly generous of you to offer, but I really don't want you to design a site for me."

"Why not?" He pulled his head back in surprise.

She let out a weary sigh. "There is a lot more to going into business than simply launching a Web site. For one thing, how would I get paid? You don't earn money simply by getting a lot of hits."

"You'd sell ads on your site."

"Which takes a lot of time and experience I don't have."

"Then hire someone to do it. I know a few people who do this sort of thing. I could help you get started."

"You're not listening to me." She pulled out of his arms. "Dylan is my top priority right now. Starting a business would consume all my energy, and leave nothing for him, which would completely negate one of the main reasons I enjoy writing the column in the first place."

He stared at her, dumbfounded. "So, you're just going to roll over and play dead? Give up something that matters to you, because it might take time away from Dylan?"

"Dylan won't be little forever. He needs me right now. And as long as he does, I refuse to put my work before him."

"I'm not suggesting that you do." *Was he?* He suddenly remembered the sacrifices his parents had made for him: his father giving up the job of his dreams, his mother giving up the stage. That was different, though. Responsible people didn't raise children on a charter boat in the Pacific. But surely sacrifices of that magnitude weren't always required. "You can love your work, and still put family first," he said as much to himself as to her.

She snorted. "That's easy for you to say."

"What, you think because I don't have a wife and kids, I've never had to sacrifice anything to be with my family?"

"Not on a regular basis. And your sacrifices couldn't have been as frequent as those you'd have to make if you had children."

He stared at her, incredulous. "Having a family doesn't mean you have to give up everything else, take some boring nine-to-five job, and be at home every night for supper. My dad worked a lot more than forty hours a week running the shipping company, but I never doubted that he cared about every one of us kids."

"Maybe you're right." A frown dimpled her brow. "Maybe it isn't the amount of time we spend with our kids, but simply being aware of their needs, and being sure we're there when they do need us. Unfortunately, when you're a single parent, the task of *being there* becomes more difficult. And even if you're married, that task nearly always falls more heavily on the mother."

"What, so mothers aren't allowed to go after their dreams? They have to put everything on hold till their kids are grown?"

"Look," she sighed, "could we talk about something else?"

"All right. Fine." He set his jaw, deciding he definitely wanted to talk about something else. The thought of her having to give up anything to be a good mother made him want to rail against the injustice of life. He wanted her to be happy. And he wanted her to have her column.

After a while, she settled back against him. His mind, however, continued to race. "I have another idea."

"Mike . . ." She started to pull away.

"No wait, just listen." He coaxed her back into his arms. "Have you ever thought about syndicating your column to print publications?"

"You mean like newspapers?"

"Sure. Why not?"

She laughed. "Because who would buy it?"

"With your talent and built-in audience, a lot of papers, I imagine. And it wouldn't take any more time than what you've spent on your column in the past."

"I don't know. It seems like an awfully big long shot. And I don't have a clue as to how to go about it."

"I have a friend who could probably help you there. She makes a living freelancing for newspapers and magazines while she's waiting for her big break in screenplays. If you like"—he trailed a finger up her bare arm—"I could give you her number."

As if tempted by the thought, Kate remained quiet for a while before she gave a defeated sigh. "Yeah, but why get my hopes up? I'd probably be better served to lower my sights and concentrate on getting a real job— And I can't believe I just said that." She covered her face with both hands. "God, I'm turning into my mother."

He laughed at that. "Then you'll give my friend a call?"

"Maybe." She settled back again. "Right now, I'd

rather not think about the future. I'd rather just enjoy the night . . . and you."

"Oh?" His ears perked up. "Now that sounds interesting."

Her low rumble of laughter surprised him. "Not nearly as interesting as the fantasies I've been having all afternoon."

"Now that definitely sounds interesting."

"Hmm." She arched her back in a stretch that drew his gaze to her breasts covered in nothing more than the thin fabric of her swimsuit.

He swallowed as his body leapt in response. "I don't suppose you'd care to elaborate?"

"I've just been thinking about the fact that we're on a boat, and you have a certain pirate appeal about you when you're handling the wheel."

"Pirate?" His hands drifted up to capture her breasts, and her nipples hardened against his palms. Her soft gasp shot straight to his groin.

"Hmm, kind of makes a woman wonder what it's like to be ravished by some dangerously attractive sea captain."

The images that statement conjured made his erection press against her back. "And here I've been hoping all day that you'd ravish me."

"Oh, no." She moved her raised knees from side to side as if to ease some tingling itch between her thighs. "I've already ravished you once. Now it's your turn."

Captivated by the sight and feel of her, he moved one hand to her knee, urging her legs to part. To his delight, she relaxed and opened herself to his touch. He ran one teasing fingertip up and down the inside of her thigh from her knee to the edge of her swimsuit while his other hand peeled the suit down her arm.

"So, you want to be ravished, do you?" he asked in the gravelly voice.

"Oh, no," she said in false alarm as he finished peeling the suit to her waist.

Kate shivered in anticipation, unable to believe how comfortable she felt playing out a fantasy with him. Closing her eyes, she savored the feel of the night air on her breasts, the building tension deep in her belly. When her arms were free, she lifted them back and linked them around his neck. "Please don't take me."

"Your struggles are useless." He lightly pinched her nipple, making her gasp. "Aboard my ship, you are at my mercy."

The hand on her thigh swept downward to cup her aching center and she whimpered in response.

"I know you want me," he whispered hoarsely. "Let me hear you say it."

"No, never," she moaned, knowing she'd die if he stopped.

His thumb moved against the dampness that seeped through her suit. "Admit you want me, or I shall give you to my men."

She shook her head in denial even as her hips lifted, pressing against his hand. One fingertip drew maddening circles over her sensitive nub until she thought she would splinter with pleasure.

"Tell me you want me," he said against her ear as his hand squeezed her breast. "I want to hear you say it."

"Yes," she cried mindlessly, opening her legs, begging with her body as well as her voice. His fingers darted beneath the swimsuit and thrust inside her. Her hips jerked upward as he withdrew and thrust again. She panted out words of wanting, telling him to take her, *now, please now*. As the climax slammed through her, the stars above burst in flashes of light.

His touch gentled, giving the world a chance to settle back into place. When she finally drifted to earth, she let out a small laugh, a little embarrassed, but too sated to truly care.

"Is that what you had in mind?" He kissed her temple sweetly, as if she hadn't just tossed her inhibitions overboard.

"Something like that." Grinning, she turned in his arms and thanked him with a languid kiss.

"Good." He cupped the back of her head and deepened the dance of lips and tongue. "Because I'm not nearly through with you."

In one swift move, he sat forward and pressed her down until she lay beneath him on the cushion. Alarm shot through her as she saw the dangerous glint in his eyes. Gone was any trace of playfulness.

"Not nearly through," he repeated as he captured her wrists in one hand and pinned them to the bench over her head. With his other hand, he grabbed one of the lines, wrapped it lightly about her wrists.

She stared at him, startled and uncertain. He gave her a devious but reassuring smile as he urged her fingers to tighten around the line to hold it in place. All she had to do to release herself was let go. Something relaxed and unfolded inside her, a liberating feeling that she was free to do anything with him. Pulling lightly on the line, she arched her breasts toward him. His eyes darkened as he peeled the swimsuit from her body.

With her stretched out naked before him, he stood and stripped with provocative slowness. Her gaze drank in the sight of his fully aroused body bathed in moonlight. He moved back onto the bench, kneeling between her thighs. Bending forward, he rested one hand beside her head, captured her face with his other. His gaze bored into her eyes as he spoke in a husky whisper. "I want everything you have, Kate." His hand trailed down her throat to cup her breast. "Everything."

Fear blended with excitement, fear that he wanted more than she was ready to give, that he would take, not just her body, but her heart. She tried to shake her head, to tell him no, but he covered her mouth with his and stole her breath, her thoughts, even her fear. All that remained was a wild wanting, a ravenous need, as he fulfilled every fantasy she'd entertained throughout the day.

Moving down her body, he suckled her breasts until the tips constricted to wet peaks against the evening air. She writhed in anticipation as he kissed a trail down her stomach. And when his mouth settled over the center of her desire, he took her places she'd only imagined, gave her pleasures beyond her dreams. Just when she thought herself beyond reason, he sheathed himself for protection, then stretched out on top of her, pinning her soft body beneath his hard planes. "I want all of you, Kate. All of you."

The fear had only a moment to flicker back to life before he drove deep. With a gasp, she arched against him, opening her body and her heart. Later she would take time to think, to pull safely away. For now, there was only Mike, and the unbearable ecstasy of having him inside her.

# Chapter 18

*A* soft whirring sound stirred Kate from sleep. She rolled over and snuggled against Mike, not ready to abandon the lazy comfort of bed. The sound came again. Raising her head, she squinted against the early dawn light that filtered through the portholes. The sound seemed to be coming from the main part of the cabin.

"Mike?" She nudged him gently, reluctant to wake him but worried that some kind of alarm was going off. "Mike, what's that noise?"

"Hmm?" His eyes cracked open a fraction. When he focused on her face, a smile tugged at his lips. "Good morning."

He moved a hand behind her neck and pulled her down for a kiss. She started to object, but the whirring noise stopped. His lips moved against hers, gentle and sweet, as opposed to the hot demanding kisses they'd shared last night. She relaxed in his arms, giving herself up to the simple pleasure of a good-morning kiss.

He turned her onto her back, deepened the kiss for a moment, then raised his head to gaze down at her. His eyes held admiration as he brushed the hair from her face.

"Kate." He whispered the name with reverence, as if savoring the sound. Elation and fear sparked at the depth of emotion she saw in his eyes—elation that he cared so deeply for her, fear that he would say the words out loud. She wasn't ready to examine her own feelings, much less deal with any monumental declarations. "Kate, I—"

The sound came again, a soft but insistent whirring.

"What is that?" She lifted her head, grateful for the distraction.

He glanced over his bare shoulder, then dismissed the noise. "My mobile phone. Ignore it. Kate, I—"

"Your mobile phone?" With her heart pounding, she pounced on the excuse, anything to stop Mike from saying something too intimate, something that would ruin the casual relationship they had. "Aren't you going to answer it?"

"My voice mail will pick it up."

"But it could be important." She tugged at the sheets to cover her breasts. "I left your number with Linda, in case Dylan needed to get a hold of me."

He studied her a moment. Then, with a resigned sigh, he climbed over her, and padded naked down the passageway that led to the galley. The minute he disappeared from sight, she breathed a sigh of relief. Surely he hadn't been about to say what she thought he'd been about to say. She didn't even want to think about words of love and commitment, of tomorrow and forever. Everything was perfect between them just the way it was. She didn't want anything more. Not now. Not yet.

He reappeared, beautifully nude in the morning light, and a small voice way in the back of her mind asked, *Would it really be so bad to have this man fall in love with you? Or for you to take that tumble with him?*

"Kate, did you hear me?" He gave her an odd frown, and she realized he was holding the phone out to her. "I said you were right. It was Linda. She's left three messages on voice mail."

"What?" She stared at him numbly, as the implication came over her in waves. Her hand shook as she grabbed the phone and dialed Linda's number. In her mind, Dylan died a thousand deaths as she waited for her friend to answer, every one violent, painful, and completely her fault. "Linda, thank God," she breathed when her friend answered. "What's happened?"

"Kate! I've been trying to get you for the past half hour."

"What's wrong?"

"Dylan's grandmother called. He's having trouble breathing and his inhaler isn't doing anything to turn it around. She says she doesn't have his nebulizer to give him anything stronger."

"What do you mean, she doesn't have his nebulizer?" Kate asked in rising tones. "And what's he doing with her anyway?"

"Apparently he spent the night with her."

Fear and fury exploded in a white flash. "Where is Edward?"

"I don't know. I was just looking up his number to call him since his mother doesn't want to bother him so early on a Sunday morning. Get this—she wants you to come into town and deal with Dylan."

*"She wants me to drive into town?"* Kate raised a shaking hand to her brow. "Does she realize he could be dead by the time I got there?"

"Oh God, Kate, are you serious?"

"Yes, I'm serious." Why didn't anyone but her own parents take Dylan's condition to heart? "Look, I've got to call Dylan. I'll call you back."

She hit the off button, then fumbled to dial the number of her former in-laws, only she couldn't figure out how to get the dial tone back. With trembling fingers, she tried again, only to have Mike take the phone from her.

"What are you doing?" She grabbed for the phone.

"Kate!" he said in a clear voice. Taking her wrist in his hand, he waited for her to look at him. "Take a deep breath."

"But—"

"I said take a breath." She did, and felt dizzy for a moment, before the world settled back into place. "Now, tell me the number."

She rattled off the number from memory. Once he'd dialed it for her, he handed her the phone. She sat, listening to it ring. And ring. Finally Edward's mother came on the line. "Good morning. Bradshaw residence."

"Anne, thank heavens. It's Kate."

"Oh, hello, Kate," the woman said as if she hadn't a care in the world. "I'm so glad you called. Dylan seems to be having a bit of difficulty breathing and claims he needs a treatment on his nebel—nubu-something?"

"Nebulizer," Kate corrected. "It's that machine that looks like a bread box. It turns his medicine into a mist. Please tell me Edward left it with you."

"A machine? I don't think so. He did bring in a bag of medicine. Perhaps one of those would help."

In the background, she heard Dylan cough. The weak, raspy sound made her chest constrict in empathy. "Have you checked his air flow on the peak flow meter?"

"You know, they really need to make the numbers on those gadgets larger. How on earth is a person supposed to read such tiny print?"

"Perhaps you could get your reading glasses?" Kate suggested through gritted teeth.

"Yes, of course. Hold on a minute."

"Anne, wait! Let me talk to Dylan while you're hunting down your glasses."

"Certainly."

"Mom?" Dylan's voice was so thin, she could barely hear him.

*Oh, God.* She bit her lip to keep from crying. If only she could reach through the phone and wrap him in her arms. In some corner of her mind, she felt a hand slip over hers and remembered that Mike sat beside her. Her fingers curled instinctively around his. "Hello, Dylan," she said in as bright a voice as she could manage. "Grandma Anne says you're not feeling too well."

"Chest . . . hurts." She heard him struggle to take in air past his constricted throat.

"I know, baby." She closed her eyes, fighting back tears. "When your grandma comes back, I want you to blow as hard as you can into the tube, okay? Can you do that for Mommy?"

She heard Anne come back into the room and sat for an eternity, rocking back and forth with one hand clasping the phone to her ear, the other clinging to Mike. At last, Anne came back on the line and gave her the three readings.

*No, please no!* Kate wanted to scream. How could any reasoning adult let a child become this weak without seeking help? "Anne," she said in a deadly calm voice. "I want you to listen to me very carefully. Dylan has got to get to the hospital. I'll call the ambulance, but I want you to keep Dylan as calm as possible until they get there."

"An ambulance?" Anne sounded offended at the thought. "Can't you simply drive into town with whatever it is he needs?"

"Dammit, Anne!" She gripped the phone. "I don't have time for one of your fits of denial. Dylan has asthma. Maybe you don't want to face that fact, but right now he needs you. Because if he gets too agitated, his air passages will close up and he won't be able to breathe. If he can't breathe, he'll die. Do you understand that? Is any of this getting through to you!"

"Well, there's hardly any need to shout."

"My son could be dying because of your negligence, and you think there's no need to shout?"

"Perhaps you should talk to Henry," Anne said, clearly ready to turn the whole situation over to her husband. But then, that was how Anne dealt with most things in life.

"No," Kate said through gritted teeth. "I don't need to talk to Henry." The last thing she needed was to have Henry Bradshaw brush her off as nothing but a hysterical female and say that Dylan was fine, the boy just needed to gut it up like a man. "All I need is for you to keep my son calm until help arrives."

"Yes, of course, but all those sirens will wake the whole neighborhood."

"Good-bye, Anne." Kate ended the call and this time managed to dial the phone by herself. She gave the emergency operator the Bradshaws' address, a quick rundown of the situation, and Mike's mobile-phone number.

Not until she hung up did the full impact of her emotions hit her. She covered her mouth with her hand and fought back a sob. She didn't have time to cry. She had to get to Dylan, but he seemed a million miles away.

"Kate?" Mike rubbed his hand in small circles over her back. "Everything's going to be fine. Just take this one step at a time."

She nodded. "Yes. Of course. I need to call Dylan's doctor. Tell him to meet the ambulance at the hospital. And my parents. I should call my parents."

"Do you need me to dial for you?"

"No. I'm fine." She straightened her back.

"All right." He rose from the bed to dress. "Take your time down here making your calls. I'll be topside getting us under way."

"Mike?" she called as he started to leave. "How long will it take? To get to my car?"

He hesitated before answering. "About two hours." Her heart fell. "I'll get you there as fast as I can, Kate," he promised.

*But would it be fast enough?*

# Chapter 19

$\mathcal{A}N$ agonizing three hours later, Kate burst into the emergency room with Mike right behind her. He'd insisted on driving her in his car, since she was too shaky to be safe on the road. "Mom," she called, seeing her parents waiting on plastic seats in the hallway.

They rose and hurried toward her, her mother reaching her first. "Katy." Her mother's arms enfolded her with gentle strength.

"I'm so glad you're here," Kate said, holding tight.

"And where else would I be, I'd like to know?" Mary Larson laughed lightly as her husband stood stoically by, offering his silent support.

Linda came up behind Kate's parents, her worried expression more eloquent than any words.

"How's Dylan?" Kate asked.

"The doctor's in with him now," her mother answered.

"No news, then?" Kate asked.

"Humph," Mary snorted. "Only from the nurses, when they have a moment to spare, and they seem to be having precious few of those, if you ask me."

For the first time, Kate noticed the chaos and noise around her. Sunday mornings in an ER were usually quiet. Yet a group of bikers filled the waiting area: some pacing, some bleeding, all of them angry and cursing. One of them, the leader she supposed, stood at the admittance counter spewing obscenities at the nurse.

"Where's Anne?" Kate asked.

"She left just a moment ago," Mary said.

"Figures," Kate snorted.

"Now, Katy." Her mother took on a stern look. "Anne did a fine job getting Dylan checked in and waiting until we arrived. Truth be told, she was that upset after talking to the doctor. I suggested she go home and wait for word there with her husband." Mary's face softened as she tucked a curl behind Kate's ear. "The last thing you needed to deal with was Anne Bradshaw's hysterics on top of worrying over Dylan."

"Thank you." Kate managed a smile of gratitude just as Dylan's pediatrician emerged from one of the treatment rooms.

"Dr. Peterson." Kate hurried toward him.

"Kate, good, I'm glad you're here."

"How's Dylan?"

"Better now." He gave her a cool look, as if wanting to voice all the things she already knew: that preventive steps in the early stages could have lessened the attack, and barring that, Dylan should have been admitted hours before he was.

"He was staying with his grandparents," she offered lamely in her own defense. "Can I see him?"

"This way." Dr. Peterson turned and led the way back toward the swinging doors. "We'll be moving him to a private room soon."

"Then you'll be keeping him overnight?" The solid footing she'd fought to maintain all morning faltered. She glanced back over her shoulder. "My parents."

"We'll let them know the room number as soon as he's been moved."

"Yes, of course." Numbly she followed the doctor down the hall, toward her son.

Mike stood for a moment, staring after Kate, before he turned awkwardly to her parents. He offered a half-smile to the tall, slender woman with smooth blond hair and soft green eyes. "You must be Kate's mother."

"Aye." The woman arched a brow. She had a quiet manner, neatly pressed clothes, and a sure, steady gaze. "And you would be . . . ?"

"Mike Cameron." He cleared his throat, wondering if Kate's parents knew where their daughter had been when she received word about Dylan. "I'm a, uh, friend of Kate's."

"Cameron?" A frown flickered across her brow. "Oh, yes. The Scotsman whose grandfather sailed out of Glasgow some years back."

"That would be me." Relief washed over him as the woman offered her hand.

"I'm Mary Larson, and this is Kate's father, Arthur." The woman turned to the man at her side. "Arthur," she repeated a bit louder.

"Hmm? What?" Kate's father pulled his attention from the door through which his daughter had disappeared.

"This is the young man Mary Pat told us about. Mike Cameron. Katy's new man friend."

Dr. Larson was a burly man with wild white hair and a steely gray beard. He looked perfectly at home in his slightly baggy pants and navy blue pullover, which he'd neglected to tuck in.

"Cameron, you say?" The surprisingly dark eyebrows came together in a frown as he gave Mike a quick once-over. "Yes, I seem to remember some mention of that name."

Mike straightened instinctively. "Yes, sir. I'm pleased to finally meet you. Though I would have preferred different circumstances."

"Yes," the professor agreed before he returned his attention back down the hall.

They waited another thirty minutes in the ER. Mike sat beside Kate's father listening absently as the women talked in hushed tones.

Finally, a nurse stopped long enough to tell them Dylan's room number before she hurried off again. By silent consent, Mike rode up in the elevator with the others. He hung back, though, as they made their way through the maze of corridors, then stopped altogether when they reached Dylan's door.

He didn't belong here, he realized. Not yet. He wasn't family, even if he longed to be the one who sat at Kate's side, held her hand, and worried along with her over her son.

That right had to be more than earned. It had to be granted. Discouraged, but far from defeated, he took a seat in the hall and began his own vigil.

Kate looked up when her parents and Linda entered. The unbearable tightness in her chest loosened some just at the sight of them.

"How is he?" her mother asked as she moved quietly toward the bed, her eyes already fixed on Dylan.

"Sleeping now, thank goodness." Kate turned back to the bed. Her son lay against the white sheets, his breathing fast and shallow. "He was so scared, though, Mom. He was so scared."

The tears rose hot and fast, clogging in her throat.

"I know." Her mother leaned down to hug her. "I know."

"How could Anne do this?" Kate pulled back to swipe the moisture from her cheeks. "How could she let him get this bad? Doesn't she have eyes and ears?"

With a patient smile, her mother brushed the hair from Kate's face. "The frailty of our children isn't an easy thing for a body to accept. For some, it's easier not to see. But I think Anne realized what she'd done when she got here."

The phrase "too little, too late" sprang to Kate's tongue, but she swallowed it down. Lashing out at Anne Bradshaw wouldn't solve anything; no matter how badly she needed to lash out at something or someone.

They settled in to wait, her mother and Linda in the chairs on the other side of Dylan's bed, her father perched on the window seat. Kate gave her mother a list of things she'd need: some juice and animal crackers for Dylan, a few storybooks, paper and a fresh box of crayons. Linda agreed to drive back out to the lake and get Kate a change of clothes, her makeup, and the magazine off her nightstand. At the moment, Kate doubted she could concentrate enough to read, but she also knew how slowly the hours passed while watching Dylan sleep.

After another gentle hug from her mother and a gruff one from her father, Kate watched her parents leave.

"Oh, Kate," Linda said as they settled back down to either side of Dylan's bed. "I feel so awful."

"What on earth for?" Kate frowned. "This wasn't your fault."

"No, but I see now that I never took Dylan's condition seriously enough. I can't believe all the times I called you overprotective."

"It's all right." Kate offered a smile she hoped was reassuring even if it felt a bit weak. "Until you've lived through it, it's hard to believe something like this can happen so quickly." She gave in to the need to take Dylan's hand in hers. Whether from the medicine or exhaustion, he lay completely still except for the rapid rise and fall of his diaphragm. His air passages had constricted to the point where he had to use his stomach muscles to pull every breath into his lungs. The sound of the effort was painful to hear.

She remembered the time, years ago, when a nurse had told her to breathe through a straw for ten minutes so she'd better understand how Dylan felt during an attack. She barely lasted the full time, had felt panicked and helpless by the end. Yet Dylan had been like that for hours, and faced hours more, perhaps even days.

"I swear," Linda said, leaning forward. "I'll never give you grief for being overprotective again."

Kate managed a more genuine smile at her friend's earnest expression. "No, but I can see I might be the one giving you grief instead."

"Maybe so." They both smiled in a moment of perfect understanding and support.

"What the hell is going on here?" a voice demanded from the doorway.

All warmth drained from Kate's face as she turned to face her ex-husband. "Well, hello, Edward. So good of you to join us."

He flushed a bit when he saw Linda. After a quick glance toward the bed, he stepped toward Kate and lowered his voice. "My mother just called, crying and spouting some nonsense about Dylan being sick and her not being able to reach you. Just where the hell were you last night?"

"Where was I?" She stared at him in disbelief. Yet, how like Edward to instantly blame her for everything. "I should think the question is, where the hell were you?"

"I had a dinner meeting with a client." He shrugged.

"You were supposed to be spending the weekend with your son, not dumping him on your parents. But, since you did, I can't believe you forgot to unpack his nebulizer."

"I didn't realize I'd be leaving him all night. But the meeting ran over."

"That's no excuse, Edward!" She raked her hands through her hair in an effort to control her temper. "Do you realize your son could have died because of your negligence?"

"What are you talking about?"

"Look at him." She pointed toward the bed. "Take a good hard look at what you've done to our son."

For the first time, he turned his full attention to the bed. His eyes widened a fraction at the sight of Dylan lying there with an oxygen tube lying across his face, and an IV snaking upward from his arm. Dylan's face appeared nearly as white as the hospital sheets. "I don't understand. He was fine when I left him."

"Somehow I doubt that," Kate snapped. "An attack this bad has warning signs. As usual, though, you were too preoccupied with yourself to pay attention."

"If y'all will excuse me," Linda said, rising. "I'll be on my way." She caught Kate's gaze and nodded toward the bed. Dylan's eyes had fluttered open. Linda came around the bed and squeezed Kate's hand. "I'll run, go get your things, then be back as soon as I can."

"Thanks." Kate nodded. When Linda had gone, she turned and found Edward still studying his son.

"Hey, Dill-man, you're going to be okay, right?" Edward asked.

Dylan managed a weak nod.

Kate bent forward and kissed Dylan's brow. "You rest here a minute, sweetie. Your father and I need to talk, but I'll be right back. I promise."

His weak, frightened look brought the tightness back to her chest. Still, she had things to say to Edward that were best said out of Dylan's hearing range. Without a word, she walked through the door, knowing her ex-husband would follow.

"Mike?" She came up short the minute she passed into the brightly lighted hallway.

Mike came instantly to his feet. "How's Dylan?"

"Better. Though not out of the woods yet." She shook her head. "What are you doing here?"

"You rode in with me, remember?" He offered her a half-teasing smile.

"Yes, but—" She glanced over her shoulder, all too aware of Edward hanging on every word of the exchange. The two men locked gazes and both of them straightened. Edward's stance turned guarded, Mike's aggressive. She immediately rejected any thought of introducing them.

"It's thoughtful of you to wait, but you really didn't need to," she said to Mike.

"Of course I did." He turned his attention back to her and the intimacy of his smile made her blush. "You rode in with me, you'll ride home with me."

Her blush grew warmer at such a possessive male statement made in front of her ex-husband. "Mike, I'll be here overnight."

Worry flashed across his face. "He's that bad, then?"

"They want to keep him on the IV and oxygen for a while. We'll know better tomorrow when he'll get to go home." She glanced again at Edward, wondering how she'd get the privacy she needed.

"I see," Mike said, and to her surprise, he seemed to understand her distress. He nodded toward the door. "Maybe I could, you know, wait for you . . . inside."

"Yes, please," she answered gratefully. "And Mike," she added as he moved past her. "Thank you. For everything."

He gave her arm a casual squeeze before turning away.

Once inside the darkened room, Mike closed the door enough to block out most of the sounds in the hall, yet still let some light through. So that was Dylan's father, he thought. The fool who'd lost Kate. White-collar wimp. No wonder she'd dumped him. The only thing he couldn't see was why someone as vibrant and lively as Kate had married a stuffed shirt like that in the first place.

"Mom?" a weak voice called from the bed.

"No." He stepped around the corner of the bathroom so Dylan could see him. "It's me, Mike."

"Oh." Dylan slumped back into his pillow.

God, the kid looked pale, and every breath sounded like a hard-won gasp. He moved closer to the bed. "Can I get you anything?"

The boy just closed his eyes, as if slipping into sleep. "They're going to . . . fight about me . . . aren't they?"

Mike shifted uneasily, not sure what to say. He knew how to talk to boys about Power Rangers and spaceships, or how he'd help make the latest action-adventure movie. But how the hell was he supposed to answer a question like that?

Looking at the boy lying in the bed, he remembered Dylan was roughly the same age as his youngest nephew, even if Dylan was much smaller. The thought of how he'd feel if this was one of his sisters' kids lying there reached inside his chest and squeezed tight.

"Well, yeah," Mike said, "it did look like they were about to light into each other, but I don't know that they were going to fight about you."

He watched the boy struggle to draw enough breath to talk. "They always fight . . . about me." Another hard breath. "Or money . . . or Dad . . . working . . . too much."

"I see." Mike took a seat in the chair by the bed. From out in the hall, he heard a masculine voice rise in anger then drop quickly to a tightly controlled rumble. Kate's voice fired back, equally angry.

"So," Mike said, loud enough to cover up the sounds from the hall. "I hear they're going to keep you here a while, eh, kid?"

"I want . . . to go home." Though Dylan's eyes remained closed, Mike saw tears wet the lashes.

"What, and miss out on all this great attention?" The voices in the hall rose and fell. The words were muffled but the fury came through all too clear. "Hey, you play your cards right, you could have these nurses eating out of your hand."

Dylan just shrugged, too weak or disinterested to respond. Mike watched him, mentally searching for a way to bridge the awkwardness between them. What would he do if this were one of his nephews?

"Hey, you like movies?" he asked.

Dylan opened his eyes enough to give him a wary look.

Mike leaned forward to brace his forearms on his thighs. "How would you like to see one being made?"

The boy's eyes widened a bit but remained guarded. "Maybe."

"Oh, well, if you're not interested . . ." Mike sat back.

"I didn't . . . say that."

"Then you are interested?"

Dylan's mouth twisted, refusing to utter a word.

"I mean, because if you are, I could get passes for you and your mom to come watch one of the location shoots. They're filming a really big stunt next Sunday."

"What kind . . . of stunt?"

"A man on horseback is going to jump from a train into a river."

Dylan closed his eyes. "That doesn't . . . sound so . . . big."

"It would if you were the guy on the back of that horse. So you interested?" He hid a smile as the boy tried not to give away his excitement.

"I guess," Dylan finally sighed. "If Mom says . . . okay."

"Hey, no sweat. You just work on getting well. I'll handle your mom."

Kate pressed her fingertips to her temples to ease the pounding in her head. "I am not going to argue with you all day about fault, Edward. Dylan being in the hospital isn't the only issue here. The fact is, you broke your promise to him. Again."

"The hell I did," Edward shot back. "I took him to the ball game."

"Then immediately dumped him on your mother."

"I told you, an important dinner meeting came up."

"Something important *always* comes up."

"You don't understand." He placed his hand over his chest, his expression earnest. "If I land this client, it could be the biggest thing that's ever happened to me. The portfolio is worth millions, Kate. It would make my career. You want me to brush that off to spend one evening with Dylan?"

"You're right. I don't know what I was thinking." She trailed a hand through the air. "Of course you should break a promise to your son, let him down for the thousandth time, in order to cement your career. After all, as long as you have money, who needs anything else?"

He gave her a condescending smirk. "I find it so ironic the way you always harp on me about my work, when you're just as bad. When we were married, you were so wrapped up in that stupid column of yours, the house could have fallen down and you wouldn't have even noticed. What was I supposed to do, come home at night so I could be ignored? I had needs of my own, you know, but did you ever take that into account?"

"Oh, grow up, Edward." She crossed her arms. "You are not the center of the universe."

A hurt frown flickered across his forehead. "No, but I used to be the center of yours."

"And you loved it, obviously. Loved it so much you married a girl you thought socially beneath you, because you thrived on all that sappy adoration. The problem is, you never gave anything back. A person can only survive on crumbs so long. You made it very clear that Dylan and I were nothing to you but ornaments for your image."

"Why do *I* always have to be the one to make sacrifices to please *you*? Why isn't it ever the other way around? If you'd given up that column, Dylan would have had plenty of attention, and we'd still be married."

"No, actually, we probably would have been divorced a lot sooner." She shook her head sadly, then held up her hand before he could continue. "Look, I admit, it wasn't all one-sided. At times, I was as self-absorbed as you. So you're right. I wasn't a very good wife. But at least I'm trying to be a good parent."

"What, by living in a shack so you can afford to spend more time playing with your kid? Great plan, Kate. Real great."

"My kid," she echoed, and felt the fight drain out of her. It was so useless. Edward didn't care about anyone but himself, and he never would. A calmness settled over her, an acceptance she'd been struggling against for years. "All right. I give up. I'm tired of putting Dylan through hell in hopes that someday you'll realize you have a wonderful, bright, sensitive son who is a sheer joy to be around. You win, Edward. You win."

"What's that supposed to mean?" His frown turned wary.

"It means I'll stop bothering you. No more calling to remind you when it's your weekend to take him. No more calling you, period. From now on, whether or not you have a relationship with Dylan is up to you. Now, if you'll excuse me, I need to see how my son is resting." She turned toward the door.

"Kate, wait a second."

"No, Edward. I'm through waiting. The ball's in your court. You can either serve or throw in the towel. Frankly, at this point, I don't even care."

She stepped into the darkened room and stopped for a moment to close her eyes and compose herself. Every encounter with Edward left her utterly drained.

An odd sound caught her ears, like someone imitating a space-age laser being fired. She stepped around the corner and found Mike sitting beside her son's bed.

"And then . . . what happened?" Dylan asked, so enthralled with Mike, he hadn't even heard her come in.

She watched in fascination as Mike, who was moving his hand like a spaceship over the bed, explained how some special effect had fallen flat, and what he had done to fix it. She'd never noticed that calming quality to his voice. He looked so natural sitting beside her son's bed that the oddest thing happened: Suddenly she couldn't imagine him *not* being there.

How on earth had he planted himself so fully in the center of her life?

Sensing her presence at last, Dylan turned to her. "Hi, Mom."

"Hi, yourself." She smiled as she stepped closer.

"Mike says . . . we can come watch . . . him make a movie."

"Oh, he did, did he?" Frowning at the weedy sound of her son's voice, she tucked the sheets around him.

"Well, it won't actually be me working on the set," Mike clarified. "I just thought you and Dylan might enjoy watching the crew film one of the horseback-riding stunts."

"Can we, Mom?" Dylan begged. "Can we?"

She raised her gaze from her son to the man who sat at his side. Those clear blue eyes caught and held her. A smile spread slowly over his face, and to her dismay, she felt her body flush with heat. How could she stand over her son's sickbed growing aroused with memories at everything she'd done the night before?

"Come on, Kate," Mike coaxed in a voice that held a hint of intimacy. "I promised the boy I'd talk you into it, if he promised to get well."

Self-preservation urged her to say no. Mike was getting too close to her heart, too quickly. She needed distance, and time to think.

"Please, Mom?" Dylan begged, his face earnest.

Her shoulders slumped. "All right, we'll go. But just this once."

"See, kid?" Mike winked at Dylan. "Like I told you, no sweat."

# Chapter 20

*KATE* battled a silly sense of excitement as she drove through the country on her way to the location shoot. True to his word, Mike had gotten them passes, and she was absurdly eager to see him again. She'd barely done more than talk to him on the phone for the past week, as busy as they both had been. The remodeling project in the kitchen was finally finished. Even though Mike was ready for her to get started on the living and dining room, she'd been too busy with other things to do more than pick out a few fabric swatches. Now that she'd lost her column, she'd agreed to take on more of Linda's accounts—a decision she was beginning to regret.

After a few days of shuttling kids to soccer practice, dance classes, piano lessons, picking up laundry, and buying groceries for other people, she missed being Dear Cupid more than ever. As much as she enjoyed people, she did not enjoy being expected to satisfy their every whim, no matter how well it paid. Plus, she'd thought working for Linda would allow her more time with Dylan than a conventional job. On that score she was sadly mistaken. While Dylan did accompany her on many of her errands, he generally sat in the car and sulked because he wanted to be home with his books and his computer games.

After one particularly grueling day, she'd finally given in and called Mike's friend, the freelance writer. The woman had generously shared her knowledge about syndicating a column. It all sounded so simple, and yet so daunting. With every day that passed, she knew she wanted to continue writing Dear Cupid, at times more than she wanted her next breath, but one question stopped her cold every time. *What if I fail?*

The question nagged at her even now as she steered the car through a series of turns. What if she submitted samples of her work, and received nothing in return but rejections?

She snorted in disgust at her own thoughts, wondering when she'd turned into such a coward. She just hoped Mike didn't ask her again if she'd followed his friend's advice. She was rapidly running out of excuses, and feared he'd recognize the truth: that she lacked the guts to go after one of the things she wanted most. Not a pleasant confession for someone with the reputation of charging headlong toward life with arms stretched wide.

Would she ever recapture that optimistic exuberance? Did she even want to? Time and time again, she'd charged toward something she wanted, only to fall flat on her face. Could she stand to take one more fall? On the other hand, could she continue to look herself in the mirror if she didn't go out on a limb for something that meant so much to her?

"Mom?" Dylan asked from the backseat, breaking into her thoughts. "Are we really gonna see a horse jump out of a train into a river?"

"That's what Mike said," she answered absently as she checked the directions Mike had given her over the phone. Either the location shoot was more remote than she'd thought, or she was lost.

"Yeah, but do you think a horse is really gonna do it?"

"Going to, not gonna," she corrected automatically, then glanced at her son in the rearview mirror and noticed the disbelieving smirk that hovered at the corners of his mouth. No one would ever guess from looking at him now that he'd been in the hospital a mere week ago. They'd discharged him late Monday and by Wednesday he was already back at school. "Why do you keep asking that?"

"I don' know." He shrugged, trying to look bored. Except, she could see the longing that lurked in the back of his eyes. "People promise kids neat stuff all the time. But when you get there, it's just some dorky thing to keep you busy while they go do something else."

"People" meaning his father, she assumed. "Well, I don't think Mike's the type to intentionally lie, but I'm with you. I say we reserve judgment till we get there, okay?"

"And if it's dorky, we can leave?"

"In a heartbeat."

At that moment, they popped over a hill and she spotted the entrance to the ranch Mike had mentioned. A burly cowboy with a clipboard jumped off the tailgate of a pickup truck as she turned onto the dirt driveway.

Kate rolled down the window and felt a wave of hot, humid air invade the air-conditioned car. "Is this where they're filming *The Seekers*?"

"Yes, ma'am. Are you with the cast or crew?"

"Neither, actually. I'm Kate Bradshaw, a guest of Mike Cameron's."

The man checked his list and nodded. "You'll need visitor's passes." He pulled two from beneath the clip

on his board and handed them to her with instructions
for her and Dylan to wear them around their necks.
"Now what you need to do is follow this dirt road here
till you get to the filming site. You can't miss it. Just
park anywhere behind the honey wagon."

"Thanks." Laughing at the term "honey wagon,"
Kate rolled up her window and headed through the
iron gate.

"Mom?" Dylan asked. "What's a honey wagon?"

"Well, I don't know what he means, but in medieval times it was the cart that went around a village,
collecting the um ... contents from people's slop
jars."

"*Uuughhh, ga-ross!* I told you this would be
dorky."

When Kate found the filming site, the number of
RVs and semis surprised her. Thick electrical cords
snaked along the ground connecting and entangling
them in a man-made web. A large tent that looked like
a makeshift dining hall sat off to one side. Since the
RVs and portable toilets were loosely formed in a line
with a makeshift parking lot to one side, she assumed
they were the "honey wagon."

"Well," she said, getting out of the car, "I guess
this is it."

"I guess so," Dylan agreed as he climbed out his
side.

"I suppose the first order of business is to find
Mike." She held a hand to her brow to shade her eyes
and searched the area. The woody scent of barbecue
drifted toward them on a light breeze, but other than
the handful of men tending the pit, the area appeared
deserted. "Got any ideas?"

Dylan's brow puckered in thought. "I'd try the
river."

Kate nodded. "Sounds like a plan."

They followed a trampled path through a field of wildflowers that led uphill. The sun beat down on her head and bare arms, making her glad she'd worn a cotton sundress that allowed air to brush her skin. When they topped the hill, they stopped and stared at the scene below. Camera crews worked along both banks, focusing their lenses on the section of tracks that spanned the river. With the recent rains, the surface of the water nearly reached the bottom of the bridge. An ambulance waited downstream, as if anticipating the worst, along with a truck bearing the name of a veterinary clinic.

In the other direction, an old-fashioned train curved around the nearest hill, looking nostalgic and impressive with its restored steam engine.

"Well," she said, "I would definitely say these people are serious."

"Yeah," Dylan agreed, clearly awed. And then he pointed toward the crowd near the train. "Look, there's Mike!"

The excitement in her son's voice caught Kate off guard. Dylan rarely warmed to people quickly, yet he seemed as excited to see Mike as if he'd spotted Jim.

Then she glanced up and caught a glimpse of the trademark Hawaiian shirt and warmth rushed through her. He stood with a small crowd gathered around Trey Evans and a massive-looking horse. Frank, the special effects supervisor, gestured with his hand as if describing how the jump should go. Trey appeared to be arguing over some point, with Jesse serving as interpreter.

Mike shifted, looking restless as his eyes searched the crowd. When he spotted her on the hill, he went still. He smiled slowly, and her body tingled with the simple pleasure of seeing him, of knowing that in a moment she'd be talking with him, laughing with him, just *being* with him.

*Katy, girl,* she told herself, *you are definitely in trouble.* The thought made her nerves jangle as she watched him excuse himself and stride up the hill to join them.

"You came," he said, sounding as breathless as she felt. Their eyes held for a moment and she wondered if he would kiss her. *Not in front of Dylan,* her panicked brain pleaded, even though her body argued strongly in the other direction.

As if sensing her quandary, he turned his attention to her son. "Hey, kid, what do you think?"

"I think Mom's right." Dylan nodded gravely. "Y'all are definitely serious."

"Nah, this here's fun and games. What I do on the computer, now that's serious work."

Kate looked about, desperate for a way to calm her pounding heart. "I can't believe it takes so many people to film one scene."

"It doesn't," Mike said, gesturing toward the river. "Most of the people here are just using the stunt as an excuse to take a little time off. It's not every day you get to see someone do something this stupid."

"Stupid?" she asked.

"Well, I ask you—would you jump off that bridge? On horseback?"

From where she stood, it didn't look that high. But then she tried to imagine standing on the bridge looking down with the added height of the train and horse beneath her. "Absolutely not."

Mike nodded in agreement. "The one thing I've learned about stunts involving horses is that anything can happen. Like, what if Trey lands in front of the

horse and gets pawed when the animal starts swimming? Or what if he gets kicked in the head on the
way down? I'm telling you, anyone who does this kind
of work for a living is nuts."

"I think you might be right," she said.

"What about the horse?" Dylan asked, and his hand
tightened around hers. "Could it get hurt?"

"Nah." Mike ruffled Dylan's hair. "Trey would
never do anything he thought might hurt one of his
horses, even if the ASPCA would let him. With all
the animal rights police running around these days,
you could beat up a kid on a film set easier than you
could abuse an animal."

Kate scowled at him. "Well, I would hope you
wouldn't abuse either."

"You sure?" He winked at her. "And here we were
talking about tossing a kid off the bridge, just to see
how he'd land." He grabbed playfully at her son.
"What do you say, Dylan? You want to go for a
swim?"

"No way!" Laughing, the boy ducked behind Kate.

"Ha, ha, very funny." She smirked at Mike.

"Oh, well, if you want to be a killjoy." Mike gestured to a row of folding canvas chairs set up behind
one of the cameras. "You want to meet some of the
crew before the action begins?"

"Actually, I think we have a better view from up
here," she said.

"You got it," he agreed easily. They settled down
amid the wildflowers with Dylan between them. Kate
tucked the skirt of her sundress about her raised knees.
In the distance, voices shouted over the drone of gen-
erators as the film crew prepared for the shoot. A burst
of laughter came from the crowd of other observers.

"So," Mike said, giving her his full attention, "did

you get those sample packets of your column off to any papers yet?"

She groaned. "No, but I will. As soon as I have time to put them together."

"Come on, Kate," he scolded her lightly. "How long does it take to write a cover letter and stick a few printouts in an envelope?"

"It's not like I haven't been busy this week."

"Kate." He gave her an exasperated look. "You'll never sell your column if you don't send it out."

*I won't get rejected either.* "I'm working on it, okay?" she snapped.

He frowned in concern, making her regret the sharpness of her tone. "Are you all right?"

"I'm fine," she sighed. "I'm just really tired."

"I know." He reached past Dylan and rubbed her shoulders. The contact relaxed her shoulders and melted something inside her. Studying his face in the sunlight, the kindness in the blue eyes surrounded by generous laugh lines, she felt the wall about her heart weaken a bit more.

As their gazes met and held, he seemed to read her mind and silently urge her to give in, to let go of her fear.

*I can't,* she wanted to tell him. Some instinct warned her that a broken heart over Mike would hurt even more than what she'd suffered over Edward. Because loving a man like Mike with all her soul would be so very easy.

"Oh, look!" Dylan pointed down the hill. "The train's moving. Is he gonna jump now?"

Mike broke eye contact, and the moment was gone. "Not yet," he said, glancing at his watch. "First Frank has to check all of the measurements from the cameras to the opening of the freight car to be sure they're right."

"What do you mean?" Kate asked.

"The animation has to be the same scale and angle as the live-action shot. This scene will be the climax of the movie when the train explodes, destroying my robot. Kevin Lee's character will barely escape by leaping from the train on horseback. In order for the effect to work, all the technical data has to be dead-on accurate."

"Cool!" Dylan's face tipped up toward Mike's. "So, we're gonna see the train blow up too?"

"Not today." Mike smiled at the boy. "That's what the audience in the theater will see. Today, all we'll see is Trey doing the stunt. The rest of the animation team will create the fireball on their computers back in California, while I finish creating the robot here. Once everything's done, a film compositor will combine all the elements to make it look as if everything happened at once."

"And it'll look real?" Dylan asked.

"As real as the dinosaurs we created for *Jurassic Park*."

"You worked on *Jurassic Park*?" Dylan's eyes widened.

"Nearly every animator I know worked on that one." Mike regaled Dylan with stories from the making of *Jurassic Park* and some other movies he'd worked on.

Watching them, Kate saw her son's eyes fill with awe, and her fear veered off in a new direction. If Dylan formed an attachment to Mike, how would he feel when his new hero disappeared? And if she couldn't give Mike what he seemed to want from her, he would definitely disappear at some point. Or, even worse, she would give him her heart, only to watch his current interest turn to disappointment.

"Oh, wait, here we go," Mike said, standing up.

Kate stood as well, forcing her attention to focus on the train as it moved onto the bridge. The director motioned with his hand and the mechanical arm holding his seat and camera rose. Downstream, near the ambulance and vet's truck, Jesse mounted a second horse, and rode to the water's edge.

"I didn't realize Jesse was in this shot," Kate said.

"She's not," Mike explained. "She's waiting out of camera range to catch Trey's horse if it gets away from him."

Someone hollered for quiet. The director spoke into a walkie-talkie and Trey appeared on foot in the doorway of the freight car, waved to Jesse, then disappeared back into the car.

"What you can't see," Mike explained in a hushed voice, "is the platform attached to the other side of the train. Trey will back the horse onto that, so the horse can take a full stride before he jumps."

Kate nodded, her gaze riveted to the train.

Then, suddenly, the horse and rider shot through the opening of the freight car to arch gracefully through the air. Trey leapt sideways, free of the saddle, his arms cartwheeling as he fell. Horse and rider landed with a splash several feet apart and disappeared beneath the water. The instant they resurfaced, Trey frantically swam toward his horse and grabbed hold of the saddle horn as the animal splashed and pawed its way toward the bank. They both appeared to struggle. Kate looked toward Jesse and the rescue team, wondering why they weren't doing anything.

Finally, the horse reached the bank, literally dragging the half-drowned Trey from the water. Kate covered her mouth with both hands when Trey collapsed face first onto the ground, his body seized by a violent fit of coughing. She took a step forward, not sure what she meant to do, but Mike grabbed her arm, holding her back. An instant later, someone yelled, "Cut," and applause broke out along both sides of the river.

Beside her, Mike clapped and whistled as Trey jumped nimbly to his feet, shaking water from his long hair. The horse, which had looked on the brink of death a moment before, tossed its head as if laughing. Trey grabbed the bridle and gave the horse a big kiss right on its nose as the crew gathered around them. Jesse rode up and tossed a towel at Trey.

"Had ya fooled, didn't they?" Mike winked at Kate.

"Scared the tar out of me is more like it." She pressed a hand to her heart.

"That was too cool!" Dylan said. "Can we go down and see the horses?"

"You bet." Mike reached down, grabbed Dylan beneath the arms, and swung the boy up to ride on his hip. Dylan giggled in response.

Kate froze, startled by the sight of Mike and her son laughing together. She would never have brought Dylan here if she'd realized the danger. After losing his father to divorce, the last thing he needed was a parade of "uncles" through his life, along with the false hope, disappointment, and grief that would follow each one.

Oblivious to her anxiety, Mike started down the hill, calling to her over his shoulder. "Come on, let's go join the party."

On wooden legs, Kate followed. All the while, her

mind raced for some way to get herself and Dylan out of this mess—with the least damage to both of their hearts.

"Mom, lookit me!" Dylan called from his perch in front of Jesse on her horse. His mother didn't hear him, though, with all the people standing between them. But he wanted her to see him sitting on a horse. An actual horse! Jesse even let him hold the ends of the reins, because he'd promised not to pull or jiggle them. He wouldn't either, because Jesse said horses didn't like that, and she knew *everything* about horses.

Just like Mike knew everything about movies. Mike had introduced him to all his friends, and even lifted him up onto the horse when Jesse said it was okay.

"Mom!" he called again. "Lookit me!"

She finally turned around, and her eyes went round. "Dylan!" she screeched, rushing toward him through the crowd. "What are you doing?"

"I'm riding, see?" He bounced up and down, wishing Jesse would make the horse go faster, instead of just walking around Mike in a slow circle.

"No, don't kick," Jesse said, placing a hand on his leg.

"Sorry." He glanced up at her and smiled. He liked the way she smiled back at him. She was really pretty. Even prettier than his teacher, Miss Marshall.

"Dylan, come down off that horse before you fall."

He glanced down and found his mom walking beside them, her arms stretched toward him.

"Nooo!" He pressed back into Jesse even as she pulled the reins and the horse quit walking.

"I'm sorry," Jesse said to his mom. "Mike said it would be okay."

"Well, Mike isn't Dylan's mother, I am. Dylan,

come down this instant." She reached for him again.

"Kate?" Mike came up on the other side of the horse. "What's wrong? Dylan's perfectly safe. Jesse's got a good hold on him."

"I don't care." His mom glared at Mike over the horse's neck. "He's allergic to nearly every kind of animal. How do I know he isn't allergic to horses?"

Dylan dropped his head so he wouldn't have to see all the people staring at him. He couldn't believe his mom would make him sound like such a wimp in front of Jesse and Mike and everybody.

"He's not sneezing or anything," Mike pointed out, then ducked his head to smile up at him. "Are you, buddy?"

Dylan shook his head.

"I don't care," his mom said. "I want him down, now!"

"All right," Mike said, patting Dylan's leg as if they really were buddies. "Us men are getting hungry anyway. What do you say, Dylan, you want to go hit the chow tent?"

After a quick glare at his mom, he reached his hands toward Mike and lunged.

"Whoa!" Mike staggered back and nearly dropped the boy on impact. Once he had him under control, he shot Kate a surprised look. Emotions flashed across her face, from disbelief, to hurt, to accusation. *Oh, boy,* he thought, *this is not a good sign.*

Jesse nudged her horse forward, breaking the moment. "See ya 'round, Magic Man," she called over her shoulder.

"Yeah, uh, thanks, Jess." Uncomfortably aware of Kate's angry glare, he lowered Dylan to the ground. "Come on, buddy, you ready for some food?"

"You bet." Ignoring his mother, Dylan took Mike's hand and started up the hill. "I'm starved."

With a helpless shrug toward Kate, he let the boy pull him along. Kate fell in step beside them.

"The next time you get the urge to put my son on the back of a horse," she said in a chilly voice, "you might want to ask me first."

"Well, gee, Kate"—he winked—"if I'd known you wanted to sit on the horse, I would have asked you first."

Her eyes narrowed a fraction. "You know what I mean."

"You're right," he said. "Next time I'll ask."

"Thank you." Kate's expression relaxed a bit. "You might also tell Jesse I'm sorry, in case she thinks I was upset at her. I was just concerned about Dylan. Although that doesn't excuse my snapping at her."

"Jess'll be okay. I'll let her know it was my fault."

She sighed. "Which doesn't excuse my snapping at you either. I'm sorry."

"Trey and Jesse live on a ranch!" Dylan told his mom, apparently over his momentary upset. "Well, not a real ranch. Jesse said it's a . . . it's a . . ."

"Rescue reserve for exotic animals," Mike supplied.

"They have camels and donkeys and ostriches." Dylan took his mom's hand and leapt forward so he swung between them, like a monkey swinging from two vines. "And they even have a tiger. Don't they, Mike?"

"They sure do," he answered.

"Can I go see it?" Dylan asked, his blue eyes pleading with his mother. "Pleeease. Mike said he'd take me."

"Oh, he did, did he?" She raised a brow at Mike, making him cringe. He'd thought she'd be pleased that

Dylan had finally decided to accept him, but apparently he'd been mistaken.

"Did I mention Rowdy, the tiger, is tame as a kitten and has no claws?" he offered hopefully.

"Can I go see him, Mom?" Dylan jumped up and down, pulling on their arms. "Can I?"

"We'll see," she said in a neutral tone.

Dylan's shoulders slumped as he turned to Mike with surprisingly adult eyes. "That means she's hoping I'll forget so she won't have to say no."

*Smart kid.* Mike nodded. "I guess we'll just have to work on her then, eh?"

"You betcha." With renewed enthusiasm, Dylan dropped their hands and raced ahead toward the tent.

"Talkative little guy, isn't he?" Mike smiled, watching the boy. "And here I actually thought he was standoffish the first time we met."

"Dylan isn't the type to give his friendship lightly."

"Gets that from his mom, I guess." He slipped his hand into hers and gave it a light squeeze. The gesture seemed so natural, he did it without thinking. But that simple contact, the mere holding of her hand as they walked up the hill, made everything inside him settle into place. This was so right.

She raised her gaze to his, and he saw the same feeling flicker in her eyes, only to be followed by a small questioning frown, a wary crease between her brows. Why couldn't she relax and let this thing between them follow its natural course?

"Mike, I—" Before she could finish, Dylan came running back.

"I found us a table," the boy panted. "But hurry up, before it's gone."

Mike stifled a sigh of frustration as they made their way into the cool shade of the tent. Later, he and Kate

would talk. They'd had very little time for that in the
last week, but sooner or later, he had to let her know
how he felt. Except, he had the nagging suspicion that
knowing how he felt would only scare her more. It
had to be done, though, because this pretense of casualness couldn't go on forever. Surely she sensed
that.

They took their seats with Dylan between them at
one of the long portable tables that had been set up
by the catering service. Bowls of potato salad, pinto
beans, and coleslaw sat on the red-checkered plastic
tablecloth.

"What would you like, sweetie?" Kate asked Dylan
as she retrieved paper plates for each of them.

"Everything," Dylan answered, arching his back to
pat his stomach. "I'm hungry."

Kate began filling his plate with side dishes as Mike
accepted one of the platters of meat being passed
around the table.

"I'm going to be in a show," Dylan announced as
he took a giant-sized bite of beans.

"You are?" Mike responded with exaggerated surprise.

"Not a movie, or anything." Dylan's mouth twisted
into a smirk with a smear of sauce on one cheek. "It's
just a dumb show at my school."

"Dylan," Kate said as she wiped the sauce from his
face. "Don't talk with your mouth full."

"What play are you doing?" Mike asked.

Dylan made a point of swallowing before he answered. "It's not a play, exactly. We're just gonna do
a bunch of skits. You know, like vawdy-villa."

"Vaudeville?" Mike dug into his own plate of
sauce-drenched brisket. "Sounds cool."

"Ya think?" Dylan's eyes brightened as he looked up at Mike.

"Absolutely. I love vaudeville shows nearly as much as the Three Stooges and old Marx Brothers movies. They're fun."

"That's what my teacher, Miss Marshall, says. She says she likes family acts best, like Eddie Boy."

"You mean Eddie Foy?" Mike asked. "I've heard of him. Didn't he have a whole bunch of kids who performed with him?"

"Yeah." Dylan's shoulders slumped as he stirred his potato salad and coleslaw together. "Some of the cool kids at school decided to do something like that. Jason's dad said he'd play Eddie. They all think they're so big, just because Jason's dad plays in a band. Sounds pretty dorky, huh?"

"Well, I don't know." Mike tilted his head to try and see Dylan's face. "Sounds pretty neat to me."

Dylan poked at his food, refusing to look at him. "I asked my dad if he'd do something with me."

"Oh?" Mike glanced uncomfortably from Dylan to Kate. She, too, refused to meet his gaze.

"Dylan," she said quietly. "Try some brisket."

Dylan heaved a big sigh, ignoring his mom. "My dad said no. He's real busy, though. You know, doing important stuff."

If Mike hadn't already decided Edward Bradshaw was an A-1 asshole, the dejected look on his son's face would have done it. "You know," he said, "if I had a son as neat as you, I'd find the time to be in your play, no matter how busy I was."

Dylan's head shot up, and the look of wonder shining from his eyes squeezed Mike's chest. "You—you mean it?" Dylan whispered. "You think I'm a neat kid?"

"Absolutely." Mike nodded.

"Only"—Dylan lowered his voice even more—"what if I wasn't your kid? Would you still want to be in a play with me?"

Mike glanced at Kate, hoping for guidance, but couldn't read her expression. She looked frightened, but was she afraid he'd say no or yes? "I—" He hesitated. Then glanced back down at Dylan's face, and caved. "I'd love to do a skit with you, I mean if your mother says it's okay." He added the last hastily, in case he'd answered wrong.

"Too cool!" Dylan kicked his feet under the table. "Since you make movies, we could do something really big, like blow up the whole stage. *Ka-pow!*" He motioned with his hands as if his plate of barbecue had exploded. Then he turned to his mom. "Isn't that neat, Mom? Mike's gonna be in my play."

"Going to, Dylan, not gonna. As for the play"—her gaze shot toward Mike—"we'll talk about it later."

# Chapter 21

KATE stared straight ahead as she drove away from the location shoot. Beside her, Mike sat sideways, listening to Dylan, who sat in the backseat, chattering on about everything they'd seen and done that day. With each mile that passed, her nerves stretched tighter, until she feared they'd snap.

Just before they reached Lakeway, Dylan's excitement finally turned to exhaustion and he fell asleep mid-sentence. Chuckling softly, Mike turned toward her. "I was wondering when his battery would wear down."

"Children don't have batteries," she said in a flat tone.

"No, of course not." He frowned at her, obviously confused by her brusque behavior. *Well, join the club,* she wanted to tell him. She was more confused than she'd ever been in her life. She needed to get away from him so she could think everything through and figure a way out of this mess.

"I appreciate your giving me a lift home," Mike said after a moment.

"Don't mention it." She tried to shrug but the gesture barely moved one shoulder. "After all, I couldn't very well have left you stranded there, now could I?"

Especially after Dylan had practically insisted Mike ride with them.

"I could have ridden back with Frank," he pointed out.

"I told you," she said with strained patience, "it's not a problem."

He drummed his fingertips on the armrest. "Look, Kate, you're obviously mad at me, so would you mind explaining why?"

She glanced in the rearview mirror to check on Dylan. The boy was dead to the world, but this was hardly the time or place for her to tell Mike she didn't want him anywhere near her son—that Dylan had been hurt enough, and she refused to stand by and let him get hurt again.

She reached for the radio as a distraction. Mike placed his hand over hers before she could turn it on, and the gentleness of his touch was almost her undoing.

"Kate," he said softly, so as not to wake Dylan, "would you please talk to me?"

She snatched her hand away. All she had to do was make it to his house, tell him good-bye, then never see him again. The thought made her throat tighten.

"It's about the play, isn't it?" he persisted. "What did you want me to do, tell him no?"

They passed through the entrance of Lakeway and she gave thanks. Just a few more blocks.

"Come on, Kate," he pleaded, barely above a whisper. "You saw how he was looking at me. There's no way I could have turned him down. And I did tell him I'd only do it if you said it was okay."

"Oh, yes," she whispered back, no longer able to keep silent, "and thank you so much for making *me* the bad guy."

"What do you mean?" He shook his head. "Are you saying you're not mad because I agreed to do the play, but because I said I'd only do it if it was okay with you?"

"I'm mad at you for both." She glanced in the rear-view mirror to be sure Dylan was still asleep and lowered her voice even more. "Now, no matter what happens, he's going to be hurt, and it will be my fault."

"Kate, you're not making any sense."

"Don't you see?" She pleaded with him to understand. "If I say no now, he'll be angry and disappointed and he'll blame me for days. But if I don't interfere, he'll be crushed when you let him down, and then it really will be my fault because I didn't interfere when I knew I should. How could you do this to me? Or him?"

"I'm not going to let Dylan down," he insisted. "All you have to do is agree to let me do the skit, and the problem is solved."

She tightened her hands on the steering wheel as she turned onto his street. When she reached his house, she braved the steep driveway to park in the shade, then lowered the automatic windows to catch the evening breeze. Without a word, she got out of the car. Mike followed suit. Neither of them spoke until they reached the protective overhang by his front door.

"Are you coming in?" he asked.

"No." She glanced toward the car where her son slept. "I just needed to talk to you away from radar ears." She took a deep breath. "Mike, I want you to call Dylan tomorrow and tell him you can't do the play."

He pulled back as if she'd struck him. "Are you forbidding me?"

"No. I just—" She looked away, feeling as if she were some kind of villain. "You know what your schedule is like. You don't have time to be in an elementary-school play."

"I'll make time," he said with absolute conviction.

She stared at him, baffled by the determination stamped into every line of his face. For a moment, she almost believed he would do it. Wanted to believe. Only— "Why would you go to so much trouble for Dylan? You barely even know him."

"Maybe I'd like to know him. And what better way than to spend some time with him one-on-one?"

"This is more than just spending time with him." She flung her arm toward the car. "You just promised a seven-year-old boy you'd get up with him in front of all his friends and their parents and do what amounts to a father-son skit. How dare you promise such a thing!"

"Maybe because he asked me."

"You had no right!" she railed, then instantly lowered her voice in deference to the open car windows. "You're not his father, and you never will be."

"Well, I could be," he insisted. "If you'd quit throwing barriers between us."

The words knocked her back a step. "Oh, my God," she whispered as the scary feeling that had swirled inside her all day swelled upward like a tidal wave. She shook her head, trying to stem the fear. "Please don't say anything else. Don't ruin things, Mike. Please? Everything is perfect the way it is."

"No it's not. I'm frustrated as hell because . . ." He took a deep breath and let it out in a rush. "I happen to be in love with you. There, I said it. I am madly, passionately in love with you."

"No." She stepped back. "That's not true. You only think you love me because you're looking for a wife and I happen to be handy."

"No, Kate, the truth is I've been in love with you since I first laid eyes on you in L.A."

"That can't be. You hired me to ..." Looking away, she tried to get her bearings as memories whirled through her head. "You lied to me. Right from the beginning. That whole nonsense about wanting a wife was a lie. Wasn't it?"

"The part about wanting a wife wasn't a lie. I just never told you that you are the only woman I've ever wanted to marry."

"And why didn't you tell me?"

"Would you have gone out with me if I had?" He reached a hand toward her, not quite touching. "Kate, you gave me no choice. Right off the bat, you made it obvious you'd turn me down if I asked you out. I didn't understand it then, but I do now. You're so damned scared of getting hurt that no man stands a chance with you."

"And with good reason, obviously!" Turning her back, she stepped away. "I can't believe I was stupid enough to fall for something so ridiculous as helping you find a wife."

"All right, I lied." He came up behind her and she closed her eyes as he rested his hands on her shoulders. "That doesn't change how I feel. I love you, Kate. I want to marry you."

A painful laugh shook her chest. The tender words and the yearning with which they were spoken sounded so tempting, yet so horribly familiar. "Why? Because you've decided it's time to settle down? That getting married is your next logical step in life? And I happen to be the nearest available female?" Shaking her head, she faced him. "I made the mistake of being a convenience once. I refuse to do it again."

"Convenience?" His brows rose. "Is that what you think you are to me?" He laughed. "Trust me, Kate, you are anything but a convenience."

"What else am I supposed to believe when you claim you fell in love with me on sight, then propose marriage after you've known me all of three weeks?"

"What does that matter? Is there some rule about how long it takes to fall in love? One year? Two years? Ten? Why can't it happen the instant two people meet?"

"I don't know!" She shook her head, wishing she could think. "Maybe it does happen that way for other people, but not for me."

He looked genuinely baffled. "Why not for you? Aren't you worth falling in love with at first sight?"

"Would you stop!" Every word he spoke tore at old wounds, making them bleed anew. She felt trapped between past and present and suddenly she couldn't breathe. "Why are you always pressuring me?"

"I'm not pressuring you." He reached for her, as if he wanted to hold her. "I'm just trying to understand."

"Well, there is nothing to understand." She stepped away. "Except that we're finished. I mean it this time. I don't want to see you again."

His face went blank as he stared at her. She stood for a moment, unable to move. By sheer force of will, she made her body turn, forced her feet to take a step toward the car.

"Wait a second." He caught her arm. "You can't just walk out on me like this. We're good together,

Kate. You've got to see that. All I'm asking is for you to give us a chance."

"I'm sorry, Mike, I can't." She pleaded with him to understand all the things she couldn't begin to put into words. "I just can't." After an agonizing moment, she turned and walked away, her legs shaking all the way to the car.

"Mom?" Dylan said sleepily when she closed the door. "Are we home?"

"Not yet, baby." She forced herself to smile even though her lips trembled. "Go on back to sleep. We'll be home in a minute."

She cast Mike one last apologetic look before she started the car and backed out of the driveway. Tears rose up in her throat as she drove. If she didn't cry or scream soon, she'd shatter into a million pieces; and this time she wasn't sure she'd be able to put the pieces back together.

When she reached the driveway to her cabin, blind impulse made her continue up the hill toward Linda's house. She needed a friend to tell her she'd done the right thing, even though she felt as if she'd just torn out a part of herself and thrown it away.

Gathering her sleepy son into her arms, she let herself in the house without bothering to knock.

"Linda!" she called, her heart pumping fast and hard. As she rounded the corner to the kitchen, she found her friend standing before the freezer holding a carton of rocky road ice cream.

When Linda turned and saw her, she dropped the ice cream on the counter and rushed forward. "Kate, what is it? What's happened?"

"Michael Cameron just told me"—she lowered her voice to a fierce whisper—"he's in love with me."

"That's wonderful!" Linda exclaimed, then frowned. "Isn't it?"

"No!" Kate nearly wept. "It's terrible."

"Why?" Linda shook her head as Kate carried Dylan to the couch and laid him down. "Kate, here, come sit down before you fall down." Linda guided her over to the breakfast bar. "Now, tell me everything that happened."

"I don't know what happened. Everything was going fine. Mike and I were"—she glanced at Dylan and lowered her voice—" 'no strings attached.' No talk about the future. And then out of the blue, he brings up the L-word."

"And?" Linda coaxed. "What did you say?"

"What do you think I said? I told him to go jump in the lake."

Linda held up a hand in the manner of an adult reasoning with a child. "He said he loved you and you told him to jump in the lake?"

"Basically, yeah." Kate sniffed.

"I'm not sure I'm following this," Linda said.

"Don't you understand? He said he wants to do the M-word!"

"Oh, well, it all makes perfect sense now." Shaking her head, Linda picked up the carton of rocky road and pried off the lid.

"I'm not ready to get M-ed," Kate tried to explain. "Not again."

"Why not? Because you made a bad choice the first time?" Grabbing two spoons, Linda held the ice cream out to Kate so they could eat right out of the carton. "How do you know Mike isn't the right choice?"

"Because he's *looking* for a wife."

"So?" Linda frowned.

"So how do I know he's attracted to me and not just the idea of getting M-ed?"

"From the smile you've been wearing the last couple of weeks, I'd say the attraction was pretty genuine, and very mutual." Linda wiggled her brows suggestively.

"Well, yeah, I mean, there is *that*." Kate blushed as memories swirled through her mind. "But how do I know that will continue?"

Linda nodded in thought as she savored a spoonful of rocky road. "I guess you could do what you tell everyone else to do—listen to your gut. What does it say?"

Kate frowned as she dug out a spoonful of ice cream with a shaky hand. Everything inside her told her that Mike was genuine. He was also caring and giving and wonderful with Dylan. "It's just happening too fast. How do I know he's serious? And even if he is, how do I know it will last?"

"Heck if I know." Linda smirked. "At the moment, I wish I'd told Jim to jump in the lake when he asked me to marry him."

"What?" Kate nearly dropped her spoon. "Good heavens, Linda, you can't mean that."

"Oh, yes I can. You wouldn't believe what a jerk Jim is being over this baby. He didn't object at all when I told him I wanted to start a family, but now that it's too late to go back, he spends all his time in that dang shop avoiding me. I swear, I'm going to burn the thing to the ground. If he didn't want this baby, why didn't he just tell me?"

"Linda." Kate gaped at her friend. "I told you that's nonsense—"

"No, I'm serious." Linda stabbed at the ice cream

with her spoon. "He's changed his mind about having a baby, but doesn't have the guts to tell me."

"Just because he's acting strange doesn't mean he doesn't want the baby. Men just have a different way of dealing with things—"

"They certainly do. And they have the gall to say we're the illogical ones." Linda waved her full spoon for emphasis. "Like the way Jim makes me feel as if getting pregnant was all my fault. As if I got this way by myself. Can you believe that?"

"Of some men, yes. But Jim's not like that. Surely."

"Oh, yes he is. You know, now that I think of it, maybe you have the right idea, Kate. Maybe we should avoid the cretins completely."

"I didn't say that—"

"You know what I think?" Linda took a bite of ice cream. "I think we'd all be better off if we divided the world in half and made all the men live in their camp, while we lived in ours." Linda licked her spoon with relish as she continued. "Of course, they'd all be living in caves and running around naked within a week. That is, if they didn't starve to death, since there wouldn't be anyone around to cook whatever meat they dragged home."

As if on cue, Jim came up the stairs, his heavy bootsteps waking Dylan. "Hi, baby," he said to Linda, removing his tool belt. Linda gave Kate a see-what-I-mean look as he skirted her and headed straight for the Crock-Pot. "What's for dinner?" He lifted the lid. The tangy scent of lemon and thyme rose with the steam. "Oh, man, don't tell me we're having chicken again."

"No." Linda jerked the lid out of his hand and slammed it back down on the pot. "*I'm* having chicken. *You're* having sawdust!"

"Sawdust?" He gave her a wary frown.

"And nails," Linda said, eyes blazing. "With wood-glue sauce."

"Uh, baby"—Jim backed up a step—"are you sure you're feeling all right?"

"No, I'm not feeling all right." To Kate's surprise, her friend blinked rapidly, against a sudden swell of tears. Out of the corner of her eye, she saw Dylan climb onto the stool next to her, looking sleepy and equally confused.

Jim glanced at Kate, then back at his wife. "Maybe I should leave you two women alone. Dylan, what do you say? You want to go sand some wood?"

"Don't you dare move, Dylan," Linda said, and Dylan froze. "I refuse to let you be corrupted by Neanderthal testosterone. You on the other hand"—she pointed to her husband—"can sleep out in the workshop for all I care."

"*What?*" His voice rose with alarm.

"I mean it, Jim, I want you out of my house, and I don't want you back until you're ready to act like my husband."

"I *do* act like your husband!" He flattened his hands against his chest, the picture of wounded innocence.

"No, you don't!" she railed at him, sniffing back tears. "You act like all those other husbands I hear about, not the one I married."

"Sweetie," he pleaded, awkwardly moving toward her. "What's this about?"

"Don't you touch me!" She fended him off with her spoon. "I mean it, Jim. You haven't touched me in weeks, so don't you dare touch me now. Not unless you mean it."

"What on earth are you talking about?"

"I'm talking about the way you've been hiding out

in your workshop for weeks rather than face me and the baby. Well, if you enjoy avoiding us so much, you can just move out there. Permanently!"

"Well, if this is the gratitude I get for working so hard, maybe I will!" He grabbed up his tool belt.

"Fine! Just don't try sneaking back in here tonight."

"Don't worry," he declared as he stomped toward the door. "The last thing I want is to get my head chewed off by someone who doesn't make a lick of sense."

"I do, too, make sense!" she shouted as he slammed the door behind him. Then quieter, to herself she added, "It's men who don't make sense."

"Mom?" Dylan said softly. "Since I'm a guy, do I have to leave too?"

"Oh, no, honey." She hugged him, as startled as he was by Linda's outburst. "We wouldn't think of banishing you."

"Certainly not," Linda sniffed. "It's our duty as women to save at least one young male from the evil influence of men."

"Oh," Dylan said, and Kate wasn't sure if he looked relieved or disappointed at the prospect of being saved.

# Chapter 22

WHEN Mike heard the doorbell, he let out a curse. The last thing he wanted was an interruption—not from his work, which wasn't going anywhere, but from the thoughts racing through his head. Although, maybe it was Kate coming back to apologize. He hit the save command on the computer, and took the stairs two at a time, debating whether to forgive her, or give her a good-sized chunk of his mind. How dare she doubt what he felt for her, just because he was smart enough to recognize an honest emotion when it slapped him in the face!

Instead of Kate, he found Jim standing on the doorstep, looking fit to chew nails. "What are you doing here?"

"I decided to get started prepping the living room walls for paint," Jim growled back.

"On a Sunday?"

"What does that matter? I can't go to my own house anymore, so I might as well just keep working round the clock."

"Another fight with the pregnant wife, I take it?" Mike asked, feeling slightly better now that he wasn't the only miserable sot in the world.

"Something like that," Jim mumbled at his boots.

"Well, come on in, but forget work." Mike headed

toward the kitchen. "After the day I've had, the only thing I'm in the mood to do is get drunk."

"Sounds good to me." Jim took a seat on one of the new bar stools, making it creak beneath his bulk. "So why are you getting drunk?"

"Because women are the most exasperating, stubborn, illogical creatures on the planet."

"I'll drink to that."

Mike perused the cabinets to see what he had left over from the last time he'd thrown a party. "You want vodka, bourbon, or gin?"

"Bourbon."

"Good. That leaves more gin for me." He managed to find two highball glasses that didn't have chips and went to the freezer for ice. As he poured the drinks, he noticed the glasses didn't match, since Kate hadn't picked up the set she'd selected yet. He guessed he could kiss that purchase good-bye. Not that he minded drinking out of glasses that didn't match, but he would have enjoyed owning a set that did.

He handed Jim a drink and clicked the rims together in a toast. "To women. May they all fall off the edge of the earth."

Jim grunted and tossed back a healthy swallow. Lowering the glass, he studied the amber liquid that remained. "So, how long you figure it takes a woman to cool off once she's good and riled?"

"Depends on the woman." Mike savored the sharp taste of gin and tonic on his tongue. "Is she as stubborn as Kate?"

Jim laughed. "No woman is as stubborn as Kate, but purt near."

"Then I'd say you may be here a while."

"No." Jim heaved a sigh. "I can't crash in on your evening. If I'm not going to do any work, I'll just finish this, then head over to my sister's. With any luck, she'll put me up for the night."

"Forget that. You think I want to sit here and drink alone?" Mike glanced around in search of a way to spend the evening. His eye landed on the big-screen TV and the cabinet of movies beside it. He had everything from old black-and-whites to the latest blockbusters. "How about we order a pizza and have a *Star Trek* marathon?"

Jim narrowed his eyes. "The old *Star Trek,* or the new one?"

"The old one, of course. I have the entire series on tape."

"Really?" Jim brightened. "I'd have pegged you as a guy who went in for all those fancy new special effects."

"Hey, I can enjoy the classics as much as the next guy." He picked up the phone and dialed the number for the nearest pizza delivery from memory. "Extra large meat-lovers okay with you?"

"With jalapeños," Jim added. "And one of those Dutch apple dessert things."

"You got it."

Hours later, they'd made their way through the pizza, a considerable amount of liquor, and several *Star Trek* episodes.

"You know," Jim said from his end of the sofa, where he'd slouched down deep into the cushions. "I sure as hell don't get it. A man busts his butt all day to give his wife a good home, and what does he get for his efforts? Nothing but grief."

"Exactly." Mike propped his feet on the coffee table and let his head rest against the back cushion. He hadn't bothered to turn on any lights as night descended, so the only light in the room came from the

TV and the blue glow from the swimming pool beyond the balcony. Only half listening to the sound of Mr. Spock's Vulcan fiancée explaining why she didn't want to marry Spock, Mike watched the squiggly blue lines play across the ceiling.

"Too bad we weren't born on Vulcan," Jim said.

"Hmm?" Mike turned his head and forced his eyes to focus on Jim.

The burly contractor gestured toward the screen with his highball glass. "At least there the women are logical."

"Yeah," Mike snorted, "and a man only gets laid what, every seven years? At least here a guy gets some compensation for his grief."

"Speak for yourself," Jim mumbled.

"What was that?"

"I said, speak for yourself." Jim glared at him, as if daring him to laugh.

Mike frowned. "Wait a second. Are you telling me your wife's already holding out on you?"

"I'm not saying anything."

"But—" Mike shook his head in an effort to clear away the alcohol haze. "I thought Kate said Linda was only in her sixth month."

Jim shrugged one shoulder, not meeting his eye.

"She is holding out, isn't she?"

"It's not that." Jim started to take a drink and found his glass empty. "It's just that . . ." He raised his gaze to meet Mike's. "You've seen my wife. She's so . . . tiny."

Mike laughed. "Last time I saw her, she was huge!" Leaning forward, he grabbed the bottle of bourbon and refilled Jim's glass.

"Now maybe. Since I got her pregnant." Jim wagged his head slowly. "Before that, though, she was skinny as a toothpick." He held up one of his thick, callused hands. "Do you know how easily I could snap a toothpick?"

Mike hesitated before setting the bottle back on the coffee table. Maybe he should change the subject to something safe, like sports. Looking at Jim, though, he saw a man who had problems weighing heavily on his mind. With a sigh, he pushed his discomfort aside. "You want to talk about it?"

"Hell, no." Jim took another drink and settled his shoulders deeper into the cushions. Several minutes passed in which neither of them spoke. "It's just . . . weird, that's all," Jim said at last. "I mean, I had a hard enough time getting over the size thing when we first met. But I got over it, and everything was fine. Then, all of a sudden, she's pregnant, and she starts blowing up like a balloon. And I look at her and think, holy shit, I did that to her. And what if something happens? What if the baby's too big, or she's too small? What if it tears her up inside? Or . . ." He looked away, his voice dropping. "What if it kills her?"

"Hey, man." Mike shifted. "She'll be all right. I mean, that's what doctors are for, right?"

Jim snorted, and took another drink. "Things still happen. I should know. My sister's a labor and delivery nurse. The stories she tells would make Stephen King read like Mother Goose."

"Yeah, but that's not with every delivery," Mike said.

"It's enough, believe me—enough to keep me up at night."

Mike tried to think of something reassuring to say, but what did he know about having babies other than sitting in a room down the hall, waiting to celebrate the arrival of his newest niece or nephew? "Have you tried talking to Linda about this?"

"Are you crazy?" Jim glared at him. "You think I want to fill her head with all this? I figure I'm losing enough sleep for the both of us."

"I take it she's not scared about it, then?"

"Who, Linda?" Jim snorted. "The pint-sized Wonder Woman? Not hardly. Besides, she's too busy being pissed off at me for not touching her for us to have a civil conversation about why."

"Then maybe you should, you know, touch her."

"Yeah." Jim scrubbed a hand over his face. "But that's the problem. I can't. It's not that I don't want to. Trust me, I want to so bad, I can't even look at her without wanting to. And God help me whenever she touches me, which she seems to do all the time now. I mean, where the hell were all these offers to give me back rubs before she got pregnant?"

Mike gave his head another shake. "I'm not sure I get the problem here."

"I'm telling you, I can't. No matter how badly I want her, the minute we start to do anything . . . well, never mind."

Mike considered the problem as objectively as possible. Since there didn't seem to be anything wrong with Jim physically, the problem had to be mental. "You know," he said, "not touching her isn't going to make her *not* pregnant. Whatever's going to happen is going to happen. The question is, are you going to waste the next few months worrying about something you can't change, or enjoying what should be one of the best times in your life? I mean, shit, a baby! That's got to be cool."

Jim frowned as he mulled that over. After a moment, the crease between his brows cleared, and his eyes widened. "You know, you're right." Laughter rumbled from his chest. "I mean, it's not like I can make her any more pregnant than she already is, right?"

"There, see, problem solved." Mike toasted him. "Now you can go home and make love to your wife."

The smile dropped from Jim's face. "Not hardly."

"What do you mean?"

"She didn't just kick me out because I wouldn't make love to her. She kicked me out because of all the time I spend out in the workshop. She's convinced I'm avoiding her—which I guess I was some—but she thinks it's because I don't want the baby."

"Which is another thing I don't understand." Mike refilled his own drink. "If you're spending all that time making a crib for the kid, why does she think you don't want it?"

Jim gave a shrug, his voice barely above a grumble. "Maybe because she doesn't know about the crib . . . yet."

"Excuse me?" Mike leaned forward. "Come again with that."

Jim flashed him a defiant look. "I said, she doesn't know about the crib."

"Why the hell not?"

"Because . . ." Jim exhaled in a rush. "It's a surprise, all right? I can't show it to her till it's finished."

Mike sat back to gape at him. "Are you nuts?"

Jim didn't answer.

"Here you could solve half your problems just by showing her the crib, and you won't do it?" Mike asked.

"I told you, it's not finished yet."

"So?"

Jim hesitated. "You really think I should?"

"I think you better, unless you want to be sleeping in the thing instead of your own bed for the rest of your life."

A thoughtful expression creased Jim's face. "You're right." He set his glass down with a thud. "I will. I'll go home and do it right now." He hefted himself up, and teetered sideways.

"Wait." Mike climbed to his own unsteady feet. "I'll go with you."

"What for?"

"To be sure you do it right. If there's one thing I've learned from the movies, it's that women like the make-up scene to be a big production."

"Yeah." Jim nodded. "Kate's always saying stuff like that in her columns. She says women are suckers for romantic gestures, so even when it makes a guy feel stupid, that's what you got to give 'em. Especially when they're mad at you." Jim scratched his head, causing his hair to stand up at an odd angle. "So, what sort of stupid gesture do you think would work?"

Mike forced his brain to work, then snapped his fingers—or tried to. "I've got just the thing."

"You don't think he took me seriously, do you?" Linda asked.

"About what?" Kate squinted in concentration as she applied a layer of Primrose Pink nail polish to Linda's toes. Only another woman who'd had a baby could fully understand the frustration of not being able to paint one's own toenails.

"About not coming home."

Kate blinked at her. "Well, you certainly sounded serious. Which is why I agreed to stay the night, in spite of the fact that it's a school night, and Dylan should be curled up in his own bed, not sacked out in your guest room."

"I know. And I'm glad you stayed." Linda reached toward her, but couldn't make contact, since she sat sideways on the sofa with her feet resting in Kate's lap. "I'd be going crazy here by myself."

Kate refrained from pointing out that Linda wouldn't be faced with this problem if she hadn't succumbed to a fit of hormone-driven emotions earlier. And surely that was all the attack had been, Kate assured herself. Although a guilty voice in the back of her mind wondered if she was partially responsible. Too many times in the last two years she'd done just what Linda had done: lumped all men into one group and blasted away at the whole lot of them. Well, if this was the sort of damage her male-bashing wreaked, she vowed never again to blame the entire sex for the sins of a few.

*But isn't that exactly what you did to Mike?* that same little voice asked. *Didn't you condemn him for Edward's sins?*

Pushing aside the uncomfortable thought, she wiped off her hand and reached for a strawberry to dip into the chocolate fondue.

"Here." She held the strawberry out to Linda. "Have some more chocolate. And remember that the whole point of this particular girls' night is to *not* talk about men."

"You're right." Linda nodded, than sank her teeth into the chocolate-covered fruit. "Mmm. God, that's good. Do you think a person can actually die from chocolate overdose?"

"Probably," Kate said as she dredged another strawberry though the warm mixture, then savored the taste as it melted in her mouth. "But what a way to go."

Linda sighed as she dropped the leafy green stem on a plate where it joined at least a dozen more. "You know, Jim really is sweet most of the time."

"I know." Kate smiled at her friend's wistful expression.

"It's just that, other times, he makes me so mad."

"I know that too." Kate remembered similar situations in her own marriage, where anger overrode reason and the two people caught up in it hurled all manner of hurt at each other. She wished she could say all the fault lay on Edward's shoulders, that she had never lashed out with the first words that sprang to her tongue, but she was equally guilty.

Was that what worried her, then? Not that Mike would become disinterested in her and Dylan as Edward had, but that getting remarried would somehow transform her back into the bitter, demanding, dissatisfied woman she'd become toward the end of her first marriage?

"I wonder where he is." Linda's gaze drifted toward the window.

"Linda," Kate said patiently. "He's a big boy, he can take care of himself."

"Maybe I should call his sister again. He could have shown up there."

"In the last five minutes?" Kate studied her friend, debating the wisdom of interfering. In the end, though, she never could keep an opinion to herself. "All right, you want my advice?"

"Of course I want your advice." Linda reached for her again, and this time managed to snag her hand.

"If you're sure." Kate hesitated. "Because I know you probably get tired of me playing Dear Cupid."

"Ka-ate!" Linda gave her an exasperated look. "Don't be ridiculous, I need your help. This isn't like Jim and me. You know we never fight. Well, not much since he got over that nonsense while we were dating."

"Okay." Kate squeezed her friend's hand, then let it go. "Dear Cupid's tip of the day is this: Never let the little cracks grow into big ones, or pretty soon your whole house will fall down around you."

"A house analogy?" Linda rolled her eyes. "I ask you for advice about my marriage, and you give me a house analogy?"

"It seemed appropriate."

"For Jim, maybe."

"For anyone," Kate insisted. "Fortunately, you and Jim have a pretty strong foundation. Even so, you have to patch the little cracks while they're still little."

"But that's the problem. I've been trying to patch this problem for weeks, as well you know."

"Are you telling me Jim still refuses to make love?"

"Something like that." Linda's mouth pursed into a pout. "And before you say one word, be forewarned that your advice about seducing him isn't working this time. In fact, I think it's making things worse."

"You're kidding." Kate frowned. "What does he say when you talk about it?"

"Talk about it?" Linda laughed. "You mean, as in get him to open up and be honest about his feelings? Yeah, right."

"Linda!" Kate scolded. "I'm serious. You know that talking things over should always be the first course of action."

"Trust me, Kate. Jim doesn't talk about his emotions, not even to me."

"Well, he's got to talk to someone," Kate insisted.

"Sometimes, merely voicing our fears out loud makes them less frightening. For example, you've read Dylan's book *A Fly Went By*, right?"

"About a thousand times," Linda acknowledged.

"Remember how all those animals are running in terror, the fly from the frog, the frog from the cat, the cat from the dog, and on and on. Only none of them are actually chasing the other, because they're all too busy trying to escape their own fear. And in the end, they all realize they're running from nothing more than a poor frightened calf who's gotten a hoof stuck in a bucket. The only reason she's chasing the others is to search for help."

"And your moral of the story would be what?" Linda asked.

"That real-life fears are no different. Sometimes all we have to do is stop running scared, turn around, and take a good hard look at what it is that has us so terrified. And when we do, suddenly those fears don't seem so bad after all. In fact, sometimes they seem downright silly."

The minute the words left Kate's mouth, she froze in amazement. Was that what she'd been doing with Mike, running scared from some imagined terror? No, the things she feared were all too real, and if she didn't watch her step, she'd make the same mistake she'd made with Edward, and wind up living through the same gut-wrenching heartache.

Or would she?

If only she could pinpoint exactly what frightened her.

"You make it sound so easy," Linda sighed.

"In theory, it is easy." Kate offered her a weak smile. "Unfortunately, reality is a great deal more convoluted."

"Which is why I don't want to push Jim to have this talk. I'm not entirely sure I want to hear what he has to say."

That startled Kate. "What could he possibly say? That he doesn't love you and he doesn't want this baby?"

Linda nodded as moisture pooled along her lashes, making her eyes look very blue and fragile.

"Linda." Kate sighed. "The man adores you, and I *know* he wants this baby."

"If only I could be as sure." Linda started to say more, but went suddenly still, listening. "What was that noise?"

Kate listened as well. "I don't hear anything." Her heart picked up speed as Linda padded over to the window, with her toes curled upward to protect her wet polish. "Is something out there?"

"I don't know . . ." Linda peered more intently into the darkness. "For a moment, I thought I heard something." She shook her head. "Probably just some deer."

Kate relaxed. "Yeah, heading down to eat my flowers again, no doubt."

Linda laughed as she hobbled back to the couch. "Honestly, I don't know why you keep planting the things."

"Because I'm a hopeless optimist?" Kate grabbed another strawberry and dipped it into the chocolate.

"True," Linda agreed as she followed suit. "Which just proves Gwen wrong. You are not the cynic she thinks you are."

"Well, you know what they say." Kate bit into the fruit, and cupped her hand beneath her chin to catch the juice. "Behind every cynic is a disillusioned optimist."

Linda held her chocolate-covered berry up in a

toast. "Well, here's to all the cynical optimists."

"May we all die of chocolate overdose, and enjoy every bite," Kate added.

"Hear, hear!"

"Shit, that was close," Jim whispered. "I swear, for a second I thought she'd spotted us."

"Is she gone?" Mike asked, trying to peer through the tangle of wild yaupon bushes they'd ducked behind when Linda had appeared in the window a mere ten feet away.

Jim rose up enough to see inside the house. "Yeah. It's all clear."

Mike reached out and grabbed Jim's arm before the man could blunder forward and spoil their surprise. "Quietly, this time, okay?"

"Hey, I'm being quiet," Jim insisted, even though he'd been the one to stumble and crash through the shrubbery with all the subtlety of an ox.

Rather than argue, Mike hefted one of the two projection units they'd brought back onto his hip, then waited a second for the ground to quit shifting beneath his feet. Even though they'd abandoned their drinking spree in favor of this new plan, he had yet to sober up completely. Although the alcohol had worn off enough for him to realize that getting in a pickup with an equally intoxicated Jim behind the wheel probably wasn't the smartest thing he'd ever done in his life.

"This way," Jim called in a loud stage whisper, then hunched forward and dashed across the clearing toward the workshop. Mike followed, cursing the nearly full moon that washed the area in pale blue light. "Watch out for the workbench," Jim cautioned once they ducked inside.

"Shit," Mike swore as his shin banged a hard edge.

"I think I just found it." With his free hand, he felt the bench and considered it as a possible surface for the projector. "Is there an outlet near here?"

"Yeah. Under the window." Jim's dark silhouette moved by a square of light. "Want me to plug it in?"

"Depends. Where's this crib of yours?"

"Over there."

"Where?" Mike peered into the darkness, barely making out the shape of a table saw and various other woodworking equipment. The place looked like the set for "Tool Time" on *Home Improvement.*

"Against that far wall," Jim finally said, apparently realizing that hand gestures didn't mean spit in the dark.

"What's on the wall behind it?"

"Nothing."

"Perfect." Mike smiled. "A nice flat surface is just what we need. Only, let's clear some of this stuff out of the way and put the crib in the middle of the room."

"What for?" Jim asked.

"Staging, man. You got to have staging."

"Oh, right."

They set to work, moving equipment out of the way as quickly and quietly as possible. When Mike was satisfied, he led Jim back over to the projector. "I've got the film already cued, so when I give the signal, all you have to do is punch this button."

"Got it."

"Good." Mike grabbed the end of the extension cord Jim had already plugged in. "Now I'll go outside and man the other projector."

"Wait. What's your signal?"

"Oh, yeah." He thought for a moment. "When Linda comes out to see what all the ruckus is about, hopefully she'll come in this direction, rather than toward me. When she gets close enough to hear you in here, I'll cut off my projector, you'll hit yours, and she'll come the rest of the way inside. From there, you're on your own."

"Right. On my own." Jim blew out a nervous breath. "Only, what happens if she doesn't come this way?"

"Don't worry," Mike insisted. "It'll work."

"God, I hope so," Jim muttered as Mike headed toward the door. "Hey, Mike," he called, then hesitated when Mike turned back. "Thanks, man."

"Don't mention it." Mike nodded, then dashed back across the moonlit clearing to where he'd left the other projector under the yaupon bushes. After plugging it in, he said a little prayer on Jim's behalf, and punched it on.

# Chapter 23

A blast of music and colored light filled the living room window.

"What in the world?" Kate said as she and Linda exchanged startled looks. Together they raced to the window and stared out in disbelief. A cartoon lit the side of the workshop, like an old-fashioned drive-in movie. Forest creatures danced about, singing cheerfully about springtime. Birds swirled and bees buzzed as apple blossoms floated through animated trees like snowflakes.

Dylan ran out of the spare bedroom wearing the pajamas he kept at Linda's. "Mom, do you see it? Do you see it?"

"I'm looking at it now," Kate answered. "I just don't know what 'it' is."

"It's a cartoon!" His eyes went wide as he joined them at the window. "Can we go outside and watch?"

Kate glanced at Linda and found her friend holding both hands over her mouth. Blinking madly, Linda turned to her and lowered her hands to reveal a big smile. "Jim."

"Jim?" Kate repeated skeptically. "Are you sure?"

"No. But I plan to find out." Linda headed for the door.

"Wait a second," Kate called. "Don't you think we

should make sure, before we go charging out there?"

Ignoring her, Linda bolted out the door with Dylan right behind her. Kate quickly followed them into the cool night air. The happy sound of animated creatures celebrating spring assaulted her ears. Dylan moved toward it, mesmerized by the colorful display while Linda looked about, searching for the source, which seemed to be the stand of trees that shielded the cabin from the main house.

"Jim?" Linda called, moving in that direction.

The screen went blank, throwing the area into darkness.

"Linda," Kate said as she grabbed Dylan's hand. "I'm not sure we should be out here."

The sound and lights resumed, this time from inside the workshop. Linda moved toward it, through the door, leaving Kate the option of following or retreating to the safety of the house.

"Come on, Mom." Dylan tugged at her hand, dragging her forward.

With a sigh, she gave in. The moment she stepped over the threshold, her heart melted. There stood Jim covered in the colored light of another cartoon. Haloing his silhouette on the wall behind him, animated birds sang a sweet lullaby to a baby nestled in the bough of a tree. Jim's face looked haggard as his eyes pleaded with Linda.

"I know you think I don't want this baby," he said just over the sound of the soft music. "But nothing could be further from the truth. I want that little fella you're carrying more than anything. Except for you. I can't stand the thought of anything happening to you, Linda. So, you have to promise me here and now that you'll stick around long enough for both of us to get plenty of use out of this." He nodded toward a crib with an intricately carved headboard and hand-turned rails.

Linda moved toward it as if in a daze. "*This* is what you've been working on all this time? A baby crib? But . . . why didn't you tell me?"

"It's not finished yet."

"I don't care. Oh, honey, it's wonderful." She ran a finger over the delicate carvings. "I love it." She lifted smiling eyes toward her husband. "Nearly as much as I love you."

Kate's eyes misted as Linda threw her arms around her husband and kissed his cheek. Jim, to her surprise, turned his head enough to bring them lip to lip, something she hadn't seen him do in weeks. As the kiss deepened, she took her son firmly by the hand. "Come on, Dylan. Show's over."

"No it isn't." Dylan strained to see the cartoon on the back wall. "It's still going. See?"

"I'm afraid we'll have to finish watching that show another time."

"Ah, Mom!" His feet dragged as he followed her outside, where they nearly ran right into Mike.

"Oh!" Kate's heart jumped into her throat. "Mike! What are you doing here?"

"Directing," he said as he glanced toward the open door of the workshop. "Did it work?"

Kate looked from him to the workshop and back again. "You? You're behind this?"

"That depends." He grinned broadly. "If it worked, it was all my idea. If it didn't, I'm blaming Jim."

"Oh, Mike . . ." Kate felt something inside her turn soft as she studied him in the faint light from the moon. "I don't know what to say, other than thank you for helping Jim and Linda. That was really sweet, and very needed."

"So, it worked?" he asked.

"Beautifully." She smiled at him. "Although I guess I should have known you were in on it. Who else would have the equipment to pull something like this off?"

"Not to mention a whole cabinet of cartoon reels to pick from," Mike added.

"True."

"You have cartoons?" Dylan asked.

"About a gazillion," Mike confirmed. "The two I brought tonight are ones I actually worked on."

"You drew those?" Dylan eyed him with awe.

"Nah," Mike said. "I just did some cell painting back when I was young enough and foolish enough to work for slave wages."

"What's cell painting?" Dylan made a face at the unfamiliar term.

"Well, I tell you what." Mike squatted down to get eye level with Dylan. "I'll explain all about how cartoons are made on one condition."

"What?" Dylan asked eagerly.

"That your mother get me a couple aspirin and a glass of water." He looked up at Kate with a sheepish smile. "My head is killing me."

She smiled, wondering how he always slipped past her defenses so easily. "Come on, you two." She swung her barefooted son up to ride her hip. "We might as well go down to the cabin, since I don't think Linda and Jim are interested in company right now."

"Let me get my projector." Mike disappeared into the trees, and emerged with a heavy-looking piece of equipment.

As they made their way down the hill, she looked back in time to see Jim and Linda walking arm in arm toward the house. An odd blend of happiness and envy settled over her. In spite of their recent turmoil, Jim and Linda had the kind of loving relationship that would endure for a lifetime. How was it that she, who helped so many other people find that kind of love, had never achieved it for herself?

She had Dylan, though, she reminded herself, as her son nestled against her. That was all she needed.

By the time they reached the cabin, Dylan was nearly asleep. She moved carefully to turn a lamp on in the living area, filling the small space with warm light. "Just give me a minute to put Dylan to bed," she whispered to Mike. "Then I'll hunt down some aspirin."

"Wait." Her son lifted his head and scrubbed his eyes. "Mike was gonna tell me how cartoons are made."

"Perhaps some other time," she suggested. "Right now, it's the middle of the night, and little boys should be in bed."

"Ah, Mom."

Mike came forward. "Why don't you let me put him to bed? I'll tell him all about my wild-and-woolly days as cell painter in lieu of a bedtime story."

She started to say no.

"Please, Mom?" Dylan begged.

She looked to an equally eager Mike. "If you're sure you don't mind."

"Of course I don't mind." Mike set his projector down, and presented his back. "Come on, buddy, climb on board."

With a squeal, Dylan leapt from her arms onto Mike's back, clinging like a little monkey. The sight brought a pang to her heart. This was how things should be, this easy intimacy at the end of the day.

Struggling against a sense of failure she feared

would never fully die, she headed for the kitchen to find the aspirin.

After the mistakes she'd made, how could she risk trying again? All the things she felt for Mike, the physical attraction, the excitement of finding someone whose company she enjoyed, the pleasure that lit within her whenever he was near, they were all things she'd felt before.

It was almost like a tangible object, like a bright shining bubble, filled with the promise of happiness and love eternal. She ached with the temptation to reach out and embrace it as eagerly as Dylan had leapt from her arms onto Mike's back. But experience had taught her that, for some, the bubble could burst the moment it was touched.

Which was so unfair! Why did other people find the one thing that eluded her? Was there something wrong with her? Was she too selfish, too demanding, too idealistic to ever make a marriage work? She didn't think so. At least she prayed that wasn't true. For, somewhere deep inside, she realized she still wanted desperately to love and be loved.

Something tickled her cheek and she raised a hand to discover a tear quivering at the edge of her jaw. Great, she thought, this was all she needed, for Mike to catch her crying. He'd no doubt think the tears were for him. But they weren't. They were for . . . well, for *everything*. The safe, solitary life she'd built so carefully for her and Dylan was crumbling around her, and she felt as if a part of her were crumbling right along with it. Swiping at a second tear, she reached for a glass, and carried it to the sink just as footsteps sounded on the ladder.

"Well, he fought hard," Mike said in a hushed tone, "but I think the champ is down for the count."

Kate closed her eyes as the mere sound of Mike's voice made the knot in her throat tighten. Wiping her cheeks one last time, she pasted on a wobbly smile and turned. "I take that to mean Dylan's asleep?"

"Dead to the world."

"Here's your aspirin." She handed them to him without meeting his gaze. If she looked at him, she really would cry.

"Thanks." After he'd swallowed the aspirin, she felt him study her face, the way she always felt his gaze. "Look, Kate, about today—"

"No, please." She turned away as her control slipped a bit more. "It's late. We're both tired. I think we should just let it lie for tonight."

He remained quiet for a long time before setting the glass aside. "You're right," he said at last, moving closer. "In fact, for tonight, I think we should forget the whole thing happened."

"Yes." She bit her lip as his hands settled on her shoulders and every muscle down her back melted. Why did his slightest touch affect her so profoundly? She fought the temptation to lean against him, to absorb his strength.

"Let's forget everything," he whispered as he bent his head to brush his lips up the side of her neck. A shiver followed the caress, and she closed her eyes. "Forget everything but this." His arms slipped around her middle as he nuzzled her ear.

How tempting that sounded, to forget everything but the feel of his arms about her, the touch of his lips on her flushed skin. To simply feel, and enjoy, and believe for one brief moment that what Mike felt for her was love. That she would find the courage to return it. And that it would last forever.

"Yes," she breathed, and turned in his arms to face

him. Trembling inside, she opened her eyes and caressed his cheek. "Yes."

He studied her face, probing for answers she wasn't ready to give. Raising up, she offered him the only thing she could give, the brush of her lips, the press of her body.

With a groan, he accepted the offering as he pulled her against him and deepened the kiss. Her heart soared as he pressed her back against the counter, fitting his hips to hers. Heat blossomed within her at the feel of his hardness nestled against her soft belly. She stroked his back, his arms, until the kiss turned greedy. His hands moved possessively over her. When he cupped her breasts at last, she broke the kiss to gasp for air.

"I want you, Kate," he growled against her neck. "God, I need you."

"Yes," she managed to rasp past her own need. She started to reach for him again, but some small part of her brain reminded her where she was: standing beneath an open loft with her son sleeping directly above her. "Not here, though," she said, nudging his chest.

He frowned in confusion as she wiggled out of his arms. Then the lines in his face melted into a smile as she took his hand and started walking backward. They moved quietly past the ladder, stopping once to embrace and kiss. Touching and turning, like dancers, they continued toward the bedroom door. The row of buttons down the front of her dress came undone, as did the ones on his shirt, giving them each access to bare skin.

The moment they entered the bedroom, darkness enveloped them. Her heart soared as his tongue swept inside her mouth, caressing and possessing by turns. Everything about him excited her, his tenderness, his strength, his control, and his hunger. She wanted and needed all of that tonight.

Pulling out of his arms, she crossed to the bed to turn on a lamp. Soft light dispelled the darkness. When she turned to face him, she found him looking at her as if she were a miracle. Slowly a smile curled his lips.

The fist that had formed in her stomach relaxed. Returning his smile, she shrugged out of her dress. His gaze followed its descent as it dropped to the floor. She reached behind her and released her bra. His eyes darkened as it, too, fell. With shaking hands, she stripped off her panties so she stood before him completely exposed.

With one hand, he reached back and closed the door before moving toward her. His expression made her feel cherished, beautiful, alluring: things she hadn't felt in a long time. Things she wanted to go on feeling forever.

She closed her eyes to savor the moment as he cupped her face and gently touched his lips to hers. *Yes,* her heart sang as he ran his hands downward, over her body, then back up to cup her breasts. They filled his palms as he circled her nipples with his thumbs. A whimper escaped her as he bent his head to suckle her, gently at first, then with growing hunger. Her head fell back as she gloried in the sharp pleasure that knifed through her, cutting clean to her soul.

Even though they'd touched before, enjoyed each other's bodies, this was the first time she'd given so deeply from herself. She captured his head in her trembling hands, brought his face back up to hers. "Love me," she whispered, thinking how he made everything seem new. "As if it were the first time."

Mike frowned at the uncertainty shimmering in her

eyes. Didn't she know how completely he did love
her? How she held his very heart in her hands? She
was the one with the power to accept or reject, yet he
saw his own vulnerability in the fathomless green eyes
that stared back at him. At a loss for words to express
what he felt, he simply cupped her face and met her
gaze steadily. "With you, it's always like the first time.
Always."

He captured her mouth and poured himself into a
kiss, into her. She responded with the honest inhibition
that enthralled him and left him shaking. The mere
feel of her in his arms, moving against him, drove him
to near madness. His heart and mind wanted to be
gentle, to show her everything he felt, but his body
overrode his better intentions.

Sweeping her into his arms, he laid her on the bed
amid the silk pillows. She looked like an erotic dream,
the bewitching kind of woman who lounged fully nude
on a Victorian couch.

"God, you drive me crazy," he said as he shed his
own clothes and joined her. Her arms wrapped eagerly
around him. He drank his fill of her perfumed neck,
her soft breasts, her quivering stomach. Every taste,
every sip left him more intoxicated than any liquor.

She touched him with equal abandon, trading gasp
for gasp, sigh for sigh. He'd always felt connected to
her in some strange way, but never so much as now.
Each time he suckled her breasts, he felt an answering
tightness in his own chest. Each time he dipped his
hand to the hot nest between her thighs, his own groin
jumped in response. And each time she ran her hands
over his taut skin, he saw her eyes go heavy and wild
with desire.

The fever swirled around them, through them, bind-ing them in a hot web of pure need. Panting for each breath, he stretched on top of her, thrilling to every soft curve that yielded beneath him. He buried his hand in her hair as their mouths joined in a frenzy and their bodies moved as if straining to get inside each other's skin.

With a curse, he broke the kiss, stared into her eyes. "I love you," he said fiercely as he settled between her legs. "And you love me," he said as he pressed at the threshold of her body.

For a second, her dazed eyes focused, and she shook her head in denial.

"You do," he said again, and nuzzled her neck. "Say it, Kate. Say it." He moved against her, teasing and enticing—and all the while hoping.

"Yes," she said at last, then gasped and arched beneath him as he drove inside her.

"Again," he whispered against her ear as he moved inside her, hard and steady. "Tell me you love me."

"I do," she wept in a choked voice. As if a dam had broken, she repeated the words as she kissed his shoulders and face. "I love you. I love you."

He wanted to shout with joy as each stroke drove them higher. The sheer, piercing pleasure mounted until the tide ripped through them both, sweeping them away. He tightened his arms about her, felt her cling to him with equal strength as they rode the crest and crashed over the other side.

The moment receded slowly, leaving behind a warm sense of contentment. A laugh rumbled in his chest. Raising his head, he gazed down at her in wonder. She smiled back, looking equally awed. *I love you,* he told her again in silence as he captured her lips in a tender kiss. She kissed him back, with the same gentle abandon, as if equally overwhelmed by what had just passed between them.

With a sigh, he settled down beside her, smiling as she snuggled in his arms. Never in his life had he felt so physically drained, yet so emotionally filled.

# Chapter 24

MIKE woke to the pleasant sensation of having Kate's body nestled in the rumpled bed beside him, her head on the opposite pillow facing him. He indulged himself a moment, watching her. Relaxed in sleep, her face wore an expression of childish innocence, which made him smile since it was framed in the orange blaze of her siren's hair. *Kate,* he thought, letting the name sink deep into his bones. *My Kate.* He could have lain like that for hours, simply watching her.

Eventually, though, the call of nature could not be put off. He eased from the bed, slipped on his pants, and went in search of a bathroom. He found it tucked between the bedroom and living area, a room no bigger than a walk-in closet and filled with fascinating feminine clutter. A floral-patterned silk robe hung on the back of the door, while talcum powder and scented deodorant crowded together with hairspray and body lotion on a shelf over the tiny sink.

After finishing in the bathroom, he couldn't resist exploring the place a bit more, as if it held secrets to the woman who lived there. He slipped silently into the living area and heard Dylan's soft snores drifting down from the loft. A few toys littered the floor, with even more stuffed into a large grapevine basket in the corner. The faint tinge of red light creeping over the horizon drew him to the windows. He looked outside, marveling at the sheer beauty of the mist-shrouded lake at sunrise. Then, he turned back and let the feel of the room settle around him. Peaceful, he decided. And welcoming.

This place had the one thing his house on Challenger didn't have. It felt like a home. The feeling had nothing to do with the structure or the décor, and everything to do with the people who lived within these walls—and how they felt about each other.

Now that Kate had admitted she loved him, she and Dylan would move into his house and help him capture this same feeling—just as soon as they married.

A smile tugged at his lips as he made his way back to the bedroom. He closed the door quietly, and tiptoed over to the bed. He found her still asleep. The morning light pressed through the sheer curtains, dusting her hair and cheeks with gold.

He crawled back beneath the covers and eased his body along hers. Rather than snuggle up to him, though, as he had hoped, she turned away.

"Kate," he whispered with a hand to her shoulder, gently trying to turn her toward him. He managed to get her onto her back, where he draped an arm about her waist. She made a sleepy sound of protest when he kissed her forehead. "Wake up, sweetheart, it's morning." With any luck, they'd have a few minutes alone before Dylan woke.

"Wha—?" she muttered and raised a hand to rub her eyes. He watched in amusement as she blinked away a few layers of sleep and half focused on his face. A smile softened her lips and turned up the corners of her eyes.

He smiled back. "Good morning, sleepyhead."

"Morning," she repeated in a contented purr. Then,

her smile faded, replaced by a look of confusion. "Morning?" Her eyes widened. "Oh, my God." She glanced about as if she were the one who had awoken in a strange room. Her gaze zipped back to him. "Mike! What are you doing here?"

He cocked a brow and waited for her to remember last night. He knew the instant memory returned.

She sat bolt upright, knocking him backward as she clutched the covers to her naked breasts. "You've got to get out of here before Dylan wakes up."

"Can't," he told her. "I don't have a car."

"What?"

"I rode over here with Jim. We sort of forgot to plan on a way for me to get home."

"What! Why didn't you tell me this last night?"

"Perhaps because the subject didn't come up?" he offered helpfully.

"Oh, never mind." She turned to the clock on her nightstand. "Look what time it is! I can't believe I didn't set the alarm last night. I've got to get you out of here. No, wait, I've got to get Dylan ready for school first."

"Kate, hey, it's all right." He rubbed her arm. "In fact, I kind of hoped we could tell him this morning."

"Tell him?" She blinked.

"You know, about us." He smiled sheepishly.

"Us?" She drew back. "I told you, Mike, there is no us."

The words were so unexpected, they took a second to sink in. He sat up, slowly. "What do you mean, there is no us? What about last night?"

"Oh, God." She hid her face in her hands. "I am not going to discuss last night, at least not now."

"Kate?" He caressed her shoulder as foreboding tightened his chest.

"No." She scrambled from the bed and ducked into the closet. "I've got to get Dylan ready for school." She reappeared an instant later, wearing shorts and a crop top and running her fingers through her tangled hair.

"Wait a second." He leapt up, still wearing his trousers, to block her way to the door. He waited until she lifted her eyes, and her frightened expression twisted his gut. "Look, Kate . . ." He rubbed her bare arms. "I know you're a little freaked out about how fast things are going between us, but—"

"No, please!" She stepped back and wrapped her arms about her middle. That simple act frustrated him to the point of anger even as her eyes pleaded with him to understand. "Promise me you'll stay in here and be quiet until I have Dylan out of the house."

She was right, of course. Dylan shouldn't know he'd stayed the night. That, however, didn't make him any less angry at the moment. Had last night meant nothing to her? Did *he* mean nothing to her? "We need to talk about this."

"Yes, we do. But not now. We'll talk as soon as I get back from taking him to school, all right?"

"Sure," he said in an even voice. "Fine."

He watched her go, grinding his teeth. How could she insist nothing existed between them after last night? She'd admitted she loved him, dammit! Did that mean nothing to her?

Kate still had no idea what she wanted to say to Mike when she returned home. Her tight stomach and shaky hands made thinking straight impossible.

She found him sitting on the far end of the sofa, his arms crossed over his chest, his feet propped on the coffee table. Even with the sullen expression on his face, he looked far too at home, and far too firmly implanted into her world for her peace of mind.

For a moment, they simply stared at each other.

"So, you're back," he said.

"And you're angry."

"I'm not sure if 'angry' is the right word."

"What do you mean?"

"Think about it, Kate. How would you feel if you told someone you loved them, if they admitted they felt the same way, and then they turned around and tried to hide you in a closet?"

"I didn't hide you in a closet. I— Never mind. You're right." She came forward and sat gingerly on the opposite end of the sofa. "I'm sorry."

"Kate . . ." He turned his head away as if he couldn't bear to even look at her. Hurt by the gesture, she watched his throat move as he swallowed. "I'm trying very hard to understand, but none of this makes sense to me." He turned back to nail her with a wounded look. "Why is it so hard for you to accept what's happening between us?"

"Because . . ." She searched for words that didn't exist. "It's happening too fast. Don't you see? I need time, Mike. I just need time."

"Time?" He looked confused. "What the hell does time have to do with anything? Ten years could pass, and I'd still feel the same way. I'm in love with you. And I have been from the moment I first met you."

Seeing the conviction in his eyes, she almost believed him—almost believed he'd fallen for her at first sight. "I'm sorry. I'm just not ready."

"Why? Because some jerk who was too stupid to realize what he had let you slip through his fingers?"

She looked away. "It was a little more complicated than that. Edward wasn't the only one to blame for our failed marriage. I failed him as much as he failed me."

"How?"

"Honestly?" She took a fortifying breath. "I'm not very good at being a wife. I'm a very selfish person, and I put my own needs first too often."

"That's pure bunk." His feet hit the floor as he leaned toward her. "You're the most self-sacrificing person I know."

A sad laugh escaped her. "I'm flattered you think so, but the truth is, sacrificing isn't natural for me. It's something I've had to work at."

He studied her a long moment. "Have you ever stopped to think that maybe you're working at it a bit too hard?"

Her back straightened. "What do you mean?"

"Kate, putting other people first, even those you love, isn't always best for them, and it damn sure isn't best for you."

"I don't know what you're talking about."

"Your career for one thing. This past week, I've watched you turn your back on something you want very badly, and I'm worried you're doing it out of some misguided belief that going after anything you want will take something away from Dylan. And I'm even more worried that that misguided belief applies to us as well. That you think letting yourself love me will somehow hurt your son."

"That's ridiculous." She shook her head. "I'm not misguided. I'm just . . ."

"What, Kate? Tell me. Make me understand."

She opened her mouth to calmly explain, but what came out surprised her. "I'm scared, all right? I'm scared!"

He stared at her incredulously as her heart pounded against her ribs. "Of what?"

"That I'll fail again."

"You mean fail at being Dear Cupid?" he asked. "Or fail at being a wife?"

"Both." Her throat closed painfully around the words. "I don't exactly have the best track record for success."

He sat back. "So, that's it, isn't it? You haven't lost faith in men, or even love. You've lost faith in yourself."

She nodded as tears welled in her eyes.

"Ah, Kate." He gathered her in his arms. "Do you have any idea how wonderful you are? Do you have a clue what I see when I look at you, what I feel when I'm around you?" He cupped her face and stared into her eyes. "You are the most incredible person I've ever met, because you're filled to the brim with life. You're intelligent, compassionate, funny, and wise. I want to spend the rest of my life getting to know your quirks and your foibles, your weaknesses and your strengths. Every time I'm with you, you simply take my breath away. And if that isn't love, then I don't know what is."

She searched his eyes, and marveled at the sincerity she saw there. "I want to believe you. But it's so hard. I don't know if I can survive letting someone else down. Especially—" Her breath caught. "Someone as wonderful as you."

His face softened as he wiped away her tears. "You could never let me down, Kate. If there were some way I could prove that to you, I would. Unfortunately, you're going to have to accept it on your own. To do that, you have to learn to believe in yourself again. To

believe in your own judgment, and believe that you
are very, very lovable."

A car horn sounded. "What's that?" She glanced at
the door, breaking the contact of his hands.

"Frank. I called and asked him to come get me."
He took one of her hands in his and squeezed. "Kate,
all I'm asking is that you give us a chance. Give yourself a chance."

"I—" She stared at their joined hands, searching
for courage, but found none. "Maybe if we took a
break. Some time apart would allow us both room to
think this through. To be sure."

"I'm afraid that's not possible."

"Why not?" She glanced up, frowning.

"Because," he sighed, "last night, Dylan asked me
again to be in his play, which is this Friday. And since
you didn't exactly forbid me from doing it, I—well, I
told him I would do it, all right?"

"Mike . . ."

"I promised him, Kate. Don't ask me to go back on
that. Ask me to do anything else, but don't ask me to
break a promise to that kid."

Pulling her hands free, she wrapped her arms
around herself as her safe world crumbled a bit more.
Outside, the car horn sounded again.

"Look, I'll make you a deal," Mike said. "If you
don't interfere with Dylan and me, I'll stay out of your
way as much as possible until Friday night." With one
finger on her chin, he turned her face toward his and
gave her a determined look. "After that, your reprieve
is over. I want to spend time with you. Hell, I want
to marry you. And I will. Even if I have to wear you
down, bit by bit, until you're finally ready to admit
that you're as crazy about me as I am about you."

Her shoulders slumped. "Mike—"

"No." He moved his finger to cover her lips. "You have all week to think about it. After that, my real campaign begins."

She hesitated, then nodded, too grateful for even a short reprieve to argue.

"All right, then." He placed a brief, chaste kiss on her lips, then rose and crossed to the door. With one hand on the knob, he turned back. "I'll see you on Friday."

She nodded weakly as he closed the door behind him.

The instant she was alone, tears slipped hot and fast down her cheeks. What was she going to do? It would be so easy to take this tumble—to believe Mike really did love her. But what if she was wrong?

*You're going to have to learn to believe in yourself again.*

His words echoed in her mind. He was so right. She had lost faith in herself. How had he seen that so clearly? The past few weeks and years played back in her mind, again and again, making her cry harder.

In an effort to escape her own thoughts, she went to the bedroom and sat at her desk. She gave a sad laugh when she realized habit alone had brought her there. She had no column to write. No e-mail to answer. The dark screen of her computer stared back at her like an eye that had gone blind.

The crushing weight of loss bore down on her chest as she lifted her hand and placed it against the cool glass.

Her eyes dropped to the stack of columns she'd printed out two days ago to appease Mike's constant nagging. On top of them lay her handwritten notes on how to submit a query to a newspaper. She realized with sudden clarity she'd never believe anyone could love her until she rediscovered her love of herself. Until she recaptured that faith, she didn't deserve Mike's love.

Some last spark of courage that had refused to die flared upward. She'd been a coward too long. And she was tired of hiding behind fear and weak excuses. With a trembling hand, she reached for the power switch and turned her computer on.

# Chapter 25

"ARE you sure she's coming?" Mike asked as he peered through a crack in the stage's backdrop.

"Of course she's coming," Dylan assured him for the tenth time. "She's my mom. You think she'd miss seeing me in a play?"

"I guess you're right." Mike glanced over his shoulder in time to catch Dylan fidgeting with the white waistcoat of his costume. Mike had borrowed the top hat and tails from one of the live theaters downtown. All around them, kids dashed about in homemade costumes that ranged from tights and tutus to sixties beads and tie-dye T-shirts. Laughter ricocheted off the hard walls, punctuated by the squeak of tennis shoes on linoleum.

After spending a week with this motley crew, Mike couldn't help but think Dylan looked and acted the most professional of the whole dang lot. He couldn't wait for Kate to see the boy onstage. Dylan was going to blow the socks off everyone in the audience.

Now, if Kate would just show up! He turned back to the crack in the backdrop. The folding chairs in the cafeteria were filling up fast, but the one between Kate's parents and the Davises remained empty. "I just don't understand why she isn't here yet. The play starts any minute."

"I told you," Dylan said with the strained patience of a seven-year-old reasoning with the inferior intellect of an adult. "She had an appointment in town. But she'll be here. Trust me. Moms live for this sort of thing."

"You're right." He let out a nervous breath. If only so much wasn't riding on this night. He hadn't talked to Kate in person in nearly a week—had only seen glimpses of her when he dropped Dylan off after their rehearsals. She'd peer at him through the kitchen window, or wave from the front porch. Every time, he longed to get out of the car and go to her. But he'd promised to give her these few days to think things over. Well, tonight her reprieve ended. From now on, he'd see her all he wanted. Unless she'd decided she didn't want to see him at all. What would he do if she told him that after the play?

"Five minutes!" Dylan's teacher, Miss Marshall, called as she hurried past, clapping her hands. "Five minutes to curtain. Amy, honey, you need to keep your costume *on*. Kyle, how many times do I have to tell you to stop putting those drumsticks up your nose?"

Mike faced Dylan, man to man. This would be Dylan's first time before an audience, and since Mike's job was all backstage, the boy would be out there alone. "Here, let me check your gear one more time." Kneeling down, he felt Dylan's rib cage to be sure the body harness was in place.

"You sure I don't look dorky?" Dylan asked.

"Would I let you go out there if I thought you looked dorky?" Mike watched Dylan's eyes travel wistfully toward Jason and Kyle in their rock 'n' roll leather and chains. "Hey." He jostled the kid affectionately. "You're gonna knock 'em dead. I promise."

"As long as people don't laugh at me."

"Just do it the way we practiced, and you'll be a hit."

Dylan nodded bravely, but still looked less than convinced.

"Last call." The teacher made another pass through the room, clapping her hands. "Places everyone. Places."

"This is it, kid. Break a leg." Mike held up his fist.

"You too." Dylan tapped his fist against Mike's. "Break a leg."

"Thanks," Mike breathed. *Tonight I need all the luck I can get.*

"Where have you been?" Linda whispered furiously as Kate made her way past purses and knees to the middle of the row. The lights had already dimmed and the opening strains of music swelled from the speakers on either side of the stage.

"I told you," Kate whispered back as she found her seat in the dark. "I had an appointment."

"Well?" Linda asked, sounding more eager than irritated. "How did it go?"

"Wonderful. Fabulous!" Excitement bubbled up inside her. "I can't wait to tell you—"

*"Shhh!"* an angry parent admonished from behind them.

"I'll tell you later," Kate whispered, and turned her attention toward the stage. Keeping her secret while she sat between Linda and her mom would require an act of sheer will. But even if her son's play weren't starting, she'd have forced herself to wait. She wanted Mike to be the first to hear her news.

Throughout the production, she fidgeted in her

chair, unable to sit still. She felt charged with confidence, and ready to tackle the world for the first time in years.

It felt good. And natural. As if she were finally back inside her own skin. For that she had Mike to thank. He'd forced her to lift the veil from her eyes and take a good, hard look at herself and her actions. As she sat through the production, she realized now how silly she'd been. About a lot of things.

Only when Linda nudged her did she realize the show was almost over. "I think Dylan's next," Linda whispered.

"So soon?" Nervous excitement shot through her.

"And now," the teacher said, "Dylan Bradshaw brings you some movie magic, with a little help from a friend."

The curtain opened, revealing a blank stage with nothing but a large blue screen for a backdrop. Something exploded in the middle of the stage, sending up a plume of smoke. When the smoke cleared, Dylan stood before the screen, dressed as a magician, with a top hat, tails, cape, and cane.

"In the theater," Dylan said in a small, nervous voice, "magic is done with a little sleight of hand." Tipping his top hat, he clumsily pulled out a bouquet of flowers. Then, making a face, he tossed the flowers over his shoulder. "Very boring."

The audience let out a small laugh, not quiet sure what to expect. Kate's heart twisted in empathy. Her son was not a natural performer, and if he bombed, he'd die of embarrassment.

"Which is why on the big screen"—Dylan held his arms out with the hat in one hand and the cane in the other—"we need something more. Something bigger. Like . . . a *big* sleight of hand!"

The blue screen came to life, and a giant hand appeared, reaching down as if to pluck Dylan off the stage. Dylan let out a holler and started to run. The hand grabbed him by the tails of his jacket, and to Kate's utter shock, lifted him into the air. The Beatles tune "Magical Mystery Tour" boomed from the speakers as Dylan swung back and forth.

Just as Kate thought she'd die of heart failure, the hand set Dylan back on the stage. Behind him flashed scenes from movies, starting with old black-and-whites and segueing to Technicolor musicals. In every scene the characters appeared to be moving in time to the music. Dylan danced right along with Fred Astaire and Ginger Rogers. He turned his cane into a gun and shot it out with cowboys and gangsters. He danced on the rooftops of London with Dick Van Dyke, and wielded his cane like a light saber against Darth Vader. As the song drew to a close, a whole chorus line of alien creatures seemed to appear on the stage, dancing and playing their bizarre instruments as Dylan played his cane like a clarinet.

When the final note of the music fell suddenly to silence, the blue screen went blank. Dylan stretched his arms out to either side and announced, "And that, my friends, is how we do magic in the movies!"

The audience burst into wild applause as Dylan took his bow with all the panache of an orchestra conductor at Carnegie Hall. Kate clapped until her hands stung.

The other children filed back onstage along with the teacher for the final number. As they sang "There's No Business Like Show Business," each act stepped forward for another bow. When Dylan's turn came, Mike jogged onstage to join him. They did a little soft-shoe shuffle, bowed to each other, then bowed to the audience. Kate's heart swelled with pride in her son and gratitude toward Mike as she watched their easy camaraderie. If any doubt had remained on how she felt about this man, it would have vanished then and there.

"Oh, Katy," her mother breathed as the curtain came down and the lights went up. "Wasn't he grand, now?"

"The hit of the show," her father agreed.

Several other parents waved at her and called out congratulations on her son's performance. Kate simply nodded, eager to get backstage.

"If y'all will excuse me," she said to her parents and her friends.

"Wait a second," Linda called. "You didn't tell me how your appointment went."

"I will," Kate assured her as she made her way through the folding chairs. "Later." First she had to see Mike.

She started toward the doors by the stage, but something caught her eye and she turned. "Edward?" she whispered in disbelief as he came up the aisle. He looked as polished and handsome as ever, but for once she felt nothing at the sight of him. No attraction, no anger, only surprise. "What are you doing here?"

He shrugged and slipped his hands into the pockets of his dress slacks. "I had an appointment with a client today who lives out here at the lake. He mentioned the show tonight, and I remembered Dylan was supposed to be in it."

She waited for him to say something more, like that he'd been thinking about what she'd said and realized she was right, he needed to spend more time with his son. Instead, after an awkward pause, he nodded toward the stage. "Hey, the kid's pretty good, isn't he?"

She laughed, though the sound held no humor. "Yeah. He is." She should have known better than to expect any verbal concessions from Edward. Even if he admitted to himself he was wrong about something, he'd never say it out loud. Well, he'd come tonight, and of his own accord. That in itself amazed her.

"Hey, look," he said, checking his watch, "I need to run, but I'd like to say hi to Dylan first."

"I'll send him out," she said, and started to step away. Realizing Edward wasn't the only one who should make some concessions, she stopped and turned back. "Edward, thanks for coming tonight. It'll mean a lot to Dylan."

"Sure, no problem." He shrugged easily, but the way he averted his eyes gave away his discomfort. Maybe there was hope for the man after all, Kate thought as she headed for the doors.

Backstage, chaos reigned as children dashed about and adrenaline filled the air.

"Mom!" Dylan shouted when he saw her, and came rushing over. "Did you see me? Did you see?"

"I certainly did." Her gaze locked with Mike's as he came up behind her son, and her stomach fluttered.

"I was really good, wasn't I?" Dylan said, bouncing on the balls of his feet.

"Yes, you were," she said.

"And Mike too. Isn't he cool?"

"Yes, he is. The absolute coolest." She smiled at Mike before giving her son her full attention. "There's some people out front who want to see you. Why don't you go show them your costume?"

"You bet!" Dylan dashed off, through the double metal doors. Her heart warmed as she imagined his reaction to seeing his father.

Pushing thoughts of her ex aside, she turned back

to Mike. He looked equal parts nervous and earnest, the same way she felt.

He nodded toward the door leading outside. "I don't suppose you'd care to get some fresh air?" A child screeched in the background, making them both wince. "And some quiet."

"I'd love to." They didn't touch as they walked side by side, and she wished he'd take her hand to stop it from shaking.

Outside, the night provided a refreshing relief from the energy-filled cafeteria. Countless stars filled the sky and the freshness of the Hill Country scented the air. Everything was perfect, exactly as it should be, except for the giant butterflies battling to escape her stomach.

"So." Mike cleared his throat. "What did you think of the show?"

"I thought you and Dylan were fabulous." A smile tugged at her lips. "Thank you."

"It was fun." He shrugged as if a week of after-school rehearsals hadn't disturbed his schedule at all. "That is one great kid you have there, you know that?"

"Yeah, I do. I'm glad you think so, though, since"— she took a deep breath—"you may be spending a lot more time with him."

"Oh?" Hope flickered in his eyes. "Does this mean you won't be pushing me away anymore?"

"It means I've done a lot of thinking the last few days."

"And?"

"And I've decided you were right." She took another deep breath. "I had lost faith in myself. Until I got that back, until I believed I was worth loving, I'd never be able to give my love to someone else."

"Kate, you are very worth loving." He moved

closer, but still didn't touch her. The golden lights from the playground showed the anxiety that lined his face.

"I know." She smiled at him, trying to tell him with her eyes that he had helped her remember that. "But first I had to prove it to myself."

"Oh?"

"So," she said, taking a breath, "last Monday, after you left, I sent out queries to every daily paper in Texas."

Panic flashed across his eyes. "You're not going to hang your self-worth on what other people think, are you? Because selling your column could take a while, even though I believe wholeheartedly that you will sell it."

"Would you wait?" She laughed at him. "And, no, I would have come to the same decision about myself, and about us, no matter what response I got from my queries."

"So?" He visibly braced himself.

"The *American Statesman* is picking up my column!" The words bubbled out of her on a burst of enthusiasm.

"What?" His face lit with excitement.

"I met with the Lifestyle editor this afternoon," she explained in a rush. "That's why I was so late getting here. He said that if my column goes over well in this market, the newspaper chain that owns them will probably run it in their other markets as well. By this time next year, Dear Cupid could be running in papers all over the country."

"That's fabulous!" He swept her up and swung her around. "I knew you could do it."

"I know." She laughed in sheer joy as he set her back on her feet. "But I had to believe it myself. Believe *in* myself. Before I could believe you really love me."

"You do believe that, though." He cupped her face as his eyes searched hers. "Don't you?"

Rather than answer, she rose up and pressed her lips to his. A week's worth of missing him, of wanting to tell him how she felt, washed over her as she poured herself into the kiss. His lips answered in the same language of eager longing. All barriers crumbled beneath the honesty and strength of the love she felt inside. Still glowing, she sighed when he ended the kiss.

"I'll take that as a yes," he breathed. "Ah, Kate, I was a goner the moment we met."

"Me too. It just took me a little longer to realize it. But no more hiding." She met his gaze evenly. "I love you, Mike. And I want to spend the rest of my life showing you how much. If you're still interested."

"If I'm still interested?" He kissed her again, long and hard, until the ground tilted beneath her feet, and the stars whirled overhead. When at last he lifted his head, she had to blink to bring him into focus.

"So," he said, smiling broadly. "What would Dear Cupid's advice be to two people who happen to be nuts about each other?"

"That they not waste any time tying the knot," she answered without hesitation. "And that from here on out, they make every second they have together count."

"I think that's one bit of advice I can easily follow." His head dipped toward hers. "Starting right now."

*Me too*, she thought as he kissed her senseless. *Most definitely, me too!*

# *Epilogue*

*Dear Cupid,*
*Do you believe in love at first sight?*
                    *Your Biggest Fan*


*Dear Fan,*
*Absolutely!*
                    *Your Loving Wife, Kate*

## YOU'LL BE CRAZY FOR
# JENNIFER CRUSIE'S
### *SEXY, SUSPENSEFUL NOVELS*

## TELL ME LIES

A hot, hilarious novel about small-town secrets, big-time betrayals, and the redemptive power of love, laughter and chocolate brownies.

"Jennifer Crusie presents a humorous mixture of romance, mystery, and mayhem."
—Susan Elizabeth Phillips, *New York Times* bestselling author of *Nobody's Baby But Mine*

## CRAZY FOR YOU

Dog-napping, petty theft, and seduction are all in a day's work for one woman who's on the run from her own unexciting life.

"CRAZY FOR YOU is filled with characters who are just plain hoots . . . She's certainly the legitimate heir to the Beach Reading Throne."
–*Los Angeles Times*